LETTERS TO BENTROCK

A DEMON'S GUIDE TO TRAPPING PREY

J B CYPRUS

Letters to Bentrock
Paperback Edition
Copyright © 2022 (As Revised) J. B. Cyprus

Published in the United States by Wolfpack Publishing, Las Vegas

CKN Christian Publishing
An Imprint of Wolfpack Publishing
5130 S. Fort Apache Road 215-380
Las Vegas, NV 89148

cknchristianpublishing.com

Paperback ISBN 978-1-63977-278-0

CONTENTS

This book is dedicated to "The Roach" whom you will meet briefly in these pages. He is based on a real person who brought the message of salvation to countless incarcerated men and women. He now rests in The Lord.

It is also dedicated to the corrections staff and chaplaincy department at the Texas Department of Criminal Justice. Life in a Texas prison is difficult for all those who live and work there. It has been even more challenging during this past year as the COVID virus raged and so many lives were lost.

In my years of volunteering, I have come to appreciate that the incarcerated men and women of Texas are blessed to have many wardens, corrections officers, and chaplains who are faithful followers of Jesus. They work in some of the most physically, mentally, and emotionally demanding jobs anywhere. They strive to live out their faith in this difficult environment and to do all they can to help the men and women in their charge find a new and better life in Christ Jesus. They are the unrecognized heroes behind the very real truth that "prison is one of the few places" where the Deceiver continues to lose ground. To them I say thank you for all you do. Your labor is not in vain.

LETTERS TO BENTROCK

INTRODUCTION

In 1942 Christian Author C.S. Lewis published *The Screwtape Letters* chronicling the fictional (?) account of a junior demon, a "tempter" named Wormwood, who had been assigned by the powers in Hell to ensure that a young British man remained on the path to damnation. Lewis' book described a world in which each person had a sort of Guardian Devil who was assigned to watch over him or her and do everything they could to ensure their "Patients" did not defect to the Christian camp.

The story in Lewis' book unfolds across a series of letters written by a senior demon named Screwtape. Through Screwtape's letters we gain insight into how the forces of temptation work to prevent the Patient from finding salvation through Jesus. After the Patient becomes a Christian, we see the tempters doing all they can to lure the Patient back from the "Enemy's camp."

The Screwtape Letters has become a classic work in Christian literature and has been continuously in print for nearly eight decades. Its unique perspective, told from the eye of the tempter, has helped generations of

Christians recognize and resist many of the temptations they encounter.

In *Letters to Bentrock* I borrow Lewis' literary device. In these pages we find a senior demon named Deumus, serving as Chief Warden of the Incarceration Services Division of the Texas Department of Corruptions where he oversees a group of tempters who are assigned to the Texas prison system.

One would think that ensuring the damnation of this bunch of criminals, thugs, and addicts would be an easy task, but, as Deumus notes, it is not. "The prison system is one place where the Enemy continues to make progress and where our own success rate is barely rising." In the letters that follow, Deumus coaches a novice tempter named Bentrock in his efforts to keep his Inmate on the wide and straight road to their Domain.

While the book was originally conceived to help our incarcerated brothers and sisters recognize and combat the temptations they encounter, I have come to realize that much of it speaks equally well to those of us in the "free world." I hope both groups may find something worth reading here.

– J.B. Cyprus

SOURCES AND METHODS

Dear Friends,

I am often asked how I came into possession of this correspondence. The observant reader will correctly guess that these letters were found in the personal effects of the late Bentrock. He had carefully catalogued and saved the notes he received from Deumus. As to how I received them, let us just say that the forces of Evil are not the only ones who have spies, and that the soldiers of the One True God are not nearly so passive as these letters might suggest.

I have not included all the letters (a few hundred were recovered), because a great many of them are repetitive, others are only a few lines long, and many are not particularly insightful for our purposes. There are also significant gaps in the timeline of letters Bentrock saved. Weeks or months would pass with nothing, only to pick up at a steady pace once again. I can only surmise that the missing letters were considered unimportant or perhaps Bentrock destroyed them for other reasons. We will never know.

I should also offer a comment about my editing. I have been asked why an other-worldly creature like Deumus would write letters in ordinary English. The answer is twofold: first, one must presume that he and Bentrock were corresponding in the language they use when communicating to their "prey" rather than their native tongue, whatever that may be; second, Deumus' letters were not written in what we might call ordinary English!

The language and style used in the original letters is a peculiar blend of modern and archaic English with odd grammatical constructions fitting for a creature who learned the language centuries ago and only uses it occasionally. Beyond the stylistic oddities, Deumus' letters are filled with bile and a deep contempt for humans that I assume is commonplace amongst these beings. I have done my best to make them more accessible to the modern reader and to eliminate the often-tedious filler material. I have also deleted much of the vile and vulgar language. I had no desire to further spread the venom of these creatures and so I have removed most of the descriptions except when I believed they were essential to convey Deumus' mood or a particular point.

There are also a great many places where Deumus uses euphemisms or odd abbreviations to communicate, especially when referring to God (whom he calls "the Enemy") and his followers. He does not use the word Christian, for example, but instead writes this as c–––. He will occasionally use the old first century name for Christianity, "The Way," and where he does, I have retained it. When he refers to Jesus, he will never use the name, only pronouns. I have translated these in most cases as "Son" to make the meaning clear while trying to avoid losing the sense that these creatures do not (cannot?) speak His name. I have adopted the convention of capitalizing pronouns He, His, and Him when referencing Our Lord.

I should say something about Deumus' temporal references. He offers several clues that he has been traveling the earth for millennia. At one point, for example, he refers to prey who sacrificed to ancient idols by offering entrails. When he uses words like "recently," I have come to realize he can mean anything from the past few years to the past few centuries. It can be a bit confusing, but I did not attempt to clarify this as in many cases even I was not certain what time period he was referencing.

Finally, I should mention something about the footnotes. Deumus would often make margin notes to highlight or expand upon a point in his letter. Where I thought these were worth keeping, I have placed them in the footnotes along with other points of clarification I thought would be useful to the reader.

Please bear in mind, dear reader, that Deumus is a liar. The letters reveal a personality that is intolerably boastful and proud (I have deleted most of this) and a creature who deeply despises the One True God, His servants, His creatures, and most everything He has created. While this correspondence is, I trust, helpful to provide insight into how Deumus and other tempters operate, be warned that it also contains a great many lies.

– Editor

PART I

A NEW LIFE

WELCOME BENTROCK

Dear Bentrock,

As this is your first assignment after training, we should set down some standard procedures for working together. You may message me here anytime, however at a minimum I expect weekly reports on your progress. While the final details are yet to be confirmed, it appears the Department of Corruptions has assigned you to the man known to the Texas Prison system as 01272226. Your mission will be to ensure he remains reliably on the expressway to our domain.

I am aware that I have a reputation among the new tempters for being demanding and uncompromising in pursuit of our mission. I make no apologies for this. I began working with these ape-gods many generations ago. In earlier centuries our work was much more difficult and demanding, but thanks to our efforts the world has become a far more tempter-friendly place. We have made great progress steering all manner of human behavior in ways that make our job easier and, as a result, our success rate is rising every year.

To help you accomplish your mission, I will advise you as I am able during this first year, but you have already received the very best training so you should be more than ready for the task. I have every confidence that this initial assignment will be a great success for you and will please our Master Below, at least so long as you remember your training and follow my advice. (Of course, if you fail the usual penalties will apply.)

Normally in our prison assignments, we have a single tempter responsible for all the inmates in a cell block. Since this is your first assignment, however, you will only be accountable for this single individual. An experienced tempter named Woertz will have charge of the other inmates in the block. You should consult with him as necessary and ensure you are working collaboratively to secure the Inmate's final destination.

I will have further instructions for you once I get word from the Texas Department of Corruptions, which oversees tempter assignments, on the details of your Inmate's arrival. It is good to have you on the team!

Chief Warden Deumus
Texas Department of Corruptions,
Incarceration Services Division

MIDNIGHT INTERVENTION

Dear Bentrock,

I have just been informed that your Inmate will be transferring to his permanent unit tomorrow morning. He was sentenced yesterday and is spending the night at a transfer unit. You should visit him there to get things started on the right path.

Since your assignment is now confirmed, there is no point in continuing to hide the truth from you: this will not be an easy mission. The prison system is the one place where the Enemy continues to make progress and where our own success rate is barely rising (we tend to do better once our assignees are released back into the "free world" as they describe it). Your classmates from training who have been assigned to the suburbs, universities, and working-class neighborhoods will all find their tasks much easier.

It will not surprise you to learn that there is a great deal of frustration among the senior staff Below about the Enemy's prison successes. Our colleagues complain that it ought to be easy to accomplish the "simple task" of maintaining our inmates' current direction. Nearly everyone they send to us, they note, is already on the fast track to our Domain. While their free world prey frequently come from good homes, have been indoctrinated in the Enemy's book, and are often professing Christians, our inmate prey tend to come from dangerous and disadvantaged circumstances with unmatched track records of what the Enemy calls "sinfulness."

All of this is true, and your Inmate is no exception. He has been reliably traveling in our direction for many years. He comes from a broken home, has received little training in the Enemy's ways, and he has adopted a personal law-of-the-jungle philosophy built around the ideas that strength is its own justification and doing "what is necessary" to thrive is the only morality that matters (at least "where he lives"). Maintaining a Hell-bound direction for someone like that *ought* to be easy, but it will not be.

What our colleagues fail to acknowledge, and what you must never forget, is that your Inmate is even now confronted by the undeniable truth that his approach to life has failed. It has failed to such an extent that he now finds himself cut off from his friends, from his romantic interests, from his remaining family, and from the personal comforts he had accumulated. He simply cannot deny the reality that his life choices have now led to him living in a small cage where even the most insignificant details of his day – from when he eats, to when and how he bathes, to if and when he may speak to his mother – are now controlled by disinterested and often hostile bureaucrats.[1]

As you will immediately recognize, our colleagues' prey among university students, executives, factory workers, teachers, retirees, and whatnot may all be easily convinced that their lives are going "just fine" and that they are, on balance, "good people" with little need to change. This has always been, and continues to be, the most reliable way to keep someone on the wide and easy road to Our Domain.

Indeed, our convict population provides an invaluable service to our free world colleagues. If one of their free world prey begin to wonder a bit too much about whether they are really "good" and "deserving," we just whisper a quiet reminder that there are plenty of thugs and thieves who are the real "bad people." Our free world colleagues point to the prisons and tell their prey that it is the inmates, not they, who need serious spiritual help. "While you may have made some 'mistakes' in life," we reassure them, "at least you have never committed any of the 'really big' sins like the ones that landed those convicts behind bars." So, we provide an important service to our free world colleagues just by being here!

Sadly, your Inmate also knows this is what most people think. He knows (and it is only now really beginning to sink in) that as of yesterday he is officially, according to the judge and the laws of Texas, just a convict. He will carry that designation for the remainder of his life, and it will affect every facet of his future. So, like most inmates, he will enter the prison system deeply troubled, on the verge of despair, and believing that he needs to "change his life" one way or another.

In other words, we are at a moment of crisis right now, tonight, even before your Inmate arrives at our unit. So, you need to do something that will be completely unnatural for our kind: you must *comfort* him. This is urgent and we do not have time to debate tactics. You must go to him now and plant the seeds for the *Seven Essential Messages* that we embed in every inmate the day they arrive. These messages will help us year after year to keep him out of the Enemy's hands. Memorize these and whisper them to him *tonight*! I will check in with you tomorrow.

Tempter's Guide: Seven Essential Messages for New Inmates[2]

1. You are in this situation because of what others did to you. (Customize for the individual. For example: unfair judge, incompetent lawyer, snitch, parent, employer, gang brother/business partner, etc.)

2. Your actions were justified or at least understandable. (For example: heat of the moment, forced by circumstances, person deserved what they got, etc.)

3. In a different context your actions would be perfectly legal. (Here you want to create "legal" analogies to underscore that while what they have done may be a crime from a *legal* perspective, from a *moral* perspective what they have done is no different than things people do all the time. Some useful pairings to reassure your Inmate: murder ~ abortion, sexual assault ~ pornography, theft ~ predatory business practices, drug dealing ~ pharmaceutical sales, etc. The point is *not* to make an airtight or even very convincing case, but to plant a seed we can nurture in the years ahead.)

4. A different future requires changing your circumstances not changing who you are.(Get

them focused on "enablers" for a better life and keep them away from thoughts about changing themselves. Examples include different friends, better education, different job, different romantic relationship, different house or neighborhood, etc.)

5. You will get out sooner than you think. (Focus on an appeal or parole or whatever is appropriate for the individual so that they become convinced this is temporary.)

6. Never let your guard down in prison, strength is power, silence is strength. (Repeat this often. Emphasize the dangers. It is important to keep them from forming real relationships inside that might connect them with the Enemy's followers.)

7. The system cannot be trusted, even in the smallest things. (This will require very little reinforcing but do not overlook it. We need to sow distrust to minimize the risk that they will seek help or trust the help they are offered.)

We will continue to reinforce these messages and build upon them in the months and years ahead. We want convicts to believe it is not their fault, they are no worse than anyone else, there is hope for getting out and getting out is what matters, the change they need is an *external* change not an *internal* change, and that befriending others is dangerous, foolish, and unnecessary. If you can plant these seeds firmly in your Inmate's mind during these first few days and weeks, it will be smooth sailing for us, and we will be on track to send him back to the free world on an expressway to our Domain.

Sincerely,
Warden Deumus

Footnotes:

[1] Do not take too much comfort in this mostly accurate description. The Enemy is skilled at slipping His own servants into these jobs with devastating effect on our work.

[2] Not to be used for those inmates who are *actually innocent* of the crimes for which they were convicted. Please see *Key Messages for the Actually Innocent* for further guidance.

THE SEVEN MESSAGES

DEAR BENTROCK,

I am encouraged to hear that the Seven Essential Messages strategy has been a success. It does not surprise me to learn that your Inmate was on the verge of falling to his knees at the transfer unit (you need to keep him off his knees!). We see so many incoming inmates rush to the Enemy's side during those first few hours after sentencing. That is why we have instituted the protocol of sharing the Seven Messages right away. I am encouraged that it has helped to settle his mind, at least a bit.

I did not have time in my previous note but allow me a few minutes now to explain why these Essential Messages are so important to our work: They are true. Well, to be more accurate, they are *partly* true, at least after a fashion. Our best lies, the ones that have the greatest impact, are always based on a truth. These lies are like that.

Take the first one, for example: "You are in this situation because of what others did to you." There genuinely were many people whose actions contributed to your Inmate being here, and a great many things that led to his breaking the law. The details of your Inmate's specific crimes aside, it is *almost always true* that the crime itself followed a long series of causes and effects set in motion long ago. Many of those causes were not of the Inmate's choosing. Some may have been things they tried to avoid. Most were things they wished had never happened. So, there is truth in this.

Never mind that many others have experienced similar challenges or temptations and *chose* not to commit the same crime! Never mind that others' actions were just one, often small, contributor to his own behavior. Keep his focus off those inconvenient facts and concentrate his attention on the causes that *were* out of his control. As long as he is not dwelling too much on his own decisions and actions, we have achieved our goal.

If you are very lucky, you will have drawn an Inmate who is seething with anger towards the people who contributed to his arrest and conviction. For this sort of (fairly rare) inmate, when he thinks about why he is incarcerated, his crimes do not even come into consideration. Instead, he cares only about the people who caused him to get caught and to get convicted. If you are lucky enough to have one of these uncommon sorts, the same point applies: keep his mind on the others who are responsible for his current situation.

The "moral equivalency" seeds that you planted – when you told him his actions were justified and that they are very like a great number of perfectly legal transgressions – is one of my favorites. It is, in fact, true that from a moral perspective there are a great many crimes which are perfectly legal according to the State of Texas (the Enemy calls them "sins," but we rarely use that word, and we do what we can to ensure the ape-gods never do either).

Make your living managing pornographic "actors"? Perfectly legal. Make your living as a pimp? Hello convict. Sell an alcoholic a bottle of whiskey? Perfectly legal. Sell an addict some cocaine? Welcome to prison. Purposely shoot and kill a teenager who startled you when he was running through your back yard? Just guarding your castle. Accidentally shoot that same kid during a robbery? Welcome to the gurney.

What is completely obvious to anyone is this: just because a particular sin (there is that word again), or a particular category of sin, goes unpunished by the State does not in the least excuse the crimes that *are* punished by the State. But with just the tiniest sleight of hand we can keep your Inmate thinking that the lack of punishment for one justifies the other.

I should mention here another seed that you may wish to plant: "You are here because people like you are treated unequally by the criminal justice system." I have been thinking about adding this to our Essential Messages list for some time.

In reality, your Inmate probably *would* have been treated better if he was from the right race and right economic class. He would almost certainly have had a different outcome if he had been better looking (or at least more harmless looking!). Judges rarely incarcerate individuals who look and sound and act like people from their immediate neighborhood. Judges rarely imprison people who look like their children.

Again, it will be obvious to most anyone that unfair

laxity on one side does not justify what your Inmate has done, but that is the whole point of planting these seeds. Get his mind focused on other things and keep him from thinking too much about how and why he should change.

And speaking of change, another lie cloaked in truth is the idea that a different future requires changing his circumstances. This is true, it does require that, but it does not require *merely* that. By pretending it is merely that, we keep his mind concentrated on the *outcomes* he desires in the future (a better job, a better place to live, more time with his kids, etc.). We keep his mind *off* questions the Enemy wants him to ponder: "Who are you?" or "Who do want to become?" or worst of all, "Whose are you?" It serves our interests to keep him asking things like "What job would I want?" or "Where would I like to live when I get out?" These things *are* important of course (the Truth), but they are not the *most* important (the Lie) much less the only thing that matters.

While we are not typically in the business of giving people hope, we delight in giving them false hope. Getting out early is a perfect case. Yes, it is based on a truth. Few inmates will serve their full sentence, and they know it. A tiny number will serve only a small portion of their sentences and fewer still will successfully get their convictions overturned. Keep your Inmate dreaming of this low-probability outcome, and he will pay little attention to the deeper problems that brought him here. (It is the same reason we enjoy sending poor people to buy lottery tickets and why our servants in State government have been pushing them so enthusiastically.) If you keep him hooked on the dream, no matter how unrealistic, he won't spend time thinking about the path he has chosen in life. So, keep him thinking that "salvation" is just one appeal hearing away.

You get the idea. These first five are the *distraction* seeds that you have planted. They should help keep his thoughts bouncing from one thing to another, each time reorienting his gaze away from thoughts that might lead to repentance and into the Enemy's arms.

The last two Essential Messages, the superhero seeds, are also built on a half-truth. It is a fact that letting his guard down or trusting the system makes him vulnerable in some (mostly unimportant) ways. So, we plant the idea that he must go it alone in this prison environment. We repeat the message that, like the lonely superhero, he will exist in a world surrounded by enemies where no one will ever truly understand or appreciate him.

The superhero knows that he must "Never let his guard down" and must always be vigilant. The superhero knows that "strength is power, silence is strength." The superhero also knows, "The system cannot be trusted, even in the smallest things." In this superhero fantasy we create, his self-isolation is noble and necessary. And conveniently enough, we know that by isolating himself he cuts off any hope of finding people who can lead him back to the Enemy.

As an aside, we have found this lonely superhero archetype to be incredibly useful in the free world as well. We convince our prey to cut themselves off from others and stand against the night in silent pride. They believe that turning to others for help or – gasp! – comfort is the worst sort of weakness. It is a delightfully useful caricature especially here in prison. (Go it alone, Convict-man, your silence is strength and blah, blah, blah.)

There is much more work to be done in all these

areas. I will try to guide you along the way. For now, it sounds as though your Inmate is off to a good start. Keep reinforcing these messages and let's keep him on our Road.

Sincerely,
Warden Deumus

DISTRACTION

Dear Bentrock,

Never forget that the most effective tool to ensure your Inmate stays on the path to Our Domain is simple *distraction*. Since you are new here, you probably imagine that prison is a place with endless hours of lonely contemplation where an inmate's thoughts can easily turn to the Enemy. While that danger exists, it is equally true that prison is a place of constant noise, commotion, and interruption. Use this to your advantage.

You will know from your training that in the free world our R&D team has been working relentlessly to develop new sources of distraction. The proliferation of video screens in recent years has been exceedingly helpful for us. Indeed, the experts Below believe these are the most helpful inventions in history of the world! Nothing has ever been as beneficial in keeping humans away from the Enemy.

The little ape-gods now have screens everywhere: on their desks, in their living rooms, on their wrists, in their pockets, in their vehicles, even in their bedrooms!

Anytime their thoughts begin to wander toward things eternal, we need only send a conveniently timed "notification" of some news, no matter how trivial, and they will be immediately drawn back to the present moment and to worldly things.

Long gone are the risks we faced for most of human history when our prey might go for a long quiet walk and be drawn into hours of quiet reflection which too often, with tragic results, turned into a prayer. Quiet walks and lazy afternoons sitting on the porch brought countless millions back into the Enemy's orbit. Today, we can just buzz the prey's phone or watch or whatever, and instantly appeal to his vanity or lust or envy or even just draw his attention with something perfectly "wholesome" like a photo of a dog wearing a cowboy hat. Almost anything will divert the attention of these filthy little creatures.

Amusingly, we have now habituated them to seek diversions to such an extent that they do most of the work for us and we rarely need to intervene. You see, Bentrock, being reflective and thoughtful is always a bit uncomfortable for them because during these moments they glimpse their true selves.

In past eras, the Enemy had taught them that personal and spiritual growth required confronting such uncomfortable subjects. Fortunately, we have spent more than a century leading a highly successful marketing campaign to persuade them that success in life is measured by their level personal happiness and that "happiness" and "personal comfort" are one in the same.

Now, anytime they feel even the least bit of mental or spiritual discomfort they believe they are doing something "unhealthy," and they rush to avoid it. With screens everywhere, they have unlimited diversions on demand so shutting down uncomfortable thoughts is impossibly easy.

Usually, I just sit back and watch the predictable progression. The Enemy will suggest something that causes them to pause and begin to reflect on their situation. After a few minutes, this reflection will begin to make them uncomfortable. Moments later they will reach for their phone or their computer or their remote control "just to quickly check something." Hours later they will be lost in the labyrinth of diversions as one link leads to another and then another. (What delicious irony that they call the diversion trap they have built for themselves a "web," and the ape-god insects rush to get stuck in it as often as possible.) It is a good thing they cannot see or hear us. I still find myself laughing uncontrollably at their foolishness. It is almost too easy.

But you will not have that advantage! Few screens are allowed in prison and even those that are allowed have far fewer options for distraction. Prisoners are generally prohibited from entering the web.

Nonetheless, you have advantages that the free world tempters do not. Your Inmate is never alone. There are always cellmates, or corrections officers, or other inmates a few feet away. Even your Inmate's bowel movements and showers are on public display. So, quiet reflection is far more difficult and there are plenty of opportunities for distraction day and night. You will, nonetheless, need to be more creative than your colleagues who chase free world prey.

Your best weapon here is your Inmate's cellmate (his "celly" they call it). They will be stuck together in a tiny space for most of the day and night. This is one reason we normally give a single prison tempter charge over everyone in a cell block. If one inmate on the block starts to gravitate toward the Enemy, you can whisper in the ear of the celly or the person in the adjacent cell. It does not have to be anything too elaborate. Just have the neighbor turn on the radio or strike up a conversation or even just cause a bit of well-timed flatulence. Any of that should be fine to divert your Inmate's attention from things eternal. As I said, these filthy creatures are very easy to distract.

This is also an instance in which the unwritten rules of prison can play to your advantage. In the free world, your Inmate could just leave the room or end the conversation. In prison, asking his celly to turn off the radio or to leave him alone is often enough to provoke a conflict and even violence. As a result, your prey will tend to be polite to a fault when it comes to tolerating, and therefore being drawn into, these little distractions.

If the minor distractions are insufficient, you can pull out the big weapons in your arsenal. Suggest to the CO that there needs to be an unscheduled inspection. Mix up the visitors list and have them call out your Inmate by mistake. There are a thousand little ways to get the staff to interrupt his reflections. The key is to remember that your Inmate is at the beck and call of dozens of minor prison staff 24 hours a day. Any one of them has power to interrupt his routine, or to demand his presence in one place or another. Use that to your advantage.

Of course, these close quarters are also your greatest danger. If your Inmate finds himself sharing a cell with a real Christian, there are few options for you to keep him continually distracted. Fortunately, you should not have any concerns in this regard. Your Inmate's celly has been a reliable member of our party for decades. So, enjoy your work and keep him distracted before his thoughts turn to anything too serious.

Sincerely,
Deumus

PS Keep your Inmate away from the one they call The Roach. I cannot emphasize this enough.

STOKE THE ANXIETY

Dear Bentrock,

I know you enjoy watching as your Inmate continues to be filled with anxiety about his new life and his new neighbors, but you are not here for your enjoyment! His anxiety can be a useful tool for us, but it requires subtlety and guidance to get it right. You need to draw upon what you learned in training to steer him through this time.

Just as in the free world, anxiety can help keep your Inmate in a perpetual state of discomfort and at the edge of despair, but it can also lead him to turn to the Enemy if you are not careful. Right now, he is anxious because the environment is not familiar, he does not know or trust the people around him, his future is uncertain, his standing with his free world family and friends is unclear, and he feels under constant threat from a set of rules he does not understand. This is all positive, but it is also temporary unless you do what is necessary to make it permanent.

The first thing you must understand about anxiety is

that its use to us is mostly as a form of distraction. Yes, it is amusing to see the discomfort it creates, but it is the distraction that is actually useful to keep your Inmate's thoughts from turning to the Enemy. We want to create a mental compartment full of anxieties that exist in the back of his mind, hidden from view. Anytime he begins to turn toward the Enemy, you can dust off one of his nearly forgotten fears and slip it into his subconscious mind. Almost immediately he will forget all about the Enemy and begin to wallow in feelings of worry and dread.

As you will know from your training, anxiety works best when the fears it is built upon are vague and hidden in the shadows. Once the fears are specific and clear, your Inmate may still fear them, but it is much more difficult to create sustained and distracting anxiety about them. Once they are known, he can measure the risk, confront the consequences, and come to terms with the reality he is facing.

Never forget that the Enemy has given these ape-gods an ability to accept even the very worst consequences once they understand them. More troubling for us, once they know what they are facing, they will instinctively turn to Him for strength and consolation. If, by contrast, you keep his fears cloaked in the shadows of his mind, they cannot be measured or confronted. They are vague, ill-defined dangers that create a fog of unease, sleeplessness, and distraction.

You will know from your history that even having wild animals tear apart His followers in the arena did little to help our cause because they *knew* and *understood* what lay before them. Worse, when faced with this terrible future, they almost inevitably turned to Him. It is a truism widely known amongst prison tempters that there is more anxiety in state jail than on death row.

In my own work, I have been able to use things as trivial and ambiguous as a fear of growing old to keep some of my free world prey anxious and distracted for decades only to reveal the truth at the moment of death when it was too late. Oh, what fun it was to pull back the curtain and reveal that a lifetime defined by unhappy anxiety was nothing more than petty vanity all along! But enough reminiscing.

The way to keep this vague in your Inmate's mind is to play anxiety like an accordion. Increase the pressure for a few days, but then pull back. Let him start "feeling better" for a short while before squeezing again. When you are ready to squeeze, remind him of one or two of the things he fears but do not overwhelm him. You want him to feel anxious, not drive him to despair. (Remember, the fears he has right now are pretty trivial, as all but one fear is, and squeezing too hard will push them out of the shadows. Once they are fully visible, they lose their power.)

Mix it up. One week you can bring to his mind a word or phrase from a family member that causes him to fear abandonment. The next you can bring to his mind an incident in the prison that causes him to fear for his safety. Another week you can bring to his mind concerns about how difficult life will be as a convicted felon once he gets out. Put these different issues into rotation and you can keep him anxious indefinitely. As I said, subtlety is the key.

You will want to keep a couple of your Inmate's greatest fears in reserve. Never raise them unless it is an emergency. If you see him wandering into the Enemy's orbit, you will be able to use these powerful distractions to redirect his gaze for days or even weeks. In the case of your particular Inmate, I see from your earlier reports that he is deeply connected to his mother. Causing her shame and disappointment is one of his greatest fears. I would certainly keep this one in reserve. I would also hold in reserve his anxiety about his daughter. He fears that his time in prison will lead her to feel as abandoned as he did when his own father left. These will give you strong ammunition should you ever need it.

One caution about these family anxieties, however: there is always a risk that his mother or his daughter will steal your ammunition. Remember that they have it in their power to forgive your Inmate. If they do that, your reserve stockpile will be worthless. Fortunately, it is unlikely they will. If they do happen to make overtures in that direction (obviously, his daughter is far too young for this right now), just be sure you quickly intervene with your Inmate to suggest that "they did not really mean it," or they "just said that out of obligation," or "she has forgiven you, but you are still a huge disappointment to her," or something similar. In other words, if you are relying on this ammunition for an emergency, you need to make sure your stockpile is clean, dry and ready at all times.

All of which brings me back to where I started: I know you enjoy watching as your Inmate continues to be filled with anxiety about his new life, but it is time for you to relieve the pressure and allow his anxiety to abate. There is no risk at the moment that he will wander onto the Enemy's path, so you need to keep these powerful weapons of distraction in your arsenal in case you need them in the future. Now is the time to help him relax and become accustomed to his new life. Help him to believe that this is "not so bad, really." Help him to believe that five years "won't seem all that long anyway" and that "it probably won't be that long in any case" (remember the seven key messages).

Never forget, Bentrock, that you are not here for your amusement. You are here to do a job for our Master. The very finest tempters are able to do their work without ever exploiting anxiety. It is always best when your Inmate does not need to be coerced down the wide and straight road. The greatest feast belongs to tempters who lead their prey happily trotting down the road to Our Domain without a care in the world.

I shall be listening for accordion music wafting through the halls of your Inmate's dorm!

Deumus

THE NICKNAME

Dear Bentrock,

You mentioned in your last note that your Inmate has acquired a prison nickname. That is great news! These nicknames can be an exceptionally useful tool for us. You need to work to reinforce this new identity and leverage the power of his new name to help you in your work.

One of the more advantageous things about prison culture is that almost no one is ever called by his given name. The institution will only refer to them by their last name or their inmate number or possibly the designation of their bunk (if I am not mistaken, your Inmate is most often called out as "Charlie dorm, A16"). With a prison nickname now also firmly attached, we can continue the process of erasing his old identity and all the problematic characteristics that came with it.

What you need to remember, Bentrock, is that when people use your Inmate's given name, what they used to refer to as his "Christian name," there is always a risk of prompting a spiritual awakening in him. That name was given to him by his mother. It symbolized to her the uniqueness and individual value of this little ape-god. It represented all her hopes and the promise she saw in his future. That name had power. When she held him and called him by that name, she was marveling at what she imagined was the "miracle" of creating a new life (never mind that, from our perspective, it is just a vulgar messy biological process). The name became, for her, synonymous with this so-called "miracle" and was worth more to her than her own life.

Each time she called out that name, whether it was in adoration or anger, through frustration or joy, said with anxiety or assurance, it always contained in it the hopes she placed in that unique individual. Even in the disgust and disappointment which your Inmate heard from her at his final sentencing, she spoke the name that was uniquely his. The disappointment was there only because it stood in contrast to the possibilities she had wrapped up in that name the day she gave it to him.

When others in his life, adults, teachers, friends, and coworkers, used his given name, they were acknowledging not just him as an individual but also him as the sum of his mother's hopes and dreams for who he might become. When someone asked him, "Who are you?" and he responded with his given name and his surname, what he was really saying was, "I am the one my mother named _____."

In prison, he is no longer that. He is, in the best of circumstances, his last name only – a nameless member of a group of people with the same surname. He is not a unique individual. Or even better, he is now the number designated by the State. But best of all, is when he becomes known by a prison nickname.

With his new prison nickname, he is once again a

unique individual but one whose name carries no hopes or promise for the future. His prison nickname is the description of who he has become. It describes who he is at this, the lowest point of his personal failures. It tells him: "*this* is who you are now."

Here is where you come in: you need to encourage him to embrace his prison nickname. Tell him it is a term of endearment. Tell him that it means he is accepted. And in truth, it *does* mean that (remember that all our best deceptions are built on a small truth), but not for who he was, much less for who he might become. It means he is now defined by this *new* name – a convict's name, with a convict's worth, and a convict's future. *This* is who he is now. All the hopes his mother wrapped into his given name are gone. You want him to take *pride* in that. Help him to reject his given name as a childish thing that he has put away. This new name is who he is.

Yes, I know that such a small thing as a nickname – especially a playful moniker like the one given to your Inmate – may feel insignificant. But it is through these seemingly insignificant changes that we help to recreate our subjects in the image of our Master. We have given your Inmate a new name. In the coming months we will give him a new purpose. He is, now more than ever, our Master's servant, even if he does not yet realize it is so.

Infernally Yours,
Warden Deumus

MONEY MATTERS

Dear Bentrock,

Your careless amusement about inmates discussing commissary money makes me wonder if you slept your way through training! Since when is it "absurd" to be "obsessed by a few dollars" in a commissary account? How did you get the impression that someone who is "dirt poor" cannot not love money? You could not be more wrong! Mark my words, your Inmate will slip through your incompetent hands if you do not start thinking more like a human.

It may look ridiculous to *you* when you overhear a group of inmates obsessing about how they can get a few extra dollars into their commissary account. It may seem to *you* incomprehensible when you see them fill with envy because someone else has enough money to buy a bag of cookies. To me it looks like Woertz is doing his job!

Loving money has nothing to do with being wealthy. Yes, back in the time when The Son came down to live with His filthy creations, most of the people who loved money were rich, or at least richer than most. He told them that the poor were "blessed," and the wealthy risked their souls by placing trust in money. His stories reinforced the message – from the Rich Young Ruler, to Lazarus and the Rich neighbor, to the Rich Fool building his barns. The wealthy fall in love with money and, as His man Paul warned, loving money is the root of all kinds of…well, let's just call it our way of thinking.

That was then. This is a new world. It is a connected world. It is *our* world. We have spent centuries devising ways to help the poor fall in love with money! We have *democratized* it, you could say.

In times past, a person's economic station was largely an inherited condition. The poor could envy the rich, but they could not possibly hope to *become* rich. When we wanted to tempt somebody to fall in love with wealth, we usually had to go through all sorts of difficulties to put them in a position where they would actually *have* money (special bargains and whatnot). It was a tremendous bother, especially in the days when ordinary people did not own property. Then along came the Enlightenment (so much good came out of that for us!) and democracy and property rights and suddenly it was possible for anyone to get rich.

Of course, very few people *did* get rich, especially in the early days, but it was possible, and that was just the thing. (I really cannot believe they did not teach you all of this in training!) Slowly, the idea of accumulating wealth seemed possible even to the subsistence farmer or the housemaid or the laborer. And we noticed, through no effort of ours, that people who were poor, and who would always be poor, started to love money as much as the purple-robe-wearing aristocrat who ignored old Lazarus.

Well, it did not take long for our marketing team to get on the case. We started spreading the word that *anyone* could get rich! We pitched "inspirational" stories of people "pulling themselves up by their bootstraps" (I know, the phrase makes no sense whatsoever, but the little ape-gods lapped it up). Over the years we reinforced the message with images, stories, and a few real "successes" of lucky gold miners, garage inventors, talentless celebrities, and the like. We also promoted the actual rags-to-riches stories that naturally occur when you have a few billion people just living their lives.

Soon enough, something *wonderful* happened. The poor loved money. The rich loved money. The poor envied the rich and the rich had contempt for the poor (who should have just grabbed their bootstraps, after all).

Now – this part is really very funny – the dirt poor, even an inmate without enough money to buy soup from the commissary, *loved* money every bit as much as the wealthiest financier. They obsessed about it. They craved it. They trusted it above all else. They put their faith in money even though they had none. No purple robes, no palace, no big barns, nothing. They just believed, with an abiding faith that filled their increasingly hard hearts, that if and when they actually *had* money, it would be the one thing that would never let them down.

Once we had them completely counting on something they did not have and would never get, things got *really* interesting. These filthy humans are stupid, but they are not completely delusional. Many of the poorest lovers of money will, after a few generations of failures, eventually come to believe they have little chance of getting the one thing they love...at least not by "legitimate" means. So, we recast the bootstrap stories with a new twist: the crooked businessman stories. These pseudo-parables (sometimes true, often fiction, always exaggerated) said that doing the bootstrap thing often, even mostly, involved some amount of cheating and stealing.

You know what happened next: the poor loved money, the rich loved money, and everyone came to believe that cheating and stealing was a common, even necessary, part of gaining money. If you were poor, stealing might involve burglary or black-market trade. If you were rich, it might involve lying on your taxes or breaking contracts or some other deceptive business practice. Our stories told them it was no big deal because pretty much everyone did this as part of pulling oneself up by his bootstraps (still makes no sense).

Think about the inmates all around you. Ask Woertz how many of them are in prison because they loved money and they believed everyone broke the rules to get it – from the richest tycoon to the neighborhood realtor. It was just part of the game. (That was another invention of ours, taking a long list of what used to be called "sins" and renaming them a "game." It is so much more friendly to say you are "running a game" than to say you are "drowning in sin," don't you think?)

By now you appreciate, I am sure, that it is ever so useful for you to keep your Inmate focused on loving money. The little miseries, like not having enough in his commissary account to buy deodorant, go a long way to keep money at the forefront of his mind. Keep whispering in his ear that it is the one thing he can trust. Keep encouraging him to believe that when he returns to the free world, money will be the one thing he can count on. Never let him doubt that money is the key to his future. (It is fine to keep it out of reach, but keep his mind focused on it nonetheless.)

Remember, our job while we have them here in prison is to prepare them for life in the free world. If they leave here loving and trusting in money, they are halfway down the road to our beloved home Below.

Your Penny-Wise Coach,
Deumus

THE LETTER PROBLEM

Dear Bentrock,

His mother's letters are indeed a nuisance for us. Sadly, there is nothing I nor Woertz can do to divert them. They are protected by the Enemy. We have previously tried to get our free world tempters to discourage her from writing, but she is protected day and night by the Enemy's forces. Woertz has tried to use our servants in the unit to "lose" them in the mail room, but those efforts always fail. The Enemy protects his mother and her correspondence in a way that puts them beyond our reach.

This is not to say, however, that there is nothing you can do. To the contrary, you still have the ear (and the heart) of your Inmate. The key to undermining these letters is already in your pocket. You just need to use it more cleverly.

One of the amusing things about the ape-gods is how often they can be persuaded that what a thing says is not at all what it means. A talented tempter, paired with the right sort of human, can routinely convince his prey that the meaning of something said or written is actually the opposite of what the author or speaker intended.

As you will recall from your training, there is an entire academic discipline in our universities called Real-Time Revisioning that studies this phenomenon and develops effective tools for tempters. This is a skill we do not normally introduce to novice tempters like you, but in this case, you will need to develop your expertise to counter the effects of his mother's correspondence.

The foundation of successful Revisioning is to create in your Inmate's mind a set of "filters" as well as a "lens" through which everything he hears or reads will pass. Just as an optical lens on a camera can be used to twist an image so it appears upside down, you can create a mental lens that will do the same. And just as optical filters can be used to block certain wavelengths of light, a well-constructed mental filter can do the same for the things your Inmate reads and hears.

To be more precise, when I say "create," I mean re-create. You will find that your Inmate, like most all humans, has already developed his own filters and a mental lens. Humans can sit in a crowded room with discussions happening all around them and not "hear" anything whatsoever. This is their filter at work. Similarly, they can listen to a spouse say, for example, "I love you" and, once it has passed through their mental lens, they will find in that statement proof that the spouse *does not* love them ("after all, the tone was not very heartfelt, and they always say that when they are heading out the door, which only shows it is just habit..."). Almost instantaneously the mental lens flips the image upside down. Our task is merely to fine-tune the instruments already in place to serve our purposes.

All this is helped a great deal, of course, by the culture of deception we have encouraged these past many years. The very useful phrase "white lie" has grown beyond its original meaning – a small and inconsequential deception that someone tells for the sole purpose of sparing someone else's feelings. White lies may now be told about most any matter and for most any reason. They have long since outgrown the limitation that they must serve to protect another's feelings. So long as the lie itself is not *too* big (in the judgement of the liar), it is a "white lie," and it is perfectly acceptable. Thanks in part to this redefinition of a white lie, it is now an article of faith among the ape-gods that "everyone lies." This is the rich soil in which we plant the seeds of Revisioning.

Before I describe our techniques, let me acknowledge that Revisioning is much easier and more effective in the free world than it is in prison (another reason why the Enemy is making inroads here). In the free world people rely mostly on videos, speech, and bits of rapidly disappearing electronic text for their information. It is far easier to filter out unwanted messages, or to adjust their meaning, when something is said aloud or temporarily appears on a screen. The prey cannot go back and re-read the sentence (at least not without effort).

Moreover, contemporary culture demands that its information sources, "just tell me the main points." It rejects any idea that the listener or the reader is responsible for considering, weighing, and processing the information. All of this is a huge help to us. The prey relies on its initial *impression* of what was said and feels no obligation to critically consider the information. This is far easier for us to manage.

In prison, by contrast, the letters your Inmate reads from his mother can be read and re-read with ease.

What is worse, he regards them as keepsakes, and saves them to re-read in the future. In these circumstances it is much more difficult to make things appear inverted. But difficult is not impossible.

We must begin with fine-tuning his filters. Dangerous words like love, hope, forgiveness, or any of their derivatives need to be filtered out. Consider these lines from his mother's most recent note, the one she wrote in that little greeting card he received last week:

We all miss you and we love you. All of us are looking forward to the day you come home.

These lines can pose significant risk for your work. They can pull your Inmate's attention back to things which would quickly lead him to the Enemy's camp. So, you need to tune his filter to ignore most of them.

We need to plant in his mind the idea that these words are just routine greetings with no real meaning. The easiest way to do this is to get him in the habit of using these phrases routinely when he is writing to his mother (I know this seems counter-intuitive). As he is writing those words you need to be whispering in his ear, "don't forget to put in there 'I love you and miss you etc. etc.'" or "put in the usual 'looking forward to coming home blah, blah, blah'."

Wrapping the sentiments with phrases like "etcetera" or "blah, blah" or "and so forth and so on" is a way for you to remind him that these are not expressing genuine feelings. They become, for him, the written equivalent of "have a nice day" – a meaningless verbal gesture. Once you have your Inmate using these words without any real meaning or emotion in his own letters, he will filter them out when reading the letters, he receives.

You also need to help him filter out the verses from the Enemy's books that she often includes in her correspondence. For your Inmate, this is not terribly difficult. You are building on work that was begun long before your Inmate ever arrived in prison.

For many years we have been telling him that "all this Bible stuff" is just an old book of nonsense from the Middle East. Like most of his peers, he thinks it is part myth, part scam, and wholly irrelevant. It has no more impact on his life than the *Egyptian Book of the Dead* (which he will have heard about, and it is a good comparison for you to keep in his mind).

The most effective technique for an Inmate like yours is to have him simply skip over these bits of the letter. (It is helpful that his mother tends to quote from a four-hundred-year-old translation of the Enemy's writings which contains language your Inmate finds difficult to comprehend.) Again, let's turn to her most recent note:

> *I pray for you always. Remember the promise of Jesus for you.*
>
> *"For God so loved the world, that he gave his only begotten Son, that whosoever believeth in him should not perish, but have everlasting life. For God sent not his Son into the world to condemn the world; but that the world through him might be saved. He that believeth on him is not condemned: but he that believeth not is condemned already, because he hath not believed in the name of the only begotten Son of God." (John 3:16-18)[3]*
>
> *I know that there is hope and there is salvation for you in our Savior. I pray that He will fill you with the Holy Spirit.*

These words are profoundly dangerous for your work and for the future of your Inmate! Fortunately, you can teach him to filter them out by simply skipping past the entire section whenever he sees a reference to a Bible book and verse. Work on this training every day. The prison is filled with little tracts and other materials that reference the Enemy's writings. Don't hide these from him, but instead point them out. Whisper in his ear phrases like "more Christian propaganda," and "at least we will never run short of toilet paper."

Encourage cynical thoughts to come to his mind as soon as he sees this material. Point out the real and imagined hypocrisy at every opportunity. I find that whispering thoughts like, "Christians seem to love prisoners as long as they are safely locked away," are very effective. The aim here is to make him dismiss the Enemy's writings in their entirety as outmoded nonsense. (It goes without saying that you do not want him to ever actually pick up one of these pamphlets or books and read it! So, remember to point them out when he is busy with other activities.)

By the way, if you do this well, he will become known around the unit for having contempt for the Enemy's writings. This is no bad thing, but sooner or later someone will challenge him by saying something like, "Have you ever *read* the Bible?" Prep him for this now. He should be ready to respond, "Have you ever *read* the Egyptian Book of the Dead? Then how do you know it's not true?"

While these two techniques are helpful and important, the most important thing you can do to undermine his mother's correspondence is to set unrealistic expectations about what they will, or more importantly what they *should*, contain. Before he receives his next letter, set his mind on specific things he is expecting to see. You can help with this by guiding the content of his own letters to his mother. Keep the focus on issues related to his legal case and his appeal. He should also pepper his letters with other requests. He should be asking for money and books. He should be asking her for news from his old friends on the outside and, of course, for news about his wife and his daughter. And he should be constantly seeking news of a visit from them (no matter how unrealistic).

As you are guiding your inmate's own letters to his mother, you are setting his *expectations* about what he *hopes* to see when she writes back. First and foremost, he should expect that his mother's letters will be, and certainly *should* be, filled with news about her progress helping him get out of prison early.

If you have done your work correctly, the moment he opens any letter from his mother the first thing he will do is scan it quickly for any news about an appeal lawyer, a parole package, or any change that might signal progress in his early release. Of course, his mother's letters will rarely contain anything about any of these subjects (legal processes run at their own, leisurely pace). If you have set his expectations correctly, within a few seconds of opening the letter he will have scanned it, realized there is no news about the "important" issues, and set it down with a feeling of great disappointment.

When he picks it up again, he will scan it for news about a visit or about money or friends, and so forth. Given her limited resources, this will also lead to disappointment, and he will once again set it aside. Just as with the humans sitting in a crowded room, if he is "listening" primarily for information about these subjects, then he will simply not "hear" the other things she writes because they will be filtered out.

By the time he resolves to read what she has written a third time, if you have set his expectations correctly, he will begin reading already frustrated, disappointed, and even a bit angry.

A quick word of warning, however, the Enemy may be guarding him when he is reading the letter, so you need to plant this idea in his mind well in advance. Whisper in his ear, "you hope that your mother will finally bring some news about a visit... but she will probably just send you a bunch of old Bible verses" or "maybe your mother will finally do her part with the appeals lawyer and not spend all her time looking up Bible verses." You get the idea. You want to firmly embed in his mind the notion that the Bible verses she includes are at best distractions and at worst convincing evidence that she does *not care* about him and is not doing the things he asked her to do.

I will talk more about this in my next letter. In the meantime, get to work on fine tuning his filters.

Deumus

_____

Footnotes:

[3] Editors' Note: In the original letter, Deumus did not quote John 3:16-18. Instead, he wrote "For the Enemy so_____," but it is my best guess that the Inmate's original letter contained this passage. I find it unsurprising that Deumus did not (could not?) write this in his own correspondence.

THE LETTER PROBLEM PART 2

DEAR BENTROCK,

As I told you, these filters are already in place and so it is not terribly difficult to modify them with a bit of effort and frequent repetition. Now that you are well on your way to teaching your Inmate to filter out large portions of his mother's letters, let's move to the more advanced work of building a lens that distorts the meaning of the words she writes.

Unrealistic expectations and heightened emotional sensitivity are essential elements to building a mental lens that changes the meaning of his mother's words. Let's start with the second element: we need to teach him to easily take offense at what his mother says. This should be easy enough since, as I noted in my letter about anxiety, one of your Inmate's greatest fears is causing his mother shame and disappointment.

Since you are inexperienced in the ways of the ape-gods it may not seem obvious, but it is a feature of these animals that they tend to deal with their own anxieties by getting angry with others for "making them feel" a certain way. It is great fun to keep a wife angry with her husband because "he makes me feel unattractive" or make a husband distant from his wife because "she makes me feel inadequate" or make a parent angry with a child because "she makes me feel like a bad parent" and so forth. They have a very natural tendency to take what they fear and blame someone else for it.

Since your Inmate fears causing his mother shame and disappointment, he is already predisposed to blame her for it. He is always on the verge of thinking, "she makes me feel like I will never be good enough." So, suggest that to him. I promise you, he will embrace it with just the slightest suggestion.

And here is the beauty of it: you will not even lessen his anxiety by turning it into anger. He will continue to think that one has nothing to do with the other. He is denying his anxiety about this anyway (and we are doing our best to keep it hidden for now). But you can present the imagined "evidence" that fuels his anxiety as "proof" that she does not think he is good enough. (Never mind that this is a completely nonsensical phrase. Good enough for what? She does not think he would make a good astronaut, perhaps? The point is to keep it vague – yes, that is a theme for us.)

If you repeat often and earnestly into his ear the idea that "she does not think you are good enough and she never did" he will begin to read her letters through a lens that completely changes their meaning. Let's return to the paragraph from her recent card:

I pray for you always. Remember the promise of Jesus for you.
...
I know that there is hope and there is salvation for you in our Savior. I pray that He will fill you with the Holy Spirit.

With his newly adjusted mental lens, he can read this and think, "what does she mean that she prays for me, and I have hope for salvation? That is just another way of saying that she is praying her God will turn me into the kind of son she always wished I was because she never thought I was good enough…" And with little effort and no drama we have turned her words upside down.

One last element of his mental lens is to read every letter carefully for the things she has *not* written. This is one of our most fertile strategies. If you can get him thinking about the things she has *not* written, subjects he had expected her to address, sentiments he thought she *would* express, then we have a clear field to fill in the blank space with material of our own.

As I mentioned in my last letter, we can set the foundation for this strategy by keeping him focused on unrealistic things over which she has no control or which are beyond her means (for example, the family visits, the appeals, money in his account). She will be reluctant to share discouraging news so she will tend not to speak about them at all. We can use this silence to encourage him to fill in the empty space with speculation that creates anger and distance from his mother.

Let's look at how this can all work together to undermine her correspondence. Below is the entire original text of that vulgar greeting card she sent last week:

Darling,

I hope this card finds you well and that things are looking up for you. I wish the food there was better but please try to eat, I do not want you losing so much weight. I hope to be able to send you a little something soon.

I pray for you always. Remember the promise of Jesus for you.

"For God so loved the world, that he gave his only begotten Son, that whosoever believeth in him should not perish, but have everlasting life. For God sent not his Son into the world to condemn the world; but that the world through him might be saved. He that believeth on him is not condemned: but he that believeth not is condemned already, because he hath not believed in the name of the only begotten Son of God." (John 3:16-18)

I know that there is hope and there is salvation for you in our Savior. I pray that He will fill you with the Holy Spirit.

We all miss you and we love you. All of us are looking forward to the day you come home.

With our various techniques in place this is how he will read this note (in other words, this is what it will say to *him* after it has passed through our fine-tuned filters and lens):

She is not even trying to talk to the attorney. Absolutely no news. She is not even mentioning my daughter, she is obviously trying to hide bad news from me. Once again, she is ignoring my need for money on my account even though she knows I am losing weight trying to eat this junk. I know she could afford twenty dollars a week. That would make a big difference.

And here she is going on again about how she is praying that I will become a different person because I was never good enough for her.

"SKIP OVER THIS crazy old myth, blah blah."

Have a nice day or whatever.

He sets down the letter disappointed, having filtered out the expressions of affection and the Enemy's words, and imagining what is "really behind" the things she neglected to say about those matters she *knew* were genuinely important to him.

Even if he sets it aside and re-reads it later, it is unlikely he will see anything close to what she intended. In fact, if you can encourage him along the way, you can build up even more resentment about the things she did *not* say and what her silence "really means."

You should continue to work on these techniques with him. Our immediate priority is his mother's correspondence but once you are effective at combatting those, you can use this same filter-and-lens Revisioning process to change what he reads and hears from any number of people and sources.

One word of caution, however, this process depends on keeping the conversation in his mind. Were he to show this card, or any of his mother's letters, to anyone who does not operate with a similar mindset they would immediately see the absurdity of his interpretation! There is a great risk that they would correct his perspective or worse, laugh at the ridiculousness of it. That laughter can shatter the lens you have carefully constructed and polished. So, it is important that you remind him these letters are *private* and should not be shared with anyone in the unit. Build upon Message Six to "never let your guard down." That should discourage him from sharing any of this.

Have a nice day,
Deumus

RESPECT

Dear Bentrock,

It was to be expected that your Inmate would eventually fall into a prison routine and begin to feel at home here. Now is a good time, therefore, to get him fixated on "respect." This one small word is among our greatest tools in the free world and even more so here in the unit. We want him to set his mind on demanding and commanding *respect*. He must believe that his very survival depends on it.

Naturally, what we mean by "respect," and what he and other inmates mean when they say this word, has very little to do with its traditional intent or meaning. You will realize by now that we use language to great advantage in our work. We will, from time to time, begin a campaign to redefine a powerful word or phrase that the Enemy has been using to teach or guide his creatures. It is an easy matter to find a few of the little ape-gods in academia, politics, and the arts to assist our efforts.

You will be familiar with some of our work. We

transformed Charity to mean donation, thereby robbing it of its moral weight and meaning. They no longer even have a word for what used to be called Charity. We have been mostly successful in redefining Hope to mean little more than a *wish* that something will come to pass. Our friend Mark Twain helped us redefine Faith to mean, in his memorably destructive phrase, "believing what you know ain't so." Today, the old phrase "Faith, Hope, and Charity," which served as a North Star for generations of the Enemy's servants, evokes little more "Fantasizing, Wishing, and a Tax Deduction."

Sometimes we dilute words by giving them a second, more ordinary meaning that robs them of power. Forgiveness, in its common business use, now means either a temporary deferral of a loan or at best eliminating a payment that is owed but saddling the beneficiary with a poor credit record they will carry with them for years. Forgiveness, in its everyday usage, means even less. When most ape-gods say, "I forgive you," they usually mean nothing more than, "I accept your apology for now, but you must live with the consequences on your own, and I will undoubtedly be reminding you of this incident in the future." Is it any wonder that the Enemy's "Good News" strikes them as less exciting than ever?

We have even transformed the shorthand meaning of literary characters (which you would think is all but impossible since their stories are written down, but no one reads anything these days). Uncle Tom went from meaning a Christ-like suffering-servant to being synonymous with cowardice and collaboration. With just the smallest bit of effort, Frankenstein is the evil monster and Pollyanna is the fool. The lessons taught by these characters, lessons that too often served the Enemy, are lost as they become caricatures that serve us.

Respect is one of those words that we have been busy transforming these past many years to mean something entirely different from what it used to mean, and now you can use this to encourage your Inmate and accelerate his destruction. As you will know, when humans said they *respect* someone, they used to mean, roughly, that they recognized and acknowledged the other person was virtuous and therefore admirable. In order to pervert this word, we shifted people's attention away from the *causes* of respect to the *effects* of respect. Since someone who was respected was often given a certain level of deference, it was a simple matter to convince people that respect *meant* deference and that it *only* meant that.

Well, as you may have observed, there are a great many ways to encourage deference among other humans. The most obvious is to have them simply fear you. We have reinforced this idea by whispering to countless inmates and others that the most *feared* person they see is the most "respected" person they see.

When you step back, you can see the process that we follow is simple enough. We redefined respect as deference. We convinced them that the cause of deference was fear. We showed them that fear was the result of power. In no time, respect meant nothing more than power, and now they were playing on *our* turf!

The humans had been told since childhood (and for generations) that people who lived admirable lives were "respected." After our redefinition program they came to believe respect equaled power. They did the rest all by themselves. It just logically follows that powerful people are admired and respected and therefore being powerful *must* be the same as living an admirable life. That is exactly how we got your Inmate to adopt his "law-of-the-jungle" philosophy I mentioned when you first arrived.

The next thing we concentrated on was, as you would expect, the word "disrespect." If respect was power and if this power is manifested in fear, then disrespect was any behavior that might indicate that one person did not show sufficient fear in the presence of another. Any slight might be an indication that your Inmate is being *disrespected*.

Having established this principle, it was obvious to everyone that when an inmate was "disrespected" (in his own mind or the eyes of another), the only way to "earn" his respect back was a raw demonstration of power. And with that we had arrived where we wished to be. What used to be the result of living a virtuous life is now transformed into a perpetual animalistic struggle to control the pack. (Our work is such great fun sometimes!)

I should address one last subject before discussing your Inmate: self-respect. It probably needs no explanation, but under our redefined concept of respect, the idea of self-respect also takes on a new meaning. Self-respect for your Inmate is now merely believing that he, himself commands enough power to instill enough fear in others that they would not dare to disrespect him. Naturally, embedded in this definition is the principle that self-respect also means *never allowing any behavior that might be interpreted as disrespectful to go unanswered*. It follows, then, that the only remedy to any real, imagined, or potential loss of self-respect is *always* a demonstration of power. In the free world this often entails complex and subtle acts of revenge. Here we prefer the straightforward path of blood and bruises.

Coming back to your Inmate then, you need to emphasize with him that being respected is essential to surviving in prison and to thriving when he leaves. His anxiety remains high, and you should be able to use this to plant the weeds of self-doubt. Have him question his self-respect. Never let even the smallest act – an accidental bump in the chow line, a mispronunciation of his unusually-spelled last name – pass without suggesting to him that this is proof the other person does not respect him. Emphasize to your Inmate that only the people in the unit who are most feared are properly respected.

These suggestions will provoke in him continued anxiety, anger, and a degree of self-loathing. He cannot possibly force the Corrections Officers, for example, to respect him (at least not under this new definition). So frequently reminding him that they do not will produce highly desirable frustration and anger. If you play your part well, you should be able to bring him into conflict with any number of other inmates and prison officials. Most importantly, you will be helping to build his character for when he returns to the free world.

Playing on his fears that he is not respected should build up a reservoir of resentment he carries with him when he leaves here. Your Inmate is certainly not the most physically intimidating person on the unit, so you may wish to play on this to increase his anxiety and encourage him to become more resentful. Remind him that others would not treat him this way on the outside if he had access to his _____ (fill in the blank with his preferred weapon). Build the resentment and try to turn it into hatred.

One note of caution as you play this game: never let

him dwell on people he *genuinely* respects. We have made great strides in redefining the word, perverting its meaning, and steering people to violence in its name. What we have *not* been able to achieve, however, is destroying the natural human instinct to admire and respect selfless, virtuous people. This is beyond our abilities (at least in the case of humans whose brains are not so damaged as to make them sociopaths – and they are of no use to us as they are beyond free will or persuasion).

From time to time the thoughts of your inmate will inevitably turn to people he truly admires and respects. It is especially important that you steer him away from these genuinely respectable people inside the unit (I have already mentioned Roach and his crew). It is also important that you employ the distraction techniques I shared previously if he begins to dwell too long on any of these or other examples he may recall from his days in the free world. You will also wish to suggest to him that such people are not *actually* respected, that they would not last fifteen minutes in *his* world, and so forth. But this will only go so far. As I have said, these humans have an instinct to respect the respectable. So, it is best to keep him distracted when his mind moves in that direction.

You should have great success with your Inmate on this matter. He seems just the sort of person who is self-conscious, anxious, and in need of other's approval. Start pushing our view of Respect. I think it will bear fruit.

Your Widely Respected Mentor,
Deumus

PS You may have heard early reports of our successes in redefining Love. We are now well into the late stages of making this word as convoluted and meaningless as

Respect. Indeed, among many humans Love is now synonymous with selfishness. I will write more about this at the appropriate time, but we believe we are making great strides in undermining one of the most important words the Enemy uses to reveal Himself to the ape-gods.

THE APE-GODS

DEAR BENTROCK,

You asked me why I so often refer to these humans as ape-gods when most of tempters tend to describe them as vermin or creatures. It is simply this: any good hunter needs to understand his prey. I call them ape-gods to remind you of the two natures of your quarry so you will be ready if and when he acts out of his (mostly dormant) spiritual nature.

You have been there long enough to see firsthand how these creatures are generally ruled by their primate instincts. (My letter on Respect should have underscored for you how easy it is, with a small linguistic sleight of hand, to get them to embrace their animal heritage.) From lust to anger to gluttony, these creatures rarely become untethered from their primate nature and most of our kind stay focused on exploiting this fact. In my experience this is a mistake, especially in prison.

Before going into the unique aspects of prison life, let me remind you of the inconvenient truth we confront:

these creatures *are* both primates and spiritual creatures that the Enemy has created. His intent is to use their primate existence to develop and shape their spiritual nature so He can have them with Him in some promised new heaven and earth. Even more outrageously, He has promised that they will be above the angels in this new creation! (Our experts tell us that such a thing will never come to pass. The falling out between the Enemy and our Master had something to do with this plan, though the details have been lost to history.) He has even promised to create for them some new and "perfect" physical body that will exist in this new creation.

Fortunately for our work, the little ape-gods spend much more of their lives living like apes than seeking to grow in stature to be able to "judge the angels." So, most tempters just keep them fixated on acting like the primate vermin they are. In the more difficult cases, we will work to corrupt their spiritual nature by concentrating especially on pride, but in today's world that is hardly necessary. We just fill them with abundant pleasures of "the flesh," as they used to say, fan their animalistic competitive embers, and our work is typically easy enough.

As often happens, the ape-gods themselves have been our greatest allies in keeping them concentrated on their primate nature. It has been popular among them to remind each other that "humans are just another animal." This humans-are-just-animals meme became popular among the educated classes in the nineteenth century as a smug comment to demonstrate that the speaker was educated and enlightened. It was shorthand amongst them to indicate that they had studied the modern natural sciences and understood the "reality" that humans were evolved apes.

Of course, if asked directly, few humans would agree that their kind are *merely* evolved apes. So, we do not put the question to them directly. Instead, we encourage them – with the invaluable assistance of their enlightened peers – to adopt language that supports the idea without being explicit about it. The educated classes have been doing our work during the past century to reinforce this in the popular mind.

They now refer to themselves as "male" and "female," for example, using the identical language to describe each other that they use to describe the lower animals (indeed, the phrase "lower animals" is no longer socially acceptable in many places). In the old, unenlightened world, they called each other "men" and "women." In doing so they were insisting that they were different than the lower animals. Horses, sheep, birds, and banana slugs were "male and female." Humans were "men and women." Happily, this is quickly becoming ancient history. Even your inmate has enthusiastically adopted the modern habit of referring to himself as a "male" rather than a "man." In doing so he reinforces the deception that he is merely an evolved ape, not any sort of ape-god. (It is delectable when the humans do our work for us!)

Unfortunately, the entire strategy is much more effective in the university than in the penitentiary. It is frequently surprising to free world tempters when they discover that it is here in prison – where humans are treated most like animals – that their spiritual nature is most likely to be exposed. When you take a person and keep him in a cage, schedule his feeding time, his bathing time, and his exercise time; when you put him on display for others to observe and monitor his every behavior; when you manage his actions with petty rewards and punishments; when you rob him of his name, stick him in a uniform, give him carefully choreographed activities to fill his day; when you strip him of the ability to make even the most basic decisions that define his daily existence; his primate nature is laid bare. Nowhere else in the Enemy's creation is he treated so much like an animal as prison.

But this has the perverse effect of causing him to rebel against this idea that he is merely another primate in a cage. In the free world, where these are all individual decisions of the humans, they feel empowered by their independence and rarely notice that they have defined themselves as just another, albeit more evolved, primate. In prison, where they are so obviously treated as animals, they begin asking questions that would have never crossed their minds when they were free: "who am I?" "what does it mean to be a human being?" and all the rest. It is very, very perilous ground for our entire enterprise. As I told you in my very first letter, the job of tempter in a prison is much more challenging.

In the free world these questions are easily sidestepped with clichéd and meaningless answers. Who am I? You are a male welder who works at... You are a female graduate of… with a degree in… You get the idea. It is easy to get them to define themselves by the insignificant "decisions" they made in their lives (never mind that most of these so-called decisions are artifacts of life's randomness and no more their doing than their height). The question of what it means to be a human being rarely comes into it. In the free world, should their thoughts ever begin to drift toward "who am I?" it is easy enough to distract them with a new hobby or a new romantic entanglement or even a well-timed "notification" on one of their ubiquitous screens.

Here in prison the answer to "who am I?" echoes from the walls of their little cage: you are primate number... residing in cage number... scheduled for work activity... and due for further evaluation on the future date of...

The answer is no different than that of their free world counterparts, but its insignificance and emptiness is terribly apparent to them. Without their ability to choose the basic activities of their lives, the illusion of meaning, significance, and purpose that keeps our free world primates distracted just melts away. Their spiritual nature is, as I said, laid bare. If they start to consider themselves – now naked and in a cage – the terrible, awful, incontrovertible truth occurs to even the hardest heart: *I was made for more than this.*

Much of my instruction, much of your work, is aimed at combatting the effects of this realization. But make no mistake, this realization is coming. It is coming for your Inmate just as it has or will for every man in this place. We do not have the tools to hide it so easily from them as we can in the free world. When this realization comes, your Inmate will have stumbled upon the great truth: he *was* made for so much more than this. He was made for more than this prison and more than this world. It is why we are interested in them (after all, we do not send tempters to the gorilla house at the zoo!).

That is why I call them ape-gods. Yes, they are vermin infecting creation and vile animal-hybrid creatures. We can make a good deal of progress with your Inmate by appealing to his animal nature, but we must never forget that the Enemy has given him a spiritual nature as well. Especially in this place, we need to always be working toward the corruption of both or we will most certainly fail. Know your Prey and don't underestimate the Enemy.

Serving The One Below, etc. etc.
Deumus

THE DROP-OUT

DEAR BENTROCK,

Your previous messages now make much more sense! A long-time contact of mine in the Ministry of Training and Selection has let me in on your little secret. Yes, I have learned that you are the grandson of His Awful Eminence Secretary Alastor. I am told by my reliable source that you were absent for much of your basic tempter training and that you skipped altogether your prison training. So be it. Family connections still carry a great deal of weight in our Realm.

Let me be clear: you should not think for a moment that you can leverage your grandfather's position and reputation to curry favor with me! I am confident, knowing old Alastor as I do, that he would be appalled (although also secretly gratified) to learn that you used his name to intimidate your instructors and avoid your training. Such petty intimidations will do no good with me. My position with your grandfather is well secured and I would not hesitate to remind you (or your grandfather) of the exceptional relationship I hold with our

Master following that special assignment I did for him some years ago (I am sure you have heard of it?).

I will, however, make this accommodation for you out of respect for my friendship with Alastor: I will do my best to coach you in the months ahead and cover some of the essential lessons you missed in training. There is no way for me to fill in all the gaps, of course, but I will do what I can to help you along.

In the end, however, your success or your failure is your own. Since you undoubtedly missed my favorite lecture, "Consequences of Failure," I would suggest you ask Woertz what happens to failed tempters. I have personally watched Alastor consume many, and I would be delighted to share the details if you ever need additional motivation to help you remain diligent in your work.

I will say no more about this but let us reset our relationship with these facts in mind. I will, out of affection for your grandfather, make my future instructions easier to follow for someone with little training and no experience in our arts.

Faithfully Serving the Master Below,
Senior Warden Deumus

THE DANGER OF DESPAIR

DEAR BENTROCK,

What does it matter what triggered your Inmate to start thinking about it? Perhaps it was the letter he received from his mother. Perhaps it was a song he heard on the radio or a comment he heard on the television. It might have been an off-hand remark from another inmate. What does it matter? I have cautioned you from the beginning that this was a danger and now it has happened. Your Inmate has drifted into full-on despair about his failure as a father.

I have warned you time and again that it is important to keep him distracted. Is it possible you misunderstood me when I wrote, "distraction is our greatest weapon?" Distraction can help prevent him from dwelling on eternal matters, from thinking too carefully about himself, and from reflecting about how he has treated others. I have cautioned you not to let him dwell too much on the things that make him anxious, and I had told you *explicitly* to hold this particular fear in reserve. Now you have made a mess of the situation.

I should not need to remind you that our free-world colleagues have, over many years, nurtured and encouraged the behaviors that have led to his failings as a father. I am particularly concerned that in this bout of despair your Inmate is getting dangerously close to recognizing their hand in his life! We must take great care to ensure that he does not begin to think along those lines. As you would have learned if you had attended training, should our prey ever truly recognize that our kind are actively steering them to Our Domain, they are usually lost to us forever. The effectiveness of our work depends on our invisibility.

As for this emotional collapse he is experiencing, there are certainly occasions when it is to our advantage to have the ape-gods stumble into the swamp of despair. When feelings of hopelessness are created by self-pity, for example, this swamp can become a wonderful life-long home in which we trap our prey. But your Inmate's despair is not born of self-pity. He is sinking under the very real weight of his own failures and mistakes. At times like these, many of our prey will call out to the Enemy for aid. Tragically, we know when they do so He inevitably sends help.

Fortunately, your description of the prey suggests to me that he is not in immediate danger. He is mostly troubled by the reality that his daughter is growing up without a father and that she will pay a price for his mistakes[4]. He fears that she will follow in his path. He is plagued by the idea that she will one day find herself living just as he is now: in a little cage like a primate in the zoo, fed by his keepers through the bars, on display twenty-four hours a day, completely reliant on the mercy, and subject to the whims, of his minders. (In this present state of despair that is how he pictures his situation.)

While this may seem especially worrying (hence the desperation in your last note), nearly every inmate in the system – or at least everyone over the age of thirty – is haunted by similar thoughts at one time or another. Sooner or later nearly all these inmates begin talking about their hope that young people, and especially their children, will not follow a similar path. It is common-place to hear them expressing a "wish" that they could do something to discourage the youngsters from making the same sort of bad decisions they made. Many fanta-size about the wise advice they would offer if only given a chance. Some even imagine dedicating their life in the free world to helping others avoid the same mistakes.

None of that is particularly problematic for us. It is mostly a meaningless emotional response that springs from their minds when the unpleasantness of prison wears on them a bit too long. I can assure you, from decades of experience, that few of them will retain this desire once they are released. Most will walk through the gates and immediately resolve to never think about prison again, the youngsters be damned (literally).

Even among those who do persist in this way of thinking, only a tiny number will ever make the effort, and even fewer are ever given the opportunity, to "make a difference," as they like to say. You may take solace that this way of thinking is mostly a harmless distraction. Indeed, we are generally able to use their "wish for better choices" in the next generation to our advantage.

As a first response, you should engage in a bit of false encouragement. Whisper to the Inmate that he is actually "a very a good person" for wishing that his daughter would choose a different path. That is often all it takes to shake the feelings of despair. Even better, encourage him to think that he not only wishes this for his daughter, but also for *all* young people and that makes him a very good person indeed! This sort of flattery will often help our prey feel magnanimous and even proud of how far they have evolved. Telling him that this proves he is well on the road to "changing his life" is an exceedingly handy tactic and it will discourage him from looking too intensely at his own spiritual health (which is, of course, the point).

As is probably beyond obvious, this approach is most effective when we are dealing with prey who have a high opinion of themselves and who imagine they have much to contribute to the world (chuckle). Your Inmate has not demonstrated particularly deep narcissistic tendencies, so I am less confident this approach will succeed in his case.

It is easy enough, however, to quickly assess if this line of attack will be effective. Whisper the idea in his ear and if he immediately perks up at the thought, you should keep pressing your case. If it seems to have little immediate effect, it is unlikely to work if you keep at it, so you are better advised to attack from a different angle.

A second, often easier, path out of despair is basic anger. The surest way to turn his despair into anger is to encourage him to blame others for his being here (essential message #1) and to blame others for failing his daughter. A combination of the two is most effective. This approach has the further advantage of helping to cultivate anger as a core personality trait.

In the case of your Inmate, I know you have been working for many months to reinforce the essential messages, including, "You are in this situation because of what others did to you." I understand from Woertz that your Inmate has decided his small group of close friends in the free world are chiefly to blame for his situation. You have done a good job of encouraging him to fault these friends for enticing him into the "lifestyle that led to prison" and encouraging him to blame them for his arrest and conviction. It is only a small step for him to now accuse these same friends of "leaving his daughter without a father." Whisper this repeatedly and in short order his anger toward them will be magnified.

Once he "realizes" that his friends are not only "responsible" for his own misery but are also to blame for his daughter "growing up without a father," you may bring other villains into the story he is constructing. The teachers and staff at his daughter's school are an obvious choice. Suggest to him that if they were "doing their jobs" properly, the effects of his absence would be minimal. Build on this theme. Tell him that there are millions of kids who grow up "just fine" without a father, and that this would not impact her life if the other adults around her would just do their part. Help him to resent them, not only for failing his daughter, but also for leaving the problem to him even though "they know full-well" he cannot do anything beyond writing a few letters and making the occasional phone call.

Once you have firmly implanted the idea that his daughter *ought* to be fine, even though he is incarcerated, if only other adults would do their job, you can build anger against any number of people who are part of her life. Parents of her friends, coaches, doctors, aunts, uncles, cousins, and, of course, her mother can all share the blame.

If you successfully plant this in his mind, you will be laying the foundation for a delightful bit of fun a few years from now. Once his daughter is older, it will be easy enough to help him start blaming her! When the day arrives (it always does) that he realizes she is a teenager who seems to be following a self-destructive path, your Inmate will be primed to say to himself, "I am tired of feeling as though this is all my fault. She needs to take responsibility. After all, there are millions of kids…" You can see how this will work, no? What joy you will feel when you persuade your Prey to blame the victim of his sin for the effects of his sinfulness!

If you can stoke his anger toward these groups, he will climb out of the swamp of despair and will no longer be at risk of turning to the Enemy. Indeed, if you do this well, anytime the idea of the Enemy crosses his mind you can just add Him to the list of those with whom your Inmate is angry. After all, the Enemy had it in His power to help your Inmate's daughter and *He chose not to*! At least the teachers were just incompetent.

Unfortunately, it is not at all clear to me that your Inmate's personality will lend itself very well to the intensity of anger necessary to climb out of despair. He seems to lean more toward resignation than the sort of seething anger that lies just below the surface in many of our prey. Once again, it should be easy enough to quickly test this. Suggest that his friends are responsible for the bleak future that he fears for his daughter. If he does not immediately begin to show signs of rage, this is not your best line of attack. Give it a try and if it does not yield results, you will need to turn to our trusted standby: self-pity. I will write more about this in my next letter.

Deumus

Footnotes:

[4] When the Enemy talks about punishing the sins of a father through three or four generations, we believe He is describing the reality that these decisions and actions have consequences beyond any individual's lifetime. (Of course, we focus our prey on the idea that the Enemy is being terribly "unfair" to the next generation rather than this more obvious point.)

A VERY UNFAIR WORLD

DEAR BENTROCK,

As I explained in my previous letter, when our prey fall into despair, we find ourselves at a very dangerous moment. At these times they will often turn to the Enemy. If the previous techniques I mentioned do not help your Inmate escape his despair, you must work to transform it into self-pity. While the swamp of despair is treacherous ground for us, the mire of self-pity is our second home.

To the casual observer, despair and self-pity look like close siblings, but we know them to be very distant relatives. Despair is born of the realization by our prey that their situation is hopeless. It steers their thoughts to the decisions and behaviors that brought them to this place. It frequently turns their attention to the impact their behaviors have had, and continue to have, on others. In other words, despair is often self-reflective and even unselfish.

Most dangerous of all, despair causes them to rethink what it means to have "hope," and to search for "real hope." In the depths of their hopelessness, they often have a rare moment of clarity. They glimpse the truth that hope cannot be found in the things of this world: not romance nor economic success nor physical strength nor intellectual acumen nor popularity nor political ideologies nor any of the many things in which the ape-gods misplace their confidence. If they glimpse that truth, they are only steps from the Enemy's camp.

By contrast, prey who are wallowing in self-pity will almost never look to the Enemy (beyond imagining Him as just one more cause for their woes). They turn outward to seek sources of blame. They concentrate on how desperately unfair life is – to them. Every source of misguided hope that despair might unmask becomes an adversary that self-pity can accuse: an unfair economic system; a rigged political system; an underprivileged family; a random genetic lottery. You get the idea. The villains of self-pity are lurking behind every rock and tree. Self-pity has become one of our most effective deceptions both in prison and in the free world.

It was not always so. In one of the tasty ironies of working with these creatures, it was the ape-gods' own efforts that made self-pity among our most effective techniques for isolating them from the Enemy.

At its core, self-pity involves helping the prey feel wronged, feel that he has been treated unfairly. Of course, he *has* been treated unfairly, or at least unequally. This great deception, like all others with us, is based on a truth.

In ages past, humans had little expectation that life was anything more than arbitrary. The pagans attributed it to the capriciousness of the gods. The Enemy's servants accepted that life's vagaries and His purposes were beyond their understanding (at least most of the time, after that well-publicized business between Our Master and Job).

For the past few centuries, however, the ape-gods have been on a mission to build a fair, just, and equal society in which people advance and are rewarded based on "merit." It is another recently invented article of faith with them – especially in the West where self-pity has become a way of life – that society is basically built on merit.

I probably do not need to tell you that this is complete nonsense. Even the word "merit" works to our great advantage. It has become synonymous with words like "deserve" or "earn" or "accomplish." They reassure one another that their promotion, or their place in university, or whatever, is based on merit. They have *earned* what they have thanks to their very enlightened and meritocratic system.

Never mind that none of these individual ape-gods have done anything to "merit" their health or intelligence or disposition or community or talents. All of those were given to them. Crediting someone with accomplishing these things is like complimenting a person's wisdom when he chooses winning lottery numbers. Never mind. Our more successful prey are not bothered by the foolishness of their conceit because it makes them feel better about themselves!

They bolster the fiction of the modern meritocracy by contrasting it with the old, unenlightened, and arbitrary world they imagine as history. "At least these days," they tell one another, "people are not born into aristocratic families where power and wealth are a genetic birthright." These days, it is all down to merit! (Chortle.)

The myth of the meritocracy serves two complementary objectives for us: the winners are filled with self-assured pride and feel almost no obligation to their fellow ape-gods, while the losers are plagued by either rage or self-pity. I won't spend time discussing how to exploit the winners' pride since it is beyond obvious that none of the inmates believe themselves to be in life's winners' circle – at least not for the moment. Rage and self-pity, on the other hand, are an easy sell to prey who see themselves in the losers' corner.

For your Inmate, guiding him into the culture of self-pity involves many of the same techniques we use for anger. The subtle difference here is that rather than emphasizing the malicious neglect of others, we emphasize the terrible unfairness of your Inmate's lot. Instead of finding people to blame, we turn his thoughts to wistful fantasies. "If only" is among our favorite phrases.

Given that your inmate already blames his friends for much of his current situation, a good starting point is to plant in his mind the idea that *if only* he had come from a slightly wealthier family, he would have never fallen in with the "wrong crowd" in the first place. (Even more, *if only* they had been from better homes, *they* would not have *become* the "wrong crowd.") *If only* he had been a bit taller, he would have realized his dream as a professional basketball player. *If only* he had turned right instead of left when the police gave chase... Really emphasize the unfairness and arbitrariness of it all. Remind him repeatedly that so much of what has happened to him was out of his control and is completely, terribly unfair.

Once the initial idea has firmly taken root, expand it to suggest that if only his mother and his brother had given him better guidance, if only they had spent more time with him, he would certainly have chosen a different path. But quickly follow this suggestion with what will seem to him a very charitable thought: "they did not know any better, they did the best they could, but that is just how they were raised as well." (If you are clever, you can sink him in the mire of self-pity while simultaneously feeling very proud of himself for pitying others.)

In any case, be cautious. We want him to feel sorry for himself, not to become angry with others. Nonetheless you need to take the risk of incorporating other people into his self-pity worldview. By expanding his list of people who have treated him unfairly, you are ensuring that if the spell of self-pity ever breaks it will naturally transform into anger towards others rather than becoming a very dangerous lurch toward self-reflection.

Remember that we are training him to adopt a self-pity mindset. The specifics matter less than the habit (you will have noted by now that the seed of every vice is a temptation, but it is watered and fully blooms through habit). You must repeat the process every day. Follow the pattern: whenever he identifies an area of disappointment, point him to an external cause or contributor, an arbitrary happenstance that left him on the wrong side of winning. Then help him to fantasize about how things might have been different, if only...

One additional note of caution: never lose sight of the fact that the entire mindset you are teaching is absurd. As with the Revisioning training we discussed previously, it is best if this conversation remains entirely in his mind. Should he share his thoughts with others, there is a risk that they will point out the obvious foolishness in his way of thinking (or worse, get him to laugh at his mindset). Yes, it is great fun to gather a couple inmates together who are trapped in the mire of self-pity and have pity-party, but even this is dangerous. I have seen instances where a couple of self-pitying ape-gods get together, the absurdity of the entire mindset becomes obvious, and the spell breaks for both. So best to keep it to himself.

I think your Inmate is just the sort who will thrive in the mire of self-pity. He tends to keep to himself; he is more reflective than most of the ape-gods; and beneath his crusty exterior he is prone to reasonably heartfelt emotions. Of course, it is true that he has suffered from a great deal of genuine unfairness (a lie based on a truth is always our firmest foundation) and life has indeed dealt him a very poor hand. You can use these things to our advantage.

I look forward to learning more about which technique proves most effective in shaking his despair. In the meantime, I will be left wondering how much easier this job would be, if only I had a properly trained tempter.

Deumus

OUR FRIEND ANGER

DEAR BENTROCK,

I am pleased to hear that your Inmate embraced his anger and that it has helped him to climb out of despair. I admit I am a bit surprised that the technique worked with him. Some humans naturally tend toward anger but, as I wrote previously, your man does not fit the typical profile. I would have thought self-pity was more his style.

Nevertheless, it is encouraging to learn that he is no longer wallowing in the mire of despair and no longer at immediate risk of turning to the Enemy. Based on your reports he appears to be on the highway to becoming one of those barely contained vessels of rage whose bitterness is aimed at the Enemy as much as anyone. That is tremendous progress and exploiting this newfound personality trait will be great fun.

You will need to work diligently to reinforce these first tentative steps he has taken. Our techniques to encourage anger have been considerably refined these past few years. As you may know, we have become exceedingly effective in the free world at creating – even in the most well-balanced prey – a reservoir of rage that we maintain just below the boiling point. If you skillfully cultivate this new tendency, the anger your Inmate has embraced can closely resemble an addiction similar to what they develop with drugs or alcohol[5].

In the same way we can create a high-functioning alcoholic or addict who is able to successfully navigate daily life while remaining handcuffed to the drug, we can fine-tune rage to ensure prey maintain civility at work and in public while routinely igniting in more private settings. We find this is especially effective to maximize damage to family and friends. You will learn that once his rage reservoir is established and well stocked, it will require only the slightest effort to increase the temperature and watch it boil over, even among the most calm and agreeable sorts of people.

As with so much of our work, building a well-constructed reservoir demands planning and considerable advance work on our part. The steps you have taken with respect to your Inmate's daughter will prove an excellent start. You now must get about the business of deepening and broadening his reservoir so it will be complete when we need it.

Given your limited experience with the ape-gods, I should begin by helping you distinguish the different sorts of behaviors we see in these creatures. First, there are the humans who are naturally quick to anger. As best we can tell (we spend very little effort trying to understand their physiology), these humans have a physical defect of one sort or another in their mental processing organ. There are several ways to spot prey with this sort of physical damage: they generally have difficulty putting their emotions into words (even in their own minds) and they tend to be volatile when it comes to other matters as well – from sadness to laughter.

Prey with this sort of hardware defect are not particularly good targets for temptation. In my experience, the Enemy makes allowances for physical infirmities of all sorts and finds other ways to reach them. With the right technique, however, we can create a similar pattern of behavior in people with perfectly functional hardware. This is the situation we have with your Inmate.

Just as anxiety is most effective when its cause remains vague, frustrations and resentments are also more corrosive when the prey cannot clearly identify the source. This leads them to a state of persistent frustration. Prey left in this state are easy to anger in most any situation.

Here in prison, just as in the free world, the most important step in constructing an anger reservoir and creating a state of persistent frustration is to develop in the prey's mind a story, or "narrative" in which groups of people and various institutions are divided into good and bad, truth-tellers and liars, victims and oppressors, light and darkness, right and wrong. When inmates arrive in prison, they already have a narrative, or worldview, that has been developed over years. Our job is to reconstruct their existing worldview to fit their new situation, but we are always building on their free-world experience, so it is best for me to begin there.

Since the Enemy first created the ape-gods, we have been in the business of dividing them into opposing groups. Our Master Below recognized right from the start that their natural desire to engage in community – which the Enemy created to help them thrive – could be twisted to create divisions. As soon as one group forms (it can be something as inconsequential as a group with similar physical characteristics, a cadre that shares a particular point of view, or a collection of ape-gods who happen to reside within a random boundary on a map) we begin to plant the idea that "other" groups are a threat. Their natural desire to protect their "own" community is easily distorted to become a very unnatural desire to despise the "other" ape-gods.

In the free world we have become expert at creating these divisions. We have perverted many popular types of entertainment to become what we've dubbed angertainment. The transformation from entertainment to angertainment has been especially successful with news programs, talk radio, and sports programming thanks to the enthusiastic support of the humans themselves.

The ape-gods who run these media enterprises have discovered that when they make their viewers or listeners angry, when they convince them to despise whatever group or person or organization is on offer for the day, the audience is all but guaranteed to "tune in again tomorrow," as they say, to learn about the latest threats and most recent offenses involving the bad people.

Our angertainment industry is sustained by blending two of our specialties: greed and pride. The ape-gods who run the media companies use these angertainment programs to sell our prey various goods. That makes the angertainment very lucrative. The angrier their viewers get, the more they tune in, the more they can sell various trinkets, the more the owners are rewarded. It is a delightfully venomous circle of animosity and greed. And then we add pride.

Part of our strategy is to encourage detailed, specific,

and clear public declarations from the angertainment celebrities. We encourage them to declare that some person or group or organization is a threat. That is where pride comes in. Once we have a public declaration, the celebrity is committed to his or her "narrative." Pride won't allow them to retreat. Pride demands that their side must be the "good" side. Pride tells them that they must be right. So, they search for, manipulate, or just fabricate examples and evidence to support their public declarations.

Nowhere has our angertainment strategy been more successful than in their "web." Here, in an absurd and banal forum they call "social media," we have created an angertainment platform where each individual ape-god can be a celebrity commentator complete with followers, fabricated examples, and public declarations of enemies.

We find that the ape-gods are surprisingly clever and inventive when they are creating profitable new mechanisms to exploit one another. They have developed various techniques to serve up the precise messages that will keep someone engaged. The tailored content is engineered so it is not too obvious, but not too subtle; not too infuriating, but not too ordinary; it is just enough to keep the individual "engaged" and, of course, angry.

As you will no doubt recognize, the social media ape-gods have finally discovered how to replicate what we have been doing for millennia: customize temptations to each individual's greatest weaknesses so they tune out the Enemy and remain engrossed in themselves. It is a beautiful thing. The ape-gods have become their own best tempters, their own best demons. And they are selling the souls of their neighbors for a pocketful of money and a few trinkets that will quickly rust away.

The cost of betrayal is now far less than thirty pieces of silver.

Sorry, I have digressed (but I do so *enjoy* my work). Obviously, you cannot leverage social media with your Inmate, but you certainly can borrow the techniques.

If we tune the level of frustration just right, we can even get the prey to fantasize about getting angry with imagined enemies. They conjure up an image of a despised "other" – sometimes while awake and other times while dreaming – and they imagine what they would say or do. They imagine the comeuppance or revenge they would exact. It is as alluring as lust with a small fraction of the complexity!

I want you to work closely with Woertz on this matter. As this letter is already long, and I am painfully aware of your short attention span, I will write more on the subject tomorrow.

Diabolically Yours,
Deumus

———————————————

Footnotes:
[5] Speaking of drugs, in a previous letter you had suggested tempting your Inmate with drugs in prison and I had meant to get back to you on the topic. Unlike our free-world colleagues, here in the prison system we do not lean much on substance abuse to soften our prey. Drugs of various sorts are certainly available here, but not in reliable enough quantities to serve our purposes beyond setting the occasional trap. It is true that your free-world predecessor relied on narcotics to steer your

Inmate to this place, but it is not a reliable tool while he is in here. When your Inmate receives notice that he will be returning to the free world, I will teach you how to reawaken those cravings. But for now, this is not a dependable technique for you to use with him.

THE ANGER MIRAGE

DEAR BENTROCK,

Yes, I understand I careened far off the subject in my previous letter. I hope you learned something! In any case, we can now see that my initial judgement was correct. Your Inmate is not leaning toward anger at all but has instead slipped into the mire of self-pity. As I told you previously, these two are closely related and your Inmate's personality lends itself far better to self-pity than anger. At this stage I will instruct you to reference my earlier note on self-pity and to give your full attention to developing this habit.

The next time you see flashes of anger in your Inmate, I trust you will better understand that these are momentary, natural outbursts for humans wallowing in the mire of self-pity. An ape-god that is fully habituated to self-pity will often become temporarily angry (even for hours or days) before he settles back into the comfortable "if only" habits to which he has become accustomed.

I will, however, take a moment to address the

concern you raised about morally justified, or "righteous," anger. Even though it is far from your Inmate's current state of mind, it is best to keep a watchful eye for the behavior. You are quite correct that not all anger works to our advantage. Even the Son Himself was given to bouts of fury when He took on the primate form and walked among them. You were also correct in identifying the trouble when your Inmate became angry after seeing the C.O. stealing from his celly. But it was, I suspect, just a one-off reaction based on a long-forgotten childhood lesson. I doubt it will be a threat to your work.

To directly answer your question: no, there is no risk that training a prey to embrace anger will lead to the sort of righteous anger endorsed by the Enemy. It is an ironic feature of these humans that those who have a well-established anger reservoir are very rarely, if ever, given to bouts of *righteous* anger. The sort of anger we foster with the help of our angertainment industry friends, is always scanning the horizon for evidence that one of their despised groups of "others" is up to its usual tricks. It is nearly impossible to bridge from this mindset to righteous anger.

The reason for this should be apparent, even to someone as uneducated as you: our sort of anger is built upon a foundation of suspicion and hatred while righteous anger arises out of love – love for their neighbors and love for the Enemy himself. If one of our "angry inmates" had witnessed the thieving C.O., it would only have sparked anger if the officer was among the groups he despised and the celly was not. In such a case, the theft itself would be nothing more than reinforcing evidence for his worldview. Otherwise, he would tend to shrug it off.

The worrying thing about your Inmate's reaction to

the theft was that it originated not from hatred toward the C.O. but from affection and concern for his celly. Even more troubling, it arose from an instinctive outrage against injustice. To be genuine righteous anger, the emotion must be spurred by a concern for others and aimed solely at ending or reversing the injustice. Righteous anger is never selfish. It is never vengeful. It is always fleeting – arising at the threat to another and subsiding when the threat has passed.

So yes, your Inmate experienced genuine righteous anger and that is something we need to carefully monitor. But as I said, it is the only time we have seen this sort of behavior from him, and I suspect it was a reflexive response based on a long-forgotten lesson from childhood.

As a precaution, I have asked Woertz to take the usual steps to change out your Inmate's celly. I think it best not to allow the affection that has grown between them to deepen. As for your own work, I expect you to give your full attention to building a habit of self-pity in your Inmate. This should keep him well out of reach of the Enemy's servants.

Your Mentor in Brevity
Deumus

SEXUAL APPETITE

DEAR BENTROCK,

You could not be more wrong about finding it "hope-less" to stoke your Inmate's sexual desire. You complain that "there is little opportunity for him to become infected by the virus of lust" since he encounters "few suitable partners and has little access to pornography." I must tell you that as I read your letter, I was left disgusted by the lack of creativity we find in your generation of tempters!

Surely even you will know that this reliance on pornography and casual sex is a recent phenomenon! It is true that over the past century we have facilitated nearly universal access to pornography, especially among young people. Our success has created generations of humans whose view of intimacy is so twisted it would feel right at home in the courts of Catherine the Great or Caligula. All this has certainly made our work easier, but it is hardly *necessary* to spread the virus.

Step back, just for a moment, from your adolescent focus on titillation and think about the fundamentals of lust. Our modern attack on chastity was not built on pornography, it was constructed on a much firmer foundation. Among our greatest achievements in this area of human behavior has been blurring the distinction between needs and desire. Sexual gratification was formerly seen as a *desire* – albeit a powerful one. Now it is well-established amongst our prey that routine sexual gratification is a basic human *need*. It is now recognized to be as essential as, say, eating (slightly less urgent, perhaps, but no less necessary). Your Inmate, like nearly all humans, believes this to be true.

Having established sexual gratification as a basic human need, we then elevated it even beyond ordinary, actual needs like eating. Among the female prey in particular we have raised the importance of the little biological function to such an extent that they speak about their "sex life" as if it were among the most fundamental aspects of their existence.

None of them – the males or females – seem to recognize the absurdity of the thing. They would not consider for a moment speaking about their "nutrition life" or their "bowel-movement life," but we have successfully persuaded them that their "sex life" is a defining characteristic of who they are.

We have elevated this single, relatively unimportant, animal behavior to be on par with the essential aspects of what it means to be an ape-god. In previous eras they spoke about their "intellectual life," their "spiritual life," their "family life," and even their "love life." All of these are things that distinguished them from the beasts. Now they speak of the "sex life" as if it were comparable.

With this success as a backdrop, we trot out our experts to offer up the latest thinking about what it means to have a "good and satisfying sex life." The standard is, as you would expect coming from us, vague and always evolving. Our experts always emphasize the key point: if one's own experience does not meet this standard of "good and satisfying" it is proof positive that their partner or their relationship is defective. Naturally, it is impossible to meet the standard since it is vague and always evolving!

In short, we have created a situation in which this little biological function carries outsized importance and is a constant source of dissatisfaction, conflict, and disappointment.

In some respects, the success of this campaign has exceeded even our greatest hopes. It is commonplace today for people to actually define themselves by the sort of sexual partner they prefer. No kidding! If you ask them to describe themselves, a great many of the ape-gods will put a description of their preferred sexual partner at the top of their list ("I am a gay man," for example). In our surrealist version of life, they have come to believe that describing the sort of sexual partner they most desire is among the very most important things about them.

Most delightfully of all, and I suspect to the great consternation of the Enemy's forces, we have been able to persuade them that all of this is somehow "empowering." They ignore the plain truth that they have become slaves to our vague and constantly changing definition of a good and healthy sex life. They instead tell themselves that this modern, enlightened culture has "empowered" them to seek out ever more satisfying orgasms with whatever sort of partner they prefer. Having a good "sex life" demands nothing less!

Never mind that sexual satisfaction is always fleeting. It almost never occurs to them that no human has ever discovered the sex act or partner that finally satisfies the desire. It cannot be satisfied, except for short periods, before it lurches in a different direction. They are enslaved to pursuing the unattainable goal we have set for them. They call this empowerment.

While they seem unable or unwilling to recognize that a satisfying sex life is an unattainable goal, they are all-too-aware that their own sex life falls short. A few minutes of hydraulic hijinks, no matter how skillfully executed, cannot possibly deliver the deep and profound satisfaction we promise. You might expect at least a few of them to question whether the promise is a lie, but they do not. This is due in significant measure to our experts reassuring them that "it's you and your relationship" that is the problem.

Lest they fall into despair over the inevitable fact that their sex life is underwhelming, we market the idea that any good and healthy relationship, built upon the foundation of a "good and satisfying sex life," ought to be supplemented by a "good and vigorous fantasy life." It is here that we begin with your Inmate.

The job of a prison tempter is to continue the work of your free world predecessors and encourage his "fantasy life." And while the external stimulus of women and pornography may make things easier for our free world colleagues, they are completely unnecessary to develop the sort of desire that will keep your Inmate shackled to our camp.

In your prison work, it is always best to begin with your Prey's personal experience. Suggest to him that a robust fantasy life involving his wife is both healthy and wholesome – and, of course, a basic biological need. Get him into a routine where he has regular time for fantasizing. When he settles in for fantasy time, he will naturally turn to his personal experiences to replay particularly satisfying memories. Your role is to make small changes to the videos he plays in his head, introducing new activities, props, locations, and other partners. Do this gradually. It will not take long before he is indulging in a healthy fantasy life that is completely disconnected from his wife and from any sort of plausible reality.

As you cycle various faces (and bodies) through his fantasies – we prefer real people he has seen or met – his view of these individuals will be subtly transformed from humans into puppets whose primary purpose is to satisfy his ever-evolving desires. If you do this well, he will eventually begin to confuse the real human and the puppet version that exists in his fantasy world.

One of the Enemy's servants[6] observed that the Enemy had intended for the ape-gods to "use things and love people," but they had instead developed a habit of doing just the opposite: "using people and loving things." It was a dangerous insight (which fortunately caught the attention of very few of them). Your objective in encouraging his "healthy fantasy life" is to reinforce the idea that people are things to be used and to create an ever-expanding library of scenarios (each one less plausible than the last) in which he uses them.

One last point on this: it is crucial that you emphasize the idea that the people who appear in his fantasies secretly *want* and *desire* exactly the sort of thing he imagines. You are aiming to create in him an expectation that the real versions of his imaginary partners are secretly fantasizing along the same lines. (Yes, we do the same with our female prey, but we tend to focus on somewhat different, though equally unrealistic, scenarios.)

If you do this well, your Inmate will indeed spend his

days in prison burning with lust for imaginary versions of partners who are well out of reach. He will come to believe that their greatest secret desire is to act out the roles he has created for them in the video library of his "healthy fantasy life." He will believe that they, too are imagining something similar in their own healthy fantasy lives. He will leave this place ready for a lifetime of disappointment, primed to treat others as objects for his personal pleasure, chasing a satisfying sex life that is unattainable, and all the while believing that if he does not achieve it, he is failing at one of the most important and basic human needs.

Yes, the tools of pornography, casual sex, suggestive language, revealing clothing, and all the rest make it far easier to spread the virus of lust amongst our prey, but they are hardly necessary. As our Master is fond of saying, it may be easier to drown a man in the ocean, but a bathtub will suffice.

La Vida Tentador
Deumus

Footnotes:

[6] Editor's Note: This comes from Rob Renfroe's *The Trouble With The Truth*

THE ROACH

Dear Bentrock,

So, you have seen The Roach. I previously warned you to keep your Inmate far away from him and now you can see why. He is the most dangerous man in the unit: a lifer with nothing left to die for. You must steer your Inmate well clear of his path.

Roach is one of the deadliest soldiers in the Enemy's army. He is not well educated, he is not particularly articulate, he is obviously not physically attractive, his manners and habits are barely civilized, and he has a tendency toward anger and violence so deeply embedded in his physiology it can never be completely overcome. You might think, with all these obvious flaws and many more besides, we could easily return him to our path. We cannot. He is lost to the Enemy.

Roach came to this unit decades ago, serving a life sentence without the possibility of parole. Before arriving, he spent many years doing our work in the free world, and he was considered an effective and reliable soldier for our Master Below. He specialized in producing petty terror in his community. Dangerous and unpredictable, even his family kept their distance. He was feared, despised, and isolated. (Or, as your Inmate would say, "respected.")

We fitted him with the full complement of our armor: the belt of Cynicism, breastplate of Anger, the helmet of Spite, and on his feet he wore the boots of Recklessness. We equipped him with the shield of Pride, the sword of Hatred and we filled his quiver with the arrows of Hopelessness (what the Enemy's servant Paul called "the flaming arrows of evil"). He was havoc unleashed, at least in the little community where he operated.

We have millions of Roach-like servants comparably equipped and living across the planet. They thrive best in the poorest communities where darkness abounds, and they can operate with less interference.

Of course, soldiers like him are inherently unreliable servants for our side. They still have free will so the best we can do is equip them with our unique armor, encourage them in a particular direction, and unleash the chaos. Sooner or later, most of them arrive in a unit like yours. Most often, especially when they are condemned to a lifetime of incarceration, they come to believe they have nothing to live for and they descend further into our ways. They lead the prison gangs, they are beacons of despair, and they are invaluable to train the next generation who are, like your Inmate, only there for a short time.

Occasionally, however, the Enemy gets His hands on one of them. Roach found his way into the Enemy's camp through a free world volunteer who arrived in the prison one weekend. (I will share more about the dangers of this in a future note, but know that while many prison volunteers are harmless, and some are even useful to us, they can have a devastating effect on our efforts if they are allowed to work in the Enemy's cause unchallenged.)

The Enemy tore off Roach's armor piece by piece. It was awful. Roach allowed himself to be stripped completely naked – shorn of his pride, his hate, his cynicism and spite, his anger, and his despair. He stood before the Enemy like a small, helpless child. It was disgusting. The man who had been Chaos Unleashed – despised and feared by all who knew him in the free world and in prison – became a disgusting, sniveling, fragile, broken, beggar, pleading "help me, forgive me."

I will not describe it further. I hope you never witness such a terrible scene. (Needless to say, it came at an indescribable cost to Woertz's predecessor, who was supposed to be guarding against this risk.)

We did not see Roach for many months after the terrible event. He was hiding behind the curtain the Enemy puts up around those who return to Him like broken children. We have tried since the beginning of time to penetrate this curtain, or even to see through it and understand what is happening, but we have never been able to do so. It is impenetrable.

When Roach finally emerged, the Enemy had clothed him in a completely different sort of armor. He was no longer the fierce warrior of Chaos Unleashed, he was now something far more dangerous: the humble servant with his gaze fixed unwaveringly on the Enemy. Our servants mocked and ridiculed him, but his pride had been ripped away. We whispered truths that would lead most people to despair – that he would be trapped here for the rest of his life, that his family had abandoned him and would never forgive him – but he was impervious.

He had placed his hope entirely in the promise of the Enemy.

Eventually we pulled together all our servants and all our tempters in the unit. We turned to our most reliable and proven strategy for winning back Roach: we put small, inconsequential little temptations in his path. For people who have stood naked and broken before the Enemy, a grand public reversal is almost impossible to achieve, but gradual indulgences in lust or envy or self-pity or doubt have proven effective in slowly leading them down that very gradual slope to our wide and straight road.

Not for the Roach! He was a lifer. He could see that none of those temptations would be real. They were not enough to pull him off the path. He said, "Nothing in this world is worth dying for." (By this he meant dying *spiritually*, the real death which these stupid humans normally discount as unimportant even as they do everything in their power to stave off physical death which is both inevitable and *actually* unimportant.)

Roach was lost. Worse, he has been an inspiration to many inside the unit who are trying to follow in his path. (Most will fail because they have never been willing to come completely naked and broken before the Enemy. That is something He seems to insist upon for reasons we do not understand, but we have used this to divert a good number of people from his path by convincing them to hold on to just one thing, like their Pride.)

As it stands, our best strategy with Roach is to get his sentence commuted. We are working on that. If we can only get him out of the prison, we have a chance of convincing him that there is hope in worldly things. But that is a long project, and it may not be successful. In the meantime, we *must* do our best to keep inmates like yours as far away from him as possible!

Fortunately, this is not as difficult as you might imagine. While Roach delights in sharing his life with anyone who will listen, there are a cadre of hangers-on who surround him in the unit and discourage others – especially new inmates – from approaching him. So, keep your Inmate far away from Roach while we work to arrange his release.

Serving the Master Below,
Deumus

GETTING OUT

Dear Bentrock,

From the very beginning of your work here we have tried to keep your Inmate's gaze fixed on getting out of prison. It is our most common and reliable tool of distraction for incarcerated men and women, and it is the one great advantage we have in the prisons that we do not have in the free world. In this place nearly everyone is hoping for and fantasizing about the day when they will leave. Now more than ever, with time dragging on and the day of his release seeming more remote than ever, we need to re-energize his hope for eventual release.

I say this is the one great advantage we have in prison, but naturally we do the same in the free world to the extent we are able. We start when they are teenagers. In those early years we keep them fixated on becoming an adult and getting out of school. As with most teens, we persuaded your Inmate that when he became an adult he would finally arrive at his destination, and he would leave his disappointment and frustration behind.

We do this generation after generation. (You would think it would have occurred to the young by now that their arrival to adulthood is always met with anxiety, disappointment, and distress, but it doesn't.) For our purposes, the false hope of adulthood is a bottomless well of distraction among people coming of age. They are easily encouraged to adopt a single-minded focus on the independence and freedom they believe to be just over the horizon.

This was not always the case, of course. In many times and places in their history young people looked toward adulthood with trepidation. It meant going to war or becoming a primary provider for the family or being married off to someone they did not know. In those cases, youth was often a time of great spiritual focus. But in the mostly comfortable and mostly peaceful modern world, their thoughts lean naturally toward anger and rebellion born of entitlement and privilege. So, our work with this group is surprisingly simple and one tempter with a smartphone can easily handle hundreds of middle-class suburban teens.

In the case of your Inmate, who could see much sooner than most that adulthood would be no oasis, we began early to reorient his gaze toward other things on the horizon. For a time, it was the imagined life he would have as a father after his daughter was born. Then it was getting the job that never materialized. Finally, we kept him occupied for several years thinking about his "business" and how achieving a level of financial success was all he needed to truly arrive and leave the streets behind.

It will no doubt seem obvious to you that this is just a variation on the same theme we use with your Inmate when encouraging self-pity. It is yet another "if only" deception but instead of coupling it with hopelessness, we combine it with the empty promise of false hope. Unfortunately, for people like your Inmate this is not our most effective strategy. Success in this world seems to them so unlikely, and the success we promise is so implausible, that it is nearly impossible for us to consume their thoughts with false hope for the future.

All of this is so much easier for our colleagues who are assigned to more privileged and successful prey. The only thing those tempters need to do is point their prey at a career ambition or a political objective or even something as trivial as a weight-loss goal, and they will race ahead with their famous tunnel vision engaged, and their trademark disregard for all those they encounter. After all, this is what makes them "successful." Their past achievements (which is what they call the mostly good fortune they have enjoyed) provide them confidence that they will be able to arrive at this new destination. Their natural optimism makes it all too easy to convince them that this new destination – whatever it is – will provide the purpose, fulfillment, and happiness that still eludes them.

I must confess that I am not entirely certain why this is the case. One would think that the "successful" prey, with their long history of hopping from one oasis mirage to another, would have long since discovered that purpose, fulfillment, and happiness cannot be found at any of them. One would think that, but one would be wrong. Back in the days when I was tormenting suburban free world prey (one of my favorite assignments) I delighted in my ability to draw them from one distraction to another. I could have them spend years striving for a new house in a different neighborhood only to see them arrive and discover it was still just a house and the new neighbors were not much different than the old. But just as the disappointment was sinking in, I could shift their gaze to the next oasis (a career objective, a milestone with their children, a vacation, almost anything would do).

As I said, however, for people like your Inmate (whose vision of a brighter future might involve not having the lights cut off next month) we have two problems: he struggles to imagine an oasis on the horizon that is particularly tempting, and a lifetime of disappointment gives him little confidence he will ever arrive.

Amusingly, when we get people like him to prison, all of that changes. Now the oasis is "getting out." For the first time in their lives, we have a perfect means of giving them false hope for the future. They finally have an imagined destination that is so much better than their current situation that it seems genuinely worthy of hope. They see enough of their peers get out to believe it is genuinely achievable – even for them. It is a mirage in the desert that even a convict can see and race towards with blinders on – at least so long as we can help him hold onto the fantasy version of what life will be like when he leaves here. Believe me when I tell you that most of the men in this place will pin their life's hope on that magical day, no matter how remote, when they walk out of the gates.

Your task, then, is to continue building up in his imagination how wonderful things will be when he leaves. But make sure these fantasies do not drift too far from reality or the mirage may evaporate. Encourage discussions among his peers about simple things like what they will eat first when they get out or what sort of bed they will sleep in or movies they might attend. These little things may seem insufficient to hold his gaze, but it is really no different than what we do with the free world types who can spend a year or more planning a wedding or a vacation. With the right encouragement, an ape-god will become endlessly distracted by food and guests and activities.

It is also important that he begin to think in great detail about how his life will be different once he returns to the free world. He should imagine that he will be treated with greater respect by the crew he left behind. He should imagine that his family will see that he is "getting his life together" and admire him for it. He should imagine that his wife will be delighted to see him (queue the mental videos from his healthy fantasy life!). He should especially imagine what a great father he will be when he arrives at home. Never doubt that even the most hardened criminal will fantasize that he has a Hollywood-style perfect parenting relationship in his future.

Remember, we are trying to do two distinct things here: we are helping him to define success and happiness in a manner that shields him from the Enemy's overtures, and we are helping him to set unrealistic expectations that can ensure his failure when he leaves. If we get this right, he will become so disappointed when he returns to the free world that he will swiftly slide into anger or despair and in no time, he will be running as quickly as he can to get back here, or at least to remain on the wide and straight road to our Domain.

Deumus

IMAGINING HIS HAPPY FUTURE

DEAR BENTROCK,

Your response to my previous letter leads me to believe I have failed to communicate the most important point about his planning for the future: he must believe that his incarceration is the *cause* of all his troubles. You can never let him imagine it is a *symptom*. This is the whole point.

Step back from your prison perspective for a moment. Nearly all our human prey – at least all of them who are not fully embedded in the Enemy's ways – are extremely predictable. They live their lives repeating the same pointless cycle: imagine some change in their situation that will make them happy; begin to fantasize about the improved circumstance and how much better it will be; embark upon a path that they believe will lead them there; arrive (sometimes); experience momentary gratification followed by disappointment followed by imagining a new change in situation that will make them happy. Repeat as necessary until time runs out.

Spend time listening to a conversation between a pair of ape-gods getting to know one another. One will invite the other to "tell me about yourself." Listen carefully to the response. They will recite a list of milestones in their lives: new towns or houses where they moved, the new jobs they accepted, the degrees they were awarded, their marriages and divorces, and so on. Each of the milestones represents an oasis they were seeking, a place or a circumstance where they believed they would find happiness.

Listen carefully and you will realize that this list of milestones is not incidental to the story of their lives, it *is* the story of their lives. Most of the ape-gods define their lives by the oases and mirages they spent their years rushing towards. Even in their own telling, it is a journey of hiking toward a hundred urgent destinations with no clear objective. Well, no clear objective except the already forgotten one we gave them when they set out to chase the latest mirage.

Underpinning this cycle is the belief that their own personal happiness is the goal of their life. When personal happiness is the goal (we assure them that it is), and their current situation is the reason they are falling short of the goal at this particular moment (we emphasize this, always), then life is spent rushing toward the next oasis.

We even fit their natural impulse to do things for others into this personal happiness framework. We talk about how there is more to *your* life than living for yourself and that by helping others you can realize *your* full potential and generate personal satisfaction that money cannot buy. See what we've done there? Even helping others is all about their own personal happiness.

In previous eras, the ape-gods would have been overwhelmed by the radical selfishness of it all. Today, however, this mindset is supported by their belief in the meritocracy I wrote about previously. The meritocratic system they have constructed means they have "earned" all the happiness they can achieve, and since life's objective is personal happiness, all we need to do is supply ever-changing images and ideas of how and why a change in their circumstance will bring happiness. Paint a picture of the next oasis and they do the rest.

Even among the so-called Christians, the your-happiness-is-life's-most-noble-goal pitch is a surprisingly easy sell to the modern ape-god. Indeed, with them we take it to an even more absurd extreme. We sell the story that the Enemy "wants you to be happy" and the modern ape-god swallows it whole. Many Christians have come to believe the entire purpose of the Enemy's program – sending the Son and the Spirit all the rest – is to help them achieve their ultimate personal happiness in what they suppose will be an unimaginably posh resort community they call Heaven. It is the final oasis they are striving to reach.

As you can see, the entire process of oasis hopping is deeply ingrained in this modern culture. Even with his modest background and low expectations, the Texas prison system has given your Inmate the perfect oasis to pursue: the free world. However, in both the free world and in prison, the success of our entire oasis-hopping program depends on the prey believing a single great lie: the source of their current dissatisfaction is their current circumstance and if that changes, personal happiness will be achieved.

Remember, we start with prey who are dissatisfied. A

content human is rarer than a humble politician in the modern world. (There was a time when contentment was a virtue that they practiced but we have well and truly done away with *that* old notion!)

In prison, we do not even spend a moment trying to stoke their dissatisfaction because there is no need. By any measure it is an unhappy place to live. In the free world, on the other hand, we spend a great deal of time sowing seeds of dissatisfaction. The job is not what it could be. The marriage is not satisfying. The "sex life" is underwhelming. Their house, neighborhood, school, physique, etcetera is disappointing. Moreover – and this is the really important part of our pitch – we emphasize that it is this circumstance or situation which is preventing the personal happiness they so richly deserve. If only they were to change the situation, personal happiness could be found (just over there at the next, even better oasis on the horizon).

What we are really doing, of course, is ensuring that they never pause long enough to consider any of the obvious questions about whether any of these things can bring happiness, if personal happiness is a worthwhile life goal, and if it is possible – at least in some small part – that the source of their dissatisfaction may be a result of their own behaviors, attitudes, and priorities. Any of these small questions will quickly lead to the big questions that would steer them straight to the Enemy's front gate.

For your Inmate, then, you must not only keep him focused on getting out, but also be sure that he sees prison itself as the main barrier to achieving happiness. We are teaching him that his problem is that he is *incarcerated* and that his problem ends when he *stops* being incarcerated. The moment he begins to think that what needs "fixing" are the behaviors, attitudes, and outlook that led to his incarceration, he already has one leg in the Enemy's camp.

Bringing False Hope to the Hopeless,
Warden Deumus

GANG LIFE FOR HIM

Dear Bentrock,

You should not be so delighted with yourself to see your Inmate getting involved with one of our prison gangs. Yes, it is a very good sign that he is on the right track, but Woertz gets at least as much credit for this turn of events as you do. It was Woertz who engineered getting your Inmate a new celly who is a faithful member of one of our gangs. Yes, your work getting him fixated on respect has been extremely helpful, but Woertz deserves at least equal credit for setting up the right environment.

Be that as it may be, your work from here is to encourage him to fully commit to his newfound prison family. To do that, you should begin by understanding the most important secret of gang culture: it is designed to mimic the Enemy's church. Once you grasp that, you can borrow many of the Enemy's own tools and techniques to encourage your Inmate to fully burrow into gang life.

Because the ape-gods spend their lives mentally

shackled to this present, material existence, they rarely grasp the obvious: much of what the Enemy encourages in this world are merely road signs that point to an eternal reality. Their concept of family is like that. They think their biological families are "real," but when the Enemy talks about His Church as a "family" they think it is an analogy to describe the abstract idea of His Church. Of course, we know it to be the other way around: the "real" thing is the eternal Church, and their earthly families are the analogy.

He has told them as much many times and in many ways. He said there was no male and female in His Kingdom, that there were no husbands and wives, that the Church is family, etcetera and so on. But they are, as I said, mentally shackled to this present, material existence. They cannot shake the idea that *this* is real and *that* is an abstraction.

The confusion stems in large measure from their steadfast refusal to appreciate that He intends for the earthly life to be a temporary, indescribably brief, moment in their existence. (This refusal is one of our greatest advantages.) The Enemy intends this moment for their training and development. Seen in the light of eternity it is obvious that the earthly families they prize so highly – all of which will be gone in the blink of an eye – are merely part of that training. They mimic the *real* family he intends for them, the eternal Church. But they insist it is the other way around.

While we had very little to do with creating this confusion (it is a defect of their nature), we have been very adept at exploiting it. Since our prey regard happy earthly families as a primary measure of success in life, and since few of our prison prey have ever known anything that comes close to a happy earthly family, we can easily tempt them to join one of our gang "families" to help mend the emotional wound.

At first glance, our gang families offer many of the features the ape-gods find in the Enemy's Church. The initiates become part of a group with shared beliefs, shared objectives, common rituals, and they pledge to care for one another. Like the Enemy's Church, members of the gang serve one lord, but in the gangs' case that lord is Our Master. (We do not make this last point explicitly, of course. They believe they serve the gang's then-current leadership, their community, and themselves. This is fine for our purposes. There is little to gain by advertising the fact that these little families serve and worship us. In any case it is obvious to anyone who wishes to see the truth and there is no point forcing it on those who do not want to know.)

To be sure, in the unholy churches of our prison gangs we do things a bit differently. The Enemy likes to invite people from all tribes into each of his little ecclesias. We prefer to keep our gangs segregated by tribe. We find this is much more natural to them. (The Enemy's communities often do the same, but it is always against His will and over His objections.) The Enemy's Church follows a ritual with bread and wine representing the broken body and blood of the Son. Our gang-church prefers actually broken bodies and blood as their initiation. We like to encourage these initiations as much for our amusement as anything: this is the body broken to prove my loyalty, this is the blood that is my new covenant with the gang. It is always rewarding to get an ape-god to embrace blasphemy.

The mandate of the Enemy's church is to serve others, love their enemies, turn the other cheek, and all the rest of His nonsense. Our gang-church's mandate is to serve the gang and yourself, to destroy your enemies, and never be disrespected. The Enemy demands that they care for those who cannot care for themselves. We demand that our associates care for other gang members so long as they remain loyal and useful.

For all the differences, being a member of each can feel similar. They have "brothers and sisters" in their Church family, and *we* have brothers and sisters in our gang families. They are engaged in a mission to infect the world with their way of life and so are we! They have little groups located in different neighborhoods but connected by a common affiliation and so do we! And, most importantly, they provide a place where people like your Inmate can feel like he belongs, and so do we.

It is this last point on which you must dwell. Your Inmate *wants* to belong to something greater than himself. He longs to feel less worthless and less helpless. The gang can provide all of this for him as long as you help maintain the illusion.

This is no simple task. Even the most thickheaded of the ape-gods will recognize instantly that being part of a gang is not worthwhile, at least not in any normal sense of the word. After all, here in prison the members are targeted by the prison administration, stuffed into segregation, and required to engage in activities that jeopardize their futures. He is *not* a part of something greater than himself, he is part of something lesser than himself. As a member of this gang, he is less empowered than ever: now under the direction of both the prison authorities *and* the gang leadership. Gang members who return to the free world are hated and hunted, they are pariahs even in their own neighborhoods and families, their lives generally play out as their philosopher Mr. Hobbes predicted: poor, nasty, brutish, and short. In exchange for signing up with the gang they learn nothing of use and gain nothing of value.

But nothing of value is not nothing, especially when we have trained them to value worthless things. They get protection from other gangs – with whom they would have had no quarrel had they not joined up in the first place. They gain "respect" in our deeply perverted sense of the term (you can see why that training was so important!). But the main reason they sign up to this obviously irrational bargain is that being in the gang makes them feel like they finally belong (though few will acknowledge this aloud).

With careful effort, the illusion can be maintained. Just as you made him feel pride in his prison nickname even though it was (and is) a badge of failure, you can help him believe that the gang makes him powerful, accepted, and part of something significant. Build on the deceptive definition of respect that you helped him adopt. Emphasize that being part of the gang means enjoying respect beyond anything he could have hoped for on his own. Constantly repeat the idea that this is an exclusive club and that he was *chosen* where so many others are not. Tell him that he belongs, and he will never be alone.

You will recognize that these are all perversions of feelings the Enemy's followers have about joining His Church. But to people like your Inmate, our church is *real*. It is here and now. It is about this world, the real world. It is focused on next week and next year, not on some abstract eternity. To an ape-god who cannot see past his momentary journey through this life, these things will all be very persuasive.

Our prison gangs offer nothing of use to your Inmate and demand a great penalty in return. They will brand him with prison ink as he sells himself into slavery in exchange for illusion of belonging, purpose, and family. Right now, that is what he *wants*! He is so desperate to be something more that he is not only *willing* to receive their brand, he *craves* it.

As I said, becoming affiliated with them is a wholly irrational act. But then again, so much of what we persuade the ape-gods to do is irrational, especially in light of eternity. Throw away a marriage for a few minutes with a prostitute? Throw away a career for just one more drink? Throw away a baby for just one more high? Throw away his future to be a member of a club no reasonable person would want to join? Why not! In the overall scheme of things, it is one of the better trades we offer.

With Malice Toward All and Charity Toward None,
Deumus

THE UNEMPLOYMENT LINE

DEAR BENTROCK,

It is no small matter that your Inmate has lost his job in the mechanic pool. Your enjoyment of his misery once again reminds me that you continue to act as though you are there for your own entertainment and not to serve our Master! Losing his job puts us in a very difficult position. His job gave him a purpose and gave him the illusion of progress. Now he risks returning to a state of despair.

For the ape-gods, a job answers three distinct objectives: one is core to who they are, the second is a perversion of the first, and the third is entirely for our own purposes. I will explain each of these below, but you must understand that a human's job affects him on many levels, and it can act for purposes both holy and demonic.

First, you must understand that the ape-gods have an innate need to be useful to other ape-gods. Hand an ape-god a lottery ticket and all the money anyone could want, and within a few short months he will be back searching for something "useful" to do. I have seen multi-millionaires tending their own gardens, maintaining their own vehicles, and cleaning their own toilets. Their neighbors will attribute that to frugality, but in most cases, it is nothing more than an unimaginative way for them to find something – anything! – that they feel is useful to do with their day.

If they cannot scratch this persistent itch one way or another, they say they are "bored." They are not bored, of course. At least not in any normal sense of the word. It is not that the novelty of life has waned or anything of that sort. It is just that their desire to be "useful" is unfulfilled and they have come to realize that the various diversions on offer (no matter how plentiful) cannot satisfy the desire.

In another time, they would have instantly recognized the source of the problem, but in this particular era the ape-gods rarely acknowledge what they used to call the "dignity of work." In fact, one of our great deceptions in the modern world was to package and sell the idea that the *only* purpose of work is to obtain luxury and leisure. So, when one of them suddenly falls into luxury and leisure they often become very confused about why they still feel a desire to do something "useful."

This can lead to all sorts of difficulties. As you might imagine, it can be a bit problematic for our side when one of the ape-gods with too much time and too little to do alights on the idea that they will "help others who are less fortunate." Suddenly they lurch toward charity work. This is generally not out of a desire to be charitable, you understand, but out of a desire to find something useful to do. And despite the entirely selfish motivation, it can and often does serve the Enemy's purposes.

Many new tempters fret that these boredom-driven acts of "charity" will risk prompting a genuinely charitable impulse in our prey. While this has been known to happen, it is rare. Mostly, this sort of thing just encourages pride. Indeed, going through the motions without a charitable motive rarely, at least in itself, leads them back to the Enemy. The biggest risk here is that the bored and selfish ape-god might find himself surrounded by genuinely charity-minded people who are firmly in the Enemy's camp.

Fortunately, we have numerous "charitable" enterprises specially designed to encourage self-satisfied pride amongst the contributors while pursuing objectives that help our cause (or at least do not run contrary to our purposes). These are run by our more reliable followers, so we usually just point them to the right sort of organization which are, helpfully, filled with the very best sort of people.

Here in prison, our inmates – in their own peculiar way – find themselves suddenly thrust into a life of leisure and luxury. It is not luxurious by any normal standard, of course, but it is as luxurious as it is going to get while they are here. In other words, improving their material position is not possible through work so that motivation is lost. And if there is one thing these inmates have in abundance, it is time. Just like the lottery winner, they quickly find themselves wishing for something "useful" to do, even if they do not recognize that this is the source of at least some of their boredom. (In prison, with the repetitive routine and all the rest, this is amplified by *actual* boredom as well.)

My main point, then, (and I would very much appreciate you not commenting once again about my long-winded replies) is that in the first instance it is in their nature to want to work. When they do not, the desire reveals itself as boredom and in the free world it leads to them creating things for themselves to do. This is no concern of ours in most instances, but here in prison where their ability to invent "useful" activities is severely constrained, it is a much greater concern as it can lead to despair. This itch must be scratched!

Beyond that, work serves two other objectives that are more useful to us. The one – a perversion of the first – I have mentioned before. We have been very effective in getting our prey to define who they are by what they do. This is both usefully dehumanizing and wonderfully distracting. Your Inmate has said these past many months "I am a mechanic" in the usual lost ape-god sort of a way. It was core to his identity. Now that he has lost his job, he has been robbed of this identity and *that* means he may begin to wonder who he really is! I do not need to remind you that this is a line of thinking we very much wish to avoid.

This habit they have of defining themselves by their jobs is as old as the race itself and has always been useful to us. When they think of themselves as "a farmer" or "a blacksmith" as opposed to a person who farms or smiths, they are inverting the Enemy's design. He wants them to think of themselves first as "image bearers" who reflect Him into the world (you may allow yourself a groan of disgust when reading that). This habit of describing themselves by their labor specialization diminishes them. They begin to see themselves a bit more the way we see them: insects managing the Enemy's hive. We like that.

In the modern world, however, this useful habit has a

gained an unfortunate side effect for us. Today, the ape-gods rarely go through life with a single vocation. They change jobs and roles as frequently as earlier generations changed clothes. Often, they will go for months or years with no job at all. None of this is our doing, mind you. It is an artifact of their own industrial progress. As a result, their vocational identity is frequently shaken, as it has been with your Inmate. In these moments, we find them too often wondering what it really means to be a person and they can stumble upon the very dangerous answer of "image bearer."

The third aspect of work that we find especially useful is that the modern workplace is delightfully hierarchical with team leaders and managers and directors and officers and whatnot. Again, this is not our doing, just an artifact of industrialization, but we find it exceptionally useful.

In the specialized modern workplace, we find that most ape-gods, at one time or another, are put in charge of other ape-gods. In this world of petty hierarchies almost all of them can eventually rise to be the prince of their little domain. It makes for an ideal training ground to develop some of our most effective habits.

Put an ape-god in charge of most anything and it takes just the slightest nudge to turn them into minor despots who exercise that power with selfishness and spite. Petty workplace hierarchies allow us to put a small portion of the corrupting power that was once reserved for princes and politicians into the hands of nearly everyone. With this we can develop in almost anyone the kind of delightfully corrupting habits that used to be reserved for the rich and powerful.

I should probably note here that these same hierarchies can be twisted to serve the Enemy. With ape-gods who are deeply embedded in the Enemy's ways, each step upwards in the hierarchy creates a greater scope for serving their neighbors. They have a ridiculous term, servant-leadership, which they use to describe this mindset. It can be very problematic. Fortunately for every one of them who truly practices servant-leadership there are tens of thousands who embrace their newfound roles as minor autocrats. So, we are happy with the trade-off.

The other incredibly useful thing about these petty hierarchies is that they create a lifetime of opportunities to keep the prey focused on scratching and clawing their way up the ladders of "success." The worker can become a team leader. The team leader can be a shift manager. The vice president can become a senior vice president. The possibilities are endless. With just the smallest bit of encouragement, each step up the petty hierarchy becomes a new oasis on the horizon which they can rush towards and a new fixation that diverts their gaze away from the Enemy. (Even in prison the inmates hold jobs where there are promotions to which they can aspire!)

As you can see, your Inmate losing his job is far from a minor setback. We need to do what we can to get him back into a role where he will have an identity, the illusion of progress, and we can keep the "boredom" at bay. There is simply no better, sustained way to distract prey from the Enemy and keep them focused on things of this world than to tightly intertwine their self-image with their job. In the meantime, make use of our other distraction techniques to keep his attention properly diverted.

Warden Deumus

PS It will not be lost on you – especially on you – that one of the very best jobs in which ape-gods can indulge their inner despot is corrections officer. Unfortunately, it is also the one job where they have a front row seat to the zoo-like treatment of their own kind. For many of them, this will often pull the officers' thoughts to the Enemy. With the right sort of ape-god it is an excellent vocation. With the wrong sort, it will lead them to throw in with the Enemy and spend their days combatting our work here.

As it stands, we already have too many of the Enemy's servants in the ranks of the officers at our unit. You need to do what you can keep your Inmate from engaging in a conversation with those we have blacklisted while we work to bring more of our own servants into the mix. Woertz can provide you a full list of the most trouble-some officers and staff to avoid.

COUCH JOCKEYS AND
CORNER BOYS

———

Dear Bentrock,

Your observation is not entirely wrong. There are indeed an entire class of ape-gods who have evolved beyond the natural desire for work which I described in my previous letter. Your inmate is not among them. It is unlikely you will be able to induct him into the tribe of couch jockeys and corner boys – ape-gods whose aversion to work is so great that they would rather subsist on scraps than suffer a day's work for a day's wage. I see no harm, however, in letting you spend a few weeks giving it a try. If nothing else, we will learn something about your Inmate that may be useful when he leaves this place.

Human laziness is nothing new, of course. We have been fostering it since the beginning of their infestation on this planet and we will continue to do so until the place dissolves. Nonetheless, several features of the current age make our work in this area easier and more effective than ever before. As you will see, however, these are most effective when used in the free world, and the tribe of idlers in prison tends to be small.

While lazy, idle humans have been a feature of their race since the beginning, life had a way of penalizing this behavior to discourage it. In previous eras, no work led quickly to starvation. Even the thief had to work diligently at his trade to fill his belly.

Ironically it was the Enemy's teaching that created the initial opening for us to grow the population of couch jockeys. His teaching about caring for others launched communities where everything was shared, and the poor never went hungry. It took us almost no time to develop a group of would-be converts who were all too happy to take advantage of His charitable mandate.

Little more than a decade after the Son was walking among them, our campaign had been so successful that His servant Paul was warning about followers who were settling into the do-nothing lifestyle (in the Enemy's name, no less!). Paul wrote to the community warning that if one of the brethren would not work then neither should he eat. We have been leveraging this weakness in the Enemy's program ever since.

While there had been couch jockeys before the Son's visit, it had generally been the occasional over-indulgent family (especially among the wealthy and powerful) supporting a do-nothing son or daughter well into adulthood. Now, with the Christian community expanding quickly and its charitable mandate firmly entrenched, the couch jockeys had an entire *community* on which to rely! Idleness was no longer an affliction of the rich, now the poor could join the ranks as well. The battle between the Enemy's charitable mandate and the idlers who take advantage of it has been raging ever since.

For us, the battle is a win-win-win situation. When a couch jockey abuses the charitable mandate, he is embracing sloth, turning away from the Enemy, and sliding onto our wide and straight road. When the Christians offering the charity see the abuse, they often get angry and begin to hate the couch jockey. Their growing contempt steers them easily back onto our path. Meanwhile, other would-be followers of the Way get frustrated by the behavior of the couch jockeys, reject the entire idea of a charitable mandate, embrace the virtue of selfishness, and abandon the Enemy's entire program. They, too, join the other groups headed our direction. (Did I mention that our road is very wide and there is plenty of room for everyone?)

With the Enemy's early success in spreading his community around the world, most societies these days have adopted the basic idea of the charitable mandate that the Son taught them. (Most no longer connect this with the Enemy's teachings because they prefer not to acknowledge His hand in it, but no matter who gets the credit it is helpful to our work.) In all but the poorest countries, the ape-gods have enshrined some version of the Enemy's charitable mandate into law. And *that* means we can encourage millions to become couch jockeys knowing that the charitable mandate will keep them fed. It also means we have endless opportunities to teach tens-of-millions to hate the couch jockeys and even more to despise the entire charitable mandate and with it the Enemy's entire teaching.

Even more delightful, the couch jockeys come to hate their benefactors. As I said in my previous letter, it is natural for them to desire to be useful. Embracing the idle lifestyle is unnatural, though surprisingly easy to encourage. In short order these ape-gods – who certainly do not wish to work – find themselves angry at the very fact that they do not wish to work. In other words, they do not want to be useful, but they *wish* they wanted to be useful because not desiring this feels unnatural, which it is! (Delightful!)

As you will well understand, especially in the free world, our distractions on demand come in very handy for the idlers. We even have various categories of these ape-gods, designated by their favorite distractions. For example: gamers, or social media mavens, or binge watchers, or sports fanatics, or corner boys, just to name a few. And, of course, our very best and most addictive distraction of all is, well, addiction. If we can get one of our prey to become dependent on narcotics or alcohol, we tie them to a life-long daily distraction that makes it near impossible to work.

Because this has become so commonplace, we are even able to remove the most effective natural process for discouraging idleness: romantic desire. In eras past, a do-nothing ape-god was the least appealing sort of mate for women or men. Being useful to other ape-gods was a basic qualification for attracting a mate. With our very enlightened views on good and healthy sex lives, however, it is now easy enough to attract temporary mates for even the most dedicated couch-jockey. After all, it is not like they are starving and begging thanks to the charitable mandate of the Enemy!

Tempting an ordinary ape-god into becoming a couch jockey is a fairly simple five-step process (at least with the right sort of ape-god). Start with a prey that thinks highly of itself. That is important. Naturally humble humans won't do at all. This is step one.

Step two is to help them fail in a few work experiences. The failure does not need to be spectacular or dramatic, but it must end in them losing their job, their business, or generally making a mess of their useful task. This is the essence of the temptation. Fear and shame in failure are the foundation on which we construct a couch jockey. Happily, if you become more expert in this area, you will learn you can accomplish step two without the effort and complexity of causing them to actually fail.

One of our recent innovations has been to convince the ape-gods that their work should be *personally fulfilling* and that they have every right to expect it to be so. This is our own modern distortion of the Enemy's idea to infuse all work – no matter how routine and ordinary – with meaning and purpose. The old Christian idea that "a dairymaid can milk cows to the glory of God"[7] was meant to suggest that they can provide meaning and significance to any work by doing it for the Enemy. It only required a slight twist from us to convince the prey that they deserve and should expect their work will *provide them* with meaning and fulfillment. Since work rarely delivers this feeling of significance of its own accord (and even then, only on rare occasion), we can often persuade them it is a failure even when it is going well. If you get this right, you do not need to cause them to fail at the job; you can let the job fail them.

Our efforts are also helped along by other ape-gods who treat a great many useful tasks as beneath contempt. Indeed, the very same ape-god who will at one moment despise an idler for his do-nothing lifestyle will in the next moment ridicule a different hard-working and useful ape-god for being engaged in unskilled menial labor. It is always easier to undermine the dignity of work when the worker is treated without the slightest dignity! (And if such workers are paid a half-day's wage for a day's work, well that is just how the very merito-cratic system operates.)

Regardless of the mechanics of the thing, after a few failures and a few encounters with their fellow ape-gods deriding their efforts, pride will discourage the would-be couch-jockey from trying again. "Best not to try than to try and fail" is their motto even if they do not say it aloud. Even better, suggest that they did not fail in their jobs, it is just that the entire "do something useful" mindset is for losers (and the jobs are unfulfilling anyway). They will latch onto that quickly enough after a few embarrassing disappointments.

Step three is our old standby: find a favorite distrac-tion. Cycle through various options until you discover at least two or three sorts of entertainment that can hold their attention. If they begin to find one distraction is becoming tedious, just move to the next.

Step four is to teach them how to source what they need – food, shelter, clothing, and so forth – without working. This typically involves teaching them how to manipulate those around them, work the "system," and run the occasional petty con. (If you are confused about how to do this just spend a day or two studying any group of teenagers, they seem to have a natural expertise in this area.) Fortunately, our kind do not need to know all the details, we just need to introduce them to the right sort of people, and we certainly know the right sort of people.

Step five is to reduce their aspirations to a level consistent with being a couch jockey. You will recall from my previous letter that we have been successfully selling the idea that the *only* purpose of work is to obtain luxury and leisure. The do-nothing can easily be taught that leisure is more important than luxury. Teach your prey to feel contempt for the wealthier ape-gods they encounter, and teach them to feel a sense of pride and superiority that they are not as shallow and materialistic as their income-producing peers (remember, you are starting with an ape-god who is a bit narcissistic so this should be an effortless sale).

With the right sort of prey, we can craft a do-nothing couch jockey in five easy steps. We create someone who has contempt for work, contempt for material success, rotates endlessly through their favorite distractions, and knows how to manipulate people and the system to meet their needs. In a delightful twist, the more accomplished a couch jockey becomes, the more he will despise the people and organizations who support him (because the charity "makes him feel" worthless). Along the way, his behavior will infuriate the people who support him as well as those who see him from afar, creating a reservoir of spite and anger that squelches their desire to follow the Enemy's charitable mandate. Win-win-win.

But, as I said, your Inmate is probably not the ideal candidate. He has shown few signs of narcissism and he has always sought ways to be useful. Moreover, this entire program is vastly more difficult in prison. The distractions available are not so entertaining and, unless you can conjure up some medical waiver, the human warden will quickly tell him that doing nothing is not an option unless he would enjoy doing it in Seg[8]. Still, it will be good practice for you and a few weeks of trial and error won't hurt anything. It's not as though he is going anywhere.

Enjoy the Work
Deumus

Footnotes:

[7] Editor's note: Deumus only wrote here "a dairymaid can milk cows to the glory..." but I surmise it was a reference to this quote from Martin Luther.

[8] Administrative segregation or solitary confinement.

SELFISH LOVE

Dear Bentrock,

So, your Inmate has finally said aloud what he has been thinking for more than a year: his wife no longer loves him. I would, as they say, roll my eyes – if I had eyes to roll. We already know what he only suspects: she has been with another man since before his trial (not that her fornication habits have much to do with love one way or another). As I told you previously, we have had great success re-defining words and terms to help further our agenda. Given the recent correspondence with his wife, it is as good a time as any to talk about love.

I will get right to the point of what we hope to accomplish with your Inmate: our objective, while we have this opportunity, is to permanently destroy his belief that love exists. We want him to believe that true love is a myth. Meanwhile, we want him to regard the word "love" in the same way the English-speaking ape-gods use the word "stuff": a term that can stand in for almost anything and means nothing. Failing that, we want him to think of the word as a synonym for self-satisfied selfishness. In other words, it will mean either nothing or roughly the opposite of what it was meant to mean.

We begin with a great advantage among our own group of ape-gods. The English language has an astonishingly impoverished vocabulary when dealing with love. Even in situations where the language has more precise alternatives, we have encouraged those to fall out of common usage in pursuit of our successful effort to undermine this once-powerful idea. Nowhere is this more helpful than in the Enemy's writings. There, the rich and varied range of Greek and Hebrew expressions are reduced to this single four-letter English word, which we have now helpfully redefined to mean something even less.

It is commonplace for the ape-gods to use the word "love" to describe the most trivial things. They might use it to explain that they enjoy a particular food as in, "I love ice cream." They can "absolutely love this song"; they can love their jobs (and sometimes they "hate" them – another word we have successfully stripped of its meaning and power); they can love a pet animal; they can love a sports team or television program or a book; they can even love an article of clothing!

Now, you may imagine that it would be impossible for them to confuse these trivial desires with something as significant as the revelation of the Enemy. Trust me, it is not! At the core of all these frivolous uses of "love" is a common definition that threads them together: when an ape-god says he loves something he means that the thing makes *him feel good*. From trivial matters like ice cream to profound matters like marriage, it is all the same. The way these things make the individual ape-god *feel* determines if he loves it or not.

This has proven especially useful with respect to romantic love. The stew of hormones and endorphins that defines romantic attraction has taken on magical qualities in their culture. When an ape-god falls "in love" with another of its kind, they are describing a deeply felt emotion that is more exciting and engaging than most anything else they can experience. They are describing the full force of romantic desire – a hormone-endorphin surge that seems to profoundly unsettle their fragile physiology[9]. We have spent centuries, however, ensuring that the average ape-god believes this romantic desire is the single most authentic version of love conceivable.

When your Inmate's wife told him she no longer loved him, what she was really saying is that she no longer feels romantic desire for him (or, more precisely, that she feels romantic desire for another). This is no surprise. The processes that produce a flood of hormones and endorphins rely on proximity and newness to do their work. In this case they had neither.

We have taught the ape-gods that when they no longer feel this romantic desire, they owe it to them-selves to seek a new partner. (YOLO and all that!) It would be unconscionable to "settle" into a long-term relationship that is "loveless" when life is short and the next, better oasis is visible on the horizon.

As will be obvious to you, this definition of romantic love integrates well with our teachings on a good and healthy sex life. If the combination of emotional enthu-siasm and hormonal craving begins to wane (which it always does), the love is obviously defective, the sex life is defective, and the entire thing is beyond repair.

We teach them that they should never engage in

physical intimacy for any reason other than because they feel a surge of emotional and physical desire for the other person. Anything else – like the Enemy's guidance that married couples have a mutual obligation not to deprive one another of physical intimacy – is inauthentic and even demeaning (unlike the fantasy-driven casual intimacy we advocate, which is, we assure them, empowering and authentic). And if the absence of intimacy degrades the emotional bond? Well, we tell them, the love has just faded, there is nothing to be done, and it is probably beyond repair. But fear not, the next oasis awaits.

The average ape-god has embraced our "love is an emotion" definition without ever considering the ridiculousness of the idea. Even when they vow to "love, honor, and cherish" one another, it does not occur to them. Do they imagine that the author of the vows, or the many generations that recited various versions of them, believed they could promise their spouse that they would always *feel* a particular way until death parts them? Yet, as they stand before friends and family (and for the religious among them before their Creator) to vow that they will love one another for all their days, it is exactly this that they have in mind. Of course, it will not last. Romantic desire always dissipates. Their fragile physiology could not tolerate a perpetual state of being in love.

The more thoughtful among them recognize this, but they adopt a no less silly notion that "true love" is that deep feeling of affection that they have for another. Indeed, among older couples and friends, the emotion they call love is often the regret and nostalgic loss they feel when they imagine life without the other. (This is likely the emotion your Inmate was describing when he talked about his faithful love for his wife.) As will be obvious to you, this is merely substituting a somewhat less volatile emotion for the original. But the bride or the groom can no more promise life-long feelings of deep affection than they can promise life-long feelings of burning romantic desire.

Among the Enemy's followers their understanding of love routinely creates amusing anxiety. They strive to generate feelings of fondness for strangers and colleagues even when they have none because they believe this is what it means to love their neighbor. They imagine that their faith is substandard when those feelings do not arise or when they encounter someone with whom they do not feel an emotional connection.

It is even more comical to watch them try to generate similar emotions toward the Enemy Himself. After all, love is an emotion. This is what we have told them, and they believe it to be true. They meditate, pray, and desperately attempt to will into existence feelings of child-like love toward an unseen omnipotent being. All the while they are spurred on by their fellow believers who ask: do you have a "personal relationship" with the Almighty? As if such a thing were possible, at least in the way most of them imagine.

Even the love parents feel for their children and children feel for their parents has been redefined as emotion. It used to be understood that feelings of positive emotion often *accompany* love, but now the emotions *are* love. If a parent or child enters a period of feeling ambivalence or even anger toward one another, they imagine the love has broken down and disappeared. (At least it keeps the therapists busy.)

This is not to say that modern ape-gods think the old definitions of love are irrelevant. To the contrary, they still believe love is patient, kind, humble, long-suffering, protective, and all the rest. It is just that they believe these things are the natural *result* of the loving emotions they feel. Should those emotions disappear, as they do, then one has fallen out of love and cannot possibly expect to feel very patient, kind, and so forth.

With our redefinition, it is simply impossible for them to see the obvious: love is supposed to mean a decision, an action, a commitment. The feelings of desire or affection or delight that may or may not accompany it from time to time are beside the point. Paul did not tell them that if they *feel* love they will naturally be patient and kind. He told them that love *is* being patient and kind. When they took vows to "love, comfort, honor, and keep" it was not a promise for one emotion and three actions, it was a commitment to four actions. When the Enemy told them to love their neighbor, he was not asking them to discover a well of hidden emotion for a Samaritan they did not know, He was calling them to action. But to suggest such a thing to a modern human is little short of blasphemy.

We have so thoroughly redefined this word as an emotion that it is simple heresy to suggest otherwise. There is no husband or wife in the modern world who would dare suggest to their spouse that deep feelings of romantic desire are not the centerpiece of their relationship. It is a romantic profanity that few would have the courage to utter and fewer still would be able to live down if they did.

In my own experience as a free world tempter, I facilitated the destruction of countless marriages by persuading my prey that the absence of sufficiently intense affection and desire was proof that the marriage was "loveless" and beyond repair. I persuaded a good number of my prey that regardless of their own emotional state, their spouse was not exhibiting sufficient evidence of the deep emotion they *ought* to be experiencing. I have seen off many a husband or wife who was patient and kind and all the rest for the crime of not demonstrating a suitably deep emotional response. "Life is too short to settle for a loveless marriage," I helpfully explained.

It will be apparent, then, that when your Inmate says in disgust, "there is no such thing as love" he will be correct. Love as we have defined it does not exist except as the most transitory of physiological and emotional states. Build on this with him. Persuade him that love is not real. Help him expand this understanding to include all sorts of love – from his friends and family to his own feelings toward his daughter. Persuade him that love is an emotion that does not last. The evidence for this will be undeniable and everywhere.

It will also be useful to continue to trivialize the word. There is little you need to do here as the culture already uses it so widely. In any case, however, do not allow him to drop the core idea that love is an emotion, and that when he says he loves someone he is really saying he values the way they make him feel. Because love is, fundamentally, a selfish act that is all about the emotions of the one who loves and is being loved.

If we can accomplish this, then he will be well insulated if he ever encounters the Enemy's message. When he hears that the Enemy so loved the world, he will be confused. When he hears that he must love his neighbor he will rightly think that there are many people in his own little cell block for whom he could never conceivably feel deep affection. None of it will make sense to him and it will be easy enough for us to encourage him to dismiss it as nothing more than feel-good platitudes.

It will be equally obvious to you that if he – or any ape-god for that matter – rediscovers the real meaning of the word it will be devastating for our work. If they come to understand love as a selfless action, commitment, and way of living, the Enemy's message regains its power and the foolishness of what they have believed will become obvious. This is unlikely though. We have spent centuries redefining love as a self-centered, self-satisfied emotional state. It is our most reliable defense against the Enemy's message.

Love,
Deumus

Footnotes:

[9] This overwhelming bio-chemical surge of emotion is another of the design defects we have observed in their physiology. It is obviously necessary, however. How else would they ever be persuaded to engage in that awkward, odorous, messy business necessary for procreation?

THE VOLUNTEERS ARE
COMING!

DEAR BENTROCK,

Woertz tells me that one of the Enemy's free world groups is coming to the unit and that your Inmate is scheduled to join their program! This is catastrophic news (you should have notified me immediately). We must take swift action to prevent him from attending.

Please understand, Bentrock, that these so-called "volunteer programs" are one of most dangerous weapons in the Enemy's arsenal. The programs represent human charity (in the original sense of the word) in one of its purest forms and even when the program itself is ineffective, the impact can be devastating to our work.

Without delving into the details of this particular event (which I have seen before), you must understand that it will have all the elements of the most challenging counterattacks from the Enemy: a group of His followers coming to assist, listen to, and care for our inmates while neither expecting nor receiving anything in return. They will be spreading what the Greeks called ἀγάπη (agape) in His name. And through their charitable act they will be able to smuggle the most dangerous elements of the Enemy's message past our defenses and directly into the hearts of our prey.

Such counterattacks are not limited to prison, of course. Disgusting examples of the Enemy's free world followers offering food, shelter, medical care, emotional support, and so forth to those in need is always perilous to our efforts. Anytime the Enemy's followers gather in His name and put their time, talents, and resources into caring for people they do not know and from whom that can expect nothing in return, we risk losing our prey.

This sort of selfless act, no matter how trivial, behaves like the worst imaginable sort of virus. It infects not only people who come in contact with it but even those who see it from afar. The effects are all the more remarkable once you realize that the ape-gods' charitable acts are usually the most insignificant sort of gesture – requiring little of the giver and offering only a brief comfort to the recipient. Yet just as a virus is at once the most insignificant and fragile of organisms but also among the most powerful forces for shaping nations, the triviality of the genuinely charitable gesture does not seem to minimize its impact. As one of our great scholars once observed, true charity is the most infectious and deadly disease ever conceived.

I am sure you will need no reminder that it was the Son's act of selfless love which infected the world two millennia ago and launched the entire pandemic of Christianity we have been battling ever since! It was not the Enemy's bold act of creation, nor demonstrations of His power, nor revelations of His character, nor even the vast evidence of His generosity and indulgence that caused this mess. Instead, it was a single act of selfless charity, performed by the Enemy himself, that sparked the revolution. It was this act that transformed His following from a small tribe in a backwater province to a worldwide movement. It was this act that pushed Our Master from his perch as the undisputed ruler of this world.

Ever since, the Enemy's revolution has spread not by war or grand gestures, but like a virus with one ape-god infecting another and then another, mostly through selfless acts of charity. And be forewarned: when they are engaging in genuinely charitable acts, even the most ill-equipped and weak-willed of the Enemy's followers can become one of our most formidable adversaries.

Naturally, we do all we can to dissuade this type of behavior among the Enemy's followers and, at the risk of seeming over-confident, we have been dreadfully effective in discouraging this sort of thing.

One of our most fruitful strategies is to recast charitable acts as an obligation rather than a privilege. When selfless care for others is depicted as a chore that needs to be done, most of the Enemy's followers avoid doing it. Of course, it helps that anytime the thought occurs to them we are standing by to remind them of the various inconveniences, demands, and difficulties the act will entail. I have successfully discouraged His followers from doing even the simplest things, like helping a neighbor clean up after a storm, by persuading my prey that he has a great many other things to do, that it comes at the worst possible time, that it will be terribly inconvenient and perhaps even a bit dangerous and that, really, charity begins at home.

Actually, that is one of our very best phrases. "Charity begins at home" brings a smile to my face whenever I hear one of the ape-gods say it. I enjoy it even more when one of their leaders says it. Best of all I truly delight when I hear it coming from one of their so-called "religious leaders" (who are busy doing our bidding by discouraging their "flock" from engaging in selfless acts and especially those that benefit someone from a different tribe).

This charity-begins-at-home deception is all the more delicious when you recall that at the beginning of all this mess one of the religious leaders asked the Son (during those days when he was walking among them) specifically about the charity-begins-at-home idea. He asked, "Who is our neighbor?" and the Son, unsurprisingly to anyone who knows anything about the Enemy (even us!), gave an answer that was precisely opposite of charity-begins-at-home. You can see why our kind find it so satisfying to persuade His present day "leaders" to proclaim loudly, "Charity...B.A.H.!"

Another well-worn phrase we favor is the one about the Enemy "helping those who help themselves." The true intended meaning of this phrase is roughly, "the Enemy expects his followers to help those who demonstrate that they deserve the help." It never occurs to the average self-absorbed, self-justifying ape-god that this would exclude all of them. Helpfully for us, in their minds the definition of "deserving" ape-gods nearly always excludes every inmate in a place like this one. I suspect that is part of the reason we find so few of the Enemy's followers here in prison despite the fact that He explicitly told them to visit the prisoner.

A somewhat different approach that has been especially successful in the past century is to encourage them to jettison the "in His name" part of the charitable act. We make it a regular part of our work these days to remind His followers that even though the Enemy calls on them to help their neighbors, there is really no need to bring Him into it. Any neighbor-helping activity is equally good. It is the action that matters, rather than the motivation for the action, much less what you tell others about the motivation for the action. Moreover, by bringing His name into it, they risk alienating unbelievers and that is not very neighborly, is it?

It seems logical enough to an ape-god and it rarely occurs to them that they are publicly denying their affiliation with the Enemy as clearly as when we whispered to Peter before the cock crowed.

When it is work done in the Enemy's name, the minds of our prey keep getting drawn back to problematic questions about whether the act is the sort of thing that brings credit to the Enemy, whether it advances His agenda, whether it is truly selfless and offered in the spirit in which He intended, etcetera and so forth. All those problems fall away once we have disconnected the act from the motivation.

Shorn of its "in His name" affiliation, a charitable action becomes much less infectious and mostly harmless. It also becomes more self-centered. Suddenly, charity is redefined to include things like financial support of your favorite theater, or your university, or your child's sports team. Why not? They are neighbors. That counts. With just this simple change we can easily have the Enemy's affiliates doing selfish acts in their own name, for their own glory, and gleefully marking the "charity chore" off their to-do list.

Sadly, these are *not* the sort of people who are going to show up to meet your inmate. They are coming with an agenda to bring the Enemy's message (in fact, the worst parts of the Enemy's message about love and forgiveness) to this prison. They are showing up not only expecting nothing in return but knowing with certainty that these convicts have nothing to give. So, our strategy over the next few days is simple: prevent him from attending.

Woertz is working to stop the program. This will likely fail as the Enemy tends to be very protective of this sort of work and we are rarely able to derail it. Woertz is also doing what he can to ensure that as many of the inmates in attendance as possible will already be at least loosely affiliated with the Enemy so they are literally preaching to the prison choir, and we can limit the damage. I am working with our free world network to send your Inmate a distraction from home (a letter or better yet the promise of a family visit) but we have little time to put that plan into action. I am not optimistic.

For your part, you must work relentlessly to discourage him from going. Remind him that he cannot be *required* to go and that it will undoubtedly be a boring, tedious waste of his time. (I know, it is absurd for an inmate to imagine that much of anything could be more boring, tedious, or a greater waste of time than his daily routine in prison, but trust me, the suggestion often works.) Suggest to him that this will be several days of the very worst parts of the church experience he had as a child. Tell him that the volunteers will believe he is a contemptible criminal and a sinner and that they are only here out of some misplaced obligation (he will remember the charity-is-a-chore message from his younger free world days). Even if you fail to persuade him to opt out of the program, planting these messages will help him adopt the right attitude.

This is a perilous time.

Deumus

THE LAST SUPPER

Dear Bentrock,

I understand you have been unable to persuade your inmate to cancel his attendance in the volunteer program. I am not surprised. Woertz tells me that the Chaplain intervened and that the Enemy placed a well-timed letter from his mother into the mail so it would arrive last evening. I am also given to understand that Roach personally contacted your Inmate in the yard to encourage him to attend (no doubt at the prompting of the Chaplain, or worse).

I fear we must acknowledge the reality that the Enemy has targeted your inmate and He is using his allies here and in the free world to pull him behind the curtain. So, it seems the time has come for us to discuss "the curtain."

You have not yet experienced this with your Inmate, but there are times and places where the Enemy shuts us off from our prey. I described some of that to you in my letter about the Roach. Now, you are about to experience it first-hand. Over the next few days your Inmate will be inaccessible to you. When he is in the room with the volunteers you will discover that you can neither speak to him nor hear his thoughts. You will be completely deaf and blind – at least until he returns to his bunk in the evening. You can only hope that the work you have done these past years will shield him from the Enemy's overtures. Distraction is no longer a tool that is available to you – at least not for the next few days.

I have seen this before and I can guide you in the evenings to help undermine the Enemy's efforts. Please use our Immediate Delivery Priority Messaging to keep me abreast of his situation and I will respond via the same channel.

For this evening, your best opportunity is to prepare him by arranging a last meal with his gang brothers. He needs to feel secure and confident in his new prison family. He needs to be reminded of the sense of belonging and purpose that he has found there. Woertz will ensure they do their part to fill him with skepticism, cynicism, and contempt for the volunteers. Remember that they will want to keep him out of the Enemy's hands almost as much as you do.

Send him to eat with the gang, encourage him to eat too much, encourage him to write a letter to his wife as that always puts him in an angry mood, and do what you can to make his night as sleepless as possible. You want him to arrive tired, angry, distracted, and secure that he has a place and a purpose in our world.

I await your communication tomorrow evening.

W. D.

PART II

A DANGEROUS DIVERSION

THERE IS ALWAYS TOMORROW

URGENT MESSAGE FOR IMMEDIATE DELIVERY

Dear Bentrock,

I am not at all surprised that your Inmate was shaken profoundly by what he encountered during his first day with the volunteers. Again, I must emphasize that all of us, me included, have no idea what is said or what happens with them. It is all hidden from us behind the Enemy's fortifications. I have learned from experience, however, that your proposed approach of trying to sow doubt about the Enemy's promises *will* fail, at least in the short run. Your Inmate is going to be swept up in the emotion as much as the argument.

Listen carefully, as this matter is urgent: Your best chance of success is to *agree* with him that these volunteers may well be right.

This evening, while you have him to yourself, you will need to work on several fronts simultaneously. First, recognize that he will probably engage in prayer for the first time since you have known him. (He may already be doing that when you receive this.) Do not be alarmed if suddenly his thoughts are inaccessible to you. This is normal (as you would have learned in training). I will write to you in more detail about this phenomenon at another time when things are less urgent.

In the unlikely event that he speaks his prayers aloud, you may find yourself driven completely from his presence. This is a painful event for our kind. You may already have experienced the wounds and the damage it does, especially if you were standing too close when he started or if you foolishly attempted to re-enter the cell while he was continuing to pray aloud. The best strategy is to wait, out of earshot from your Prey, until he is finished.

If he is praying silently (and given your Inmate's natural tendency toward embarrassment I suspect that is the method, he will choose) you may hover just outside the cell door and attempt to listen in. As I said, you will not be able to access his thoughts while he is talking with the Enemy, but in my experience the ape-gods are generally incapable of keeping their minds from wandering during their first attempts to pray. You may be able to detect useful snatches of information while his thoughts are wandering. But be prepared to swiftly withdraw if he begins to speak aloud. The impact on us is a bit like a small explosion if your Inmate suddenly cries out to the Enemy.

When he has finished praying you need to swoop in immediately and begin to speak to him. Do not be startled if he cannot hear your voice right away – that happens sometimes when they have finished communing with the Enemy. Just stay persistent. You should repeat messages about how weary he is from the day until you have his attention. He will be exhausted from the disruption of his routine, from the unfamiliar food, and from the emotional aspects of the event. Once you have him settled in his bunk, you can get to work.

Your first line of attack is embarrassment. You need to emphasize with your Inmate how foolish he appeared in front of his fellow inmates. Even though we do not know what happens in these meetings we have learned that this is often effective. You should be able to quickly assess whether this will be successful: if you detect his anxiety beginning to rise when you put the thought in his mind, then keep pressing your advantage. Remind him of the cost of losing "respect" in a place like this. Remind him that the volunteers are only here for a few days, and he will be stuck right back in this cell come Monday. Remind him that he will have to live with the consequences of acting foolishly.

Your next line of attack is discrediting the volunteers. As with all groups of the Enemy's servants, we can be sure that there are some who are deeply committed and acting out of a selfless desire to serve the Enemy, but there will also be others who are acting out of vanity or pride. They imagine themselves to be the liberators riding in to save the "bad people" from themselves. In almost every group like this you will find both sorts. You need to assess which sort of volunteers your Inmate encountered.

Again, your best approach is to simply suggest something like, "Many of those volunteers seemed genuine, but a few seemed completely phony." Make the suggestion, and see what images come to his mind. If one or more of the volunteers seemed disingenuous to him, he will think of them immediately. You can then focus his attention on those images and keep pressing the point. Ask questions like, "I wonder what is in it for him to be here?" Build on his other anxieties and suggest, "This is just another person who thinks you are not good enough and never will be." You get the idea. But be cautious! If at the first suggestion no particular images come to his mind, then you must cease your attack. Pressing the point if he is not already skeptical of their motives will cause him to rebel against the ideas you are placing in his mind. It might lead him back to prayer – which is something you very much wish to avoid.

Finally, and most importantly, is your third line of attack: there is always tomorrow. You want to be very reassuring to him. You want to tell him that these volunteers, just like his mother, are probably right. (I know this will be difficult for you, but it is essential.) Tell him the Enemy probably *is* real and that He probably *does* want him back. Tell your Inmate that the Enemy may indeed forgive even someone as wayward and hopeless as him.

Then, when he has relaxed, ask a simple question: But at what price?

Tell him that the Enemy will require him to give up everything. The Enemy will make him change who he is, renounce his friends, and surrender his future. No more women. No more gang. No more fun! He will have to become one of those losers in the Chapel who walk around with a stupid grin and act so much holier than everyone else. Does he really want to be *that* guy? At what price does this come?

Once you have thoroughly sowed these doubts – pay attention, this is the key to the entire strategy – tell him that, actually, it probably IS worth it. Tell him that, after all, they are talking about eternity. Let him dwell on that thought…

As he is about to settle on this, his guard down, his

mind relaxed, introduce a final thought: In any case, this is not a decision you need to make *today*! After all, there is always tomorrow, and the next day, and the next week. If the Enemy is happy to have him back today, He will certainly be happy to have him back next week. It is not as though your Inmate is going anywhere. Sometime before he gets out of prison, he can take this step. Perhaps it should be part of starting a new life. It is something he should consider, but certainly not *now*.

Remind him that this is all a bit hasty in any case. Remind him that hasty decisions are what led to his incarceration, and hasn't he outgrown those? Remind him that he probably needs to do a great deal more investigation on his own before making this sort of decision. Leave him with the thought that there is always tomorrow, and the next day, and the next week. And with that let him rest.

In the morning re-emphasize all three messages: he is embarrassing himself, some of those volunteers are exceptionally self-absorbed, and there is no rush, just listen to what they have to say, and remember he has years ahead of him to think about all of it.

Our objective is to get through the day and get him back into our carefully curated routine.

Deumus

TOMORROW

URGENT MESSAGE FOR IMMEDIATE DELIVERY

BENTROCK, YOU ARE A FOOL.

I understand from Woertz that you became so pleased about the reaction you provoked in your Inmate that you decided to short-circuit the Always Tomorrow strategy. My message was not meant as a suggestion, it was meant as an *instruction*.

I am not at all surprised that once you started getting your Inmate to think about the price the Enemy would require, he started having second thoughts. Yes, I give you credit from raising the issue of his girlfriend and the prospect that he might have to surrender that relationship in favor of his wife and child. Yes, it was clever to bring up the stolen money he has hidden. But I am telling you – and I have seen this too many times – it will not be enough!

You will know soon, but I can assure you that in these circumstances the best thing to do is persuade our prey that the Enemy is always open to their return and that both prudence and practicality dictate that they put off any decisions, and not do anything too rash!

He has now returned behind the Enemy's barriers for the day, in a room filled with Christian volunteers and Christian inmates, armed only with the idea that he may not wish to give up his girlfriend and his money. You did not even emphasize the embarrassment and loss of respect! Trust me, it will not be enough.

I am turning over this message, as well as my previous message, to the Tempter Enforcement Division. They can deal with your disobedience.

Senior Warden Deumus

TURNING HIS LIFE OVER

DEAR BENTROCK,

I enjoyed coming up to see you. I particularly enjoyed seeing for myself the damage done by the Enforcement Division which was plainly evident. I can assure you it won't heal. I trust you will think twice before ignoring my advice in the months ahead. I can promise that it will not go nearly so easy for you next time.

Returning to the matter of your Inmate, the outcome with the volunteers is terrible, but it is not unrecoverable. We have had considerable success in pulling inmates back from the Enemy's camp following this sort of conversion process. I am especially encouraged that he did not strip himself bare when turning to the Enemy. (Remember what I said about the Roach.)

I see from your report that your Inmate is now bouncing around the prison telling people he has "turned his life over" to the Enemy. As irritating as this may be to you, there is good news in this for us. With his language and his enthusiasm, he is setting himself an impossibly high standard that is bound to fail. When his exuberance gives way to reality, he will once again be vulnerable.

This idea – popular among some of the Enemy's followers – that a spiritual experience culminating in a public expression of devotion to Him will suddenly change everything about them, is nearly magical in its thinking. The Enemy does not work that way anymore than we do. He could not do so even if he wished, as it is contrary to the free will He prizes so highly. Exercising their free will is what got the ape-gods into their current situation, and an exercise of free will is required to extract them (or, if you do your job correctly, it will be the thing that returns your Inmate right back to us).

I am not sure where the idea originated that speaking aloud a special incantation called the "sinner's prayer" would suddenly and irrevocably transform the prey. It does not work that way, it never has, and your Inmate will discover this fact soon enough. For now, it is far better for you to *step back* and let him trumpet his conversion as far and as wide as he chooses. With a bit of luck and skill, this very loud and obnoxious public affir- mation will allow us to drag him back into our camp with several other inmate converts in tow.

Let me be clear, however, that while your Inmate's disappointment and disillusionment is certain to come, that is no guarantee that he will return to our path. Walking the Enemy's straight and narrow road requires a constant and diligent application of the prey's free will, to be sure, but it also requires the generous and ongoing assistance of the Enemy Himself (something He calls "grace").

The Enemy has promised to provide such assistance as necessary, and He does so reliably when the prey seek it. He has also warned them clearly that they cannot enter His Kingdom without His help (so that none of them can boast of their accomplishment)[10]. If your Inmate follows these simple instructions faithfully – diligently seeking to live in the Enemy's will and seeking His help as needed – then he is lost to us, and you are doomed. (I do so enjoy watching the slow, terrible, and complete destruction of a failed tempter in the hands of Our Master.)

But all is not hopeless for you. As I said, we have had great success in pulling inmates like yours back onto our wide and easy road. Let us begin by encouraging him to continue to trumpet his conversion for the next several days. This phrase that he has "given his life over" to the Enemy is particularly useful to us. Especially since we both know it is a lie.

Your Inmate has held back from exposing to the Enemy some of his greatest (and most embarrassing) failures and weaknesses. It is not uncommon to see prey hold these back. They do not wish to confront their most painful and difficult failings. They certainly do not wish to confess them aloud, and they generally prefer not to admit them even to the Enemy. Your prey comforts himself by noting that the Enemy "already knows" about all that – which He does, and so do we – as if the purpose of exposing it before the Enemy was to convey some news He might not otherwise know. (These ape-gods are so astonishingly simple-minded. One does wonder what He sees in them.)

Soon enough your Inmate will confront the reality that there are a great many aspects of his life he has decidedly *not* "turned over" to the Enemy! He will have to deal with these piece by piece, painful truth by painful truth. It will be your job to make the pain as intense as possible and to make the process of slipping away from the Enemy's side seem as simple and ordinary as possible. We will need to work on this over the coming weeks and months.

You should also begin to plant another useful seed for us. Like a great many Christians, your Inmate harbors a belief – which even he does not fully realize or acknowledge – that there is a *quid pro quo* with the Enemy. If he is a good person, then he will be rewarded. When things are going well for him, as they seem to be at the moment, he rests confidently in the idea that he is doing well because he is doing good. He has decided that things went badly for him in the past because he was living a "sinful" life and now that he has decided to live a "good" life, things will go well.

None of that is true, of course. The Enemy has never provided such assurance. To the contrary, he told them the rain falls on the wicked as well as the righteous and so on and so forth. But that does not deter the ape-gods. They cannot help themselves. They latch onto the *quid pro quo* because that is how they run their own lives (they have pithy sayings like "you scratch my back and I'll scratch yours"). Soon enough he will discover that doing good is no guarantee of doing well and that many of those who never attempt to do good seem to do very well indeed.

So, subtly encourage your Inmate to think along these lines. Encourage him by whispering, "Look how much better your life is all because you are in the Enemy's camp." I appreciate it is difficult for our kind to even formulate such a thought, much less to share it with our prey, but it will yield great benefits in the months ahead. In the meantime, let him trumpet his conversion and reinforce the idea that his incantation has "saved" him. This will all be useful to us later.

Make no mistake, Bentrock, your life is hanging by the thinnest of threads. You may yet come out of this more or less intact, but to fail on your first outing is not something Our Master takes lightly. (By the way, I would not mention any of this to old Alastor. If you do, you will discover that he is very far from the indulgent grandfather you imagine him to be. Yes, you may put that in the category of friendly advice that very much ought to be heeded.)

Warden Deumus

Footnotes:

[10] We think this combination of free will being necessary but insufficient is what confused their pea-brains.

GET HIM OFF HIS KNEES!

BENTROCK!

I cannot tell you how tired I am of getting all the important news about your Inmate from Woertz. Your Inmate was spotted on his *knees* this evening. You must get him off his knees! You have too many other battles to fight and cannot add another one.

I have emphasized to you before that your Inmate is part animal part spirit. When his mind and body are in harmony and focused together on the Enemy, His influence is at its highest. You must do everything in your power to discourage your Inmate from getting on his knees when he prays.

Yes, I am well aware that there is "nothing to be done" when your Inmate is actually praying. When he is communing with the Enemy, he is shielded from our voices behind the Enemy's curtain just as he was during his volunteer program. We do not actually *know* what happens during these times of prayer since none of us have ever seen or heard it (though we have some ideas which I will explain below).

While all of that is fairly inconvenient for us, we are hardly powerless to influence your Inmate's prayer practices. As with much of our other work, a subtle and persistent attack can be extremely effective, and when done well you can even lead your Inmate to stop praying altogether. But this takes time to accomplish and right now you need an emergency intervention.

While the ape-gods are shielded from us when they are praying, we have learned a great deal by watching and listening when they are in a "prayerful mood." This is quite common with them. They imagine what they *would* be praying about *if* they were praying. You would think, at moments like this, that they would simply turn to the Enemy and begin to pray, but often they do not. Instead, they mull over the things they *ought* to pray about or *intend* to pray about in the future. (Yes, I know it makes no sense.)

They generally think to themselves things like, "Next time I must remember to pray about…" or "I should have prayed about…" and so forth. In the same way they tend to wallow in anxiety and uncertainty about ordinary daily life, even experienced Christians will often spend time replaying, planning, critiquing, and worrying about what they failed to bring before the Enemy in prayer.

By watching this behavior, we have developed a good understanding of at least some of what happens behind the prayer veil. We believe that they tend to ask the Enemy for help with all manner of petty little concerns (it is incomprehensible why He invites such nonsense, but He does). They also appear to spend a lot of time asking for forgiveness of one thing or another. They seem to spend some time praying for family and for neighbors (though our research suggests they spend a great deal less time on this than on themselves) and on very rare occasions they pray for their adversaries. The Enemy has also provided them with some prayer formulas that they tend to memorize (although it has been our observation that they frequently skip the step of genuinely understanding the words they are committing to memory).

It appears that they may also, on rare occasion, spend their prayer time worshiping the Enemy, but this appears to be very rare indeed. There are hardly any documented cases of our kind hearing them think to themselves something like, "I must spend more time praising and worshiping next time." By contrast, there are countless billions of documented examples of the ape-gods saying things like, "I must remember to pray for..." my health or my job or my marriage or my children or my country or my pets or my whatnot. So, it seems that ape-gods spend most of their time in communion with the Enemy speaking about themselves, which is perfectly in character with what we know about them.

Be that as it may be, the Enemy has told them to bring their concerns to Him in prayer. Just as you have seen with your Inmate, when they enter their prayer time with these concerns on their mind, they emerge from behind the prayer veil a short time later with greater assurance, acceptance, and peace. We have seen on countless occasions where months of work creating anxiety, or years of manipulation stoking vanity, or decades of effort encouraging self-pity, are undone in thirty minutes behind the prayer veil. And when they are on their knees, and they are focused both mind and body on the Enemy, the damage to our work is particularly acute. You must remember that these creatures are animal-hybrids!

Your primary weapon to discourage prayer is your

Inmate's natural inclination to laziness and procrastination. (I know that your Inmate is not more inclined to these things than most humans, but they all have this tendency.) You need to build up in his mind the idea that prayer is a task that he is duty-bound to complete. Perversely, frequent reminders from us that they ought to pray more can often *discourage* prayer. Pick a time when he is busy – perhaps in the early morning when he has been called out to work – and remind him that he has not prayed yet today (or that he has cut his prayers short). Keep reminding him at inopportune times. If he does stop for a prayer, wait for a few hours, and then plant the question, "Did you really pray for all that you *ought* to have prayed for?" We cannot be too specific since we do not know what he has said but given the natural tendency of these humans to worry, just the general idea is usually enough to get his mind circulating through the list of things he has failed to bring before the Enemy.

After some weeks of this, your Inmate will begin to think of prayer as a task he is generally failing to do well and failing to do diligently. Once he begins to think along those lines, you should pivot to a different angle of attack and begin encouraging him to *wait* until just before he goes to bed, when there is "peace and quiet" and he can "really concentrate" on his prayers. Tell him there is just not a good time or place to pray during the day. We have found this to be a very effective strategy as the ape-gods who put off prayer until the end of the day often fall asleep before going to the Enemy or at the least, they have trouble concentrating because they are tired.

If your Inmate becomes the sort who will take time out in the middle of the day to pray, especially if he is doing it in a place where others can see him, you should suggest to him that it certainly appears to others like he is just putting on a show to impress his fellow inmates. Even if there is no truth to this whatsoever, they are sensitive to the suggestion. The Enemy has warned them against engaging in show-prayers to make themselves look good before their peers. Since there is nowhere in prison to be alone, we find that Christian inmates are especially vulnerable to this suggestion.

Prayer is a dangerous habit that can destroy our work and solidify his new commitment to the Enemy. It is important that you begin to undermine this practice immediately. The Enemy is pulling him closer; I do not need to remind you what it will mean for you if He succeeds.

Warden Deumus

BLOOD OUT

Dear Bentrock,

The beating was worse than expected but we all knew it was coming. Your Inmate expected it the day he threw down his flag and quit the gang. This is not good for you.

As I told you at the beginning, prison is one of those places where the Enemy is making substantial progress. We have seen far too many "bangers" throw down their flags in His name.

I know you have seen cases where the retribution for members who leave the gang is more modest. That is more typical with the older members who have served for years before switching their allegiance to the Enemy. Your Inmate had been a new initiate. I think they decided to make his beating a warning to others who might join the gang in prison.

Once your Inmate has healed, he can expect more of the same. He has disrespected some of our best servants in the unit. I do not think they will let up anytime soon. This is all a very troubling turn of events.

By the way, you could not be more wrong in thinking that "at least this will discourage others" from switching to the Enemy's camp. As you would know if you had attended your training, we have seen this happen many times before. Your Inmate is telling anyone who will listen, through his wired jaw, that he "counts it as joy" that he is suffering for the Enemy. (Sycophantic dolt!) If your Inmate keeps this up, he will be the best recruiter the Enemy has in the unit.

We need to do something to intervene. I will have a word with Woertz and with the rest of our team up there. We will suggest to his other gang "brothers" that he is not worth it, that the message has been sent, and that it is best to limit future reprisals to ridicule. But they are a headstrong bunch, and I am not sure we will succeed.

For your part, you should do whatever you can to discourage him. I am well aware that he is spending most of his days in prayer and that you are completely unable to reach him when he is talking to the Enemy but keep a close watch and try to whisper in his ear if you see him at a vulnerable moment. (Just after they wake in the morning is often a good time to whisper to them.) However, the Enemy will be guarding him closely during these days of trial so I doubt you will get much opportunity.

I do not need to tell you that your incompetence in this matter is having ramifications across the unit. Other inmates are talking about him. While some are deriding him, others admire his "courage," and still more are wondering what he discovered that led to his current state. It is very bad news for our side.

In any case, your own consequences will be far worse than your Inmate's, but I will leave that to the Enforcement Division down Below. They are experts in their craft. I look forward to their report, which truly *will* serve as an example to others you may be sure. Whatever torments they have in store for you, they will not damage you to such an extent that you are incapable of doing your work. I expect a revised report when you return.

Senior Warden
Deumus

THE SEEDS OF DOUBT

DEAR BENTROCK,

While I feel no sympathy for your recent difficulties, I am glad to finally have you back to work. As Woertz has no doubt explained during the re-engagement briefing, while you were busy with correction and re-education your Inmate has become more deeply embedded in the Enemy's ranks. We need someone dedicated full-time to pulling this man back to our path and, while neither of us are delighted by the prospect, you have been re-appointed to the task.

You must now begin the long process of discrediting Christianity for your Inmate. Rather than trying to drive him back to our side through fear or enticements, the process of discrediting his new faith – if effective – will see him gradually and quietly walk away from the Enemy's camp of his own accord. I would wager that at least half of our Returnees come back to us by this proven method. (Many return to us without ever acknowledging, or even realizing, they abandoned the Enemy's side.)

You will require the assistance of Woertz and the other tempters in the unit, and we will need the help of our human followers to execute the strategy. With this in mind, we will be giving you limited direct access to certain other ape-gods, beginning with the Chaplain's Assistant, so you can use them to help mount a coordinated attack on your Inmate's newfound faith.

Before discussing specifics, you need to familiarize yourself with a few of our fundamental tactics for discrediting Christianity. There are a great many more that we use in the free world, but we find these six to be especially effective in prison. I will provide more detail for each of these in due course, but for now the following is a short summary of the techniques we are going to use:

1. Moderation in all things…
2. With all these hypocrites around…
3. The entire thing is a fantasy…
4. If the Enemy really cared…
5. Just forgiven…
6. Come back tomorrow…

Remember that through these techniques we are working to *discredit* the faith; to make the prey believe it is not real or, at the least, not something deserving of their deepest allegiance. Unfortunately, we begin this phase of your work with a great disadvantage: we do not know where the core of your Inmate's faith lies. Because so much of his communing with the Enemy is hidden from us – his prayers, his time of worship, his study, and of course his time with the volunteers – we can only pick up snippets from his conversations with others.

We know from experience that the Enemy's followers – especially in these early days following conversion – tend to latch onto certain aspects of His message, and that this forms the initial core of their faith. For some it will be intellectual assent – they have come to believe the historical truth of the Son and the evidence of the Creator that is all around them. For others it will be a more heartfelt response – finding in His message the hope, purpose, and answers for which they have been searching. Others will be drawn in by the community of faith and the example of His followers. Still others will find comfort and confidence from childhood memories reawakened.

It is infuriating that the Enemy seems completely disinterested in the path they take back to Him. I have even seen people return to his side on the strength of nothing more than watching the sun set. He does not seem to care (you would think He would require a basic entrance exam of some sort). Regardless of where they begin, over time His followers will broaden and deepen the basis of their faith, at least so long as they follow His program.

If we had a better understanding of your Inmate's personal journey and his specific path back to the Enemy, we could launch a targeted attack. Should you pick up any clues about this from your Inmate or another ape-god in the unit, you must contact me immediately and we will adjust our strategy. Barring this unlikely opportunity, however, we will take a broad approach to discrediting the faith and drawing your Inmate back to us.

Understand that pursuing prey who have turned to the Enemy is like walking through the forest trapping birds with a net. You must operate by stealth and each throw must hit its mark the first time or the prey will swiftly fly out of your reach and back to safety behind the Enemy's curtain. With each failed attempt the prey will become more wary. In short, patience is more important than ever, and you must time your attacks with the greatest of care.

Rather than trying to capture your Prey outright, I am going to teach you how to launch subtle assaults that your Inmate will barely notice. Over time he will become more relaxed when he hears you rustling in a nearby bush, convinced that it is little more than the wind. If you are careful, you can use these stealth attacks to steer him in the direction of our net and let him fly into it of his own accord. In any case, the clumsy temptations and threats you used in the past will no longer be effective. Even distraction – which will continue to be our best weapon – must be deployed with greater sensitivity.

In the coming weeks we need to tamp down his enthusiasm and his urgency. Both work against our strategy. We suspect (we do not know) that he is pouring himself into broadening and deepening the foundation of this newfound faith. During this initial rush of post-conversion enthusiasm, we have learned that followers will typically have one of two initial reactions: basking in the joy they have found or remaking themselves to fit into their new life. It will come as no surprise that we prefer the "basking" sort of converts rather than the "remaking" sort.

One theologian early in the last century told his fellows that when the Son calls a person, "he bids him come and die." The remaking sort of converts are following that path. They are engaged with the Enemy's program of abandoning the attachments to their former lives and letting "the old person die." The remaking sort of converts understand that they have enlisted in the Enemy's army to be a *servant* for Him. They understand that this is the meaning of those memorized words about "thy will be done." (As I wrote previously, a great many of His followers memorize the words of the prayers but not their meanings.)

The basking converts are an entirely different sort. You can usually spot them busy telling others something along the lines of "I have been saved" and "I am redeemed" and "I am heaven-bound." These things may be true enough for the Enemy's servants, but when you hear one of the ape-gods talking in this way it is often a sign that they never enlisted to be a servant in the Enemy's army, but instead think they enlisted the Enemy to serve them!

I know it sounds ridiculous but believe me when I tell you that a good number of converts have somehow twisted the entire thing around. They think that professing their faith is like rubbing the genie's lamp in that old fairy tale. They have now been granted their original wish of redemption and the genie is standing by to grant other wishes as and when necessary. All they must do is ask and it shall be given to them. Now they bask in the warmth, overjoyed about the benevolent genie they've unleashed into their lives. When the genie does not deliver in the manner and at the time they expect, their faith withers.

Sadly, in speaking to Woertz during these weeks you have been indisposed, your Inmate has shown no signs that he is basking. To the contrary, the hints we have gleaned from conversations he has had with our servants suggest that he is delving deeply and enthusiastically into the business of remaking himself. It appears he is purposefully shedding some of the most helpful traits we cultivated during his pre-conversion life. (I warned you that the entire gang business would work against us.) We need to surround him with our kind of Christians.

It is here where the Chaplain's Assistant will come to our aid. The Assistant was one of those basking-converts who quickly lost confidence in the genie. He is a shrewd sort, however, and he quickly realized that prison life hanging around the chapel was much more tolerable than prison life in the laundry. He readily adopted the Christian vocabulary, and he is one of those ape-gods who was genetically gifted with an engaging smile and a welcoming disposition. He used these advantages to align himself with the former Chaplain at the unit (a long-time servant of ours who was sadly replaced last year) and landed one of the Chaplain's Assistant jobs.

You may directly contact the Assistant this evening. Your first task is to teach your Inmate *moderation*. The Assistant should be useful in this regard, but I must offer a word of caution before you begin: The Assistant does not know that he is our servant. In fact, he does not think we exist at all. To reach him, you will need to appeal to him indirectly. Suggest to him that your Inmate is a good guy who he should get to know. Tell the Assistant that your Inmate, "the poor guy," is getting smothered by the God Squad and he needs a friend who has "been there" and "knows what it's like." That should appeal to his vanity and get him started.

On the other side of the equation, you should suggest to your Inmate that he ought to befriend the Assistant. Remember that your Inmate is still naïve in spiritual matters and is not yet able to recognize the Assistant for who he is. Tell him that the Chaplain's Assistant is just the sort of experienced Christian who can help him grow in his faith.

Give this a try tonight and let's see if our little match-making works out. I suspect it will.

Warden Deumus

THE SPECTATOR

DEAR BENTROCK,

I hear from Woertz that our matchmaking has worked out better than you could have hoped. Who knew that your Inmate and the Assistant would have so much in common? Well, I did, of course, but that is owing to my insight and expertise.

The Assistant is already becoming a moderating influence on your Inmate. Most helpfully, they are attending chapel services together. The Assistant is introducing your man to everyone, doing his usual glad-handing with his big smile, and is busy transforming your Inmate's view of the so-called "worship service" into just another social gathering. "Don't take it so seriously, be joyful," the Assistant croons. His message seems to be resonating with your Prey. This is all very encouraging.

In no time, he will be like those many Christians we see both in prison and in the free world who come to Sunday Show for the "spiritual boost" and an emotional pick-me-up. And why not? It *should* be all about them!

The basking-in-joy converts embrace this attitude with little effort. They have recognized right from the start that the entire purpose of church and worship is to give them a good spiritual experience. They come seeking entertaining music, quality oration, and a well-produced and smooth-running program of 60 minutes or less. Even here in prison – where services are less like a spectator activity than most anywhere in the modern world – they have these expectations.

Out in the free world, these sorts of Christians think of themselves as the church's customer, and, of course, the customer is always right. Here in prison, they might not be able to head down the street to a different congregation, but they are no less certain that the purpose of the show is to keep them engaged, give them a spiritual boost, and provide a venue to "fellowship" with like-minded friends. It comes so naturally to the basking-Christians because in their theology the Enemy is there to serve them (though they would never quite put it that way). And the baskers' joyful enthusiasm is contagious – as your Inmate is now learning.

Along with teaching your Inmate to expect a good show, the Assistant is teaching him how to be a spectator. This approach to his faith will yield lifelong benefits for us. In fact, we love spectator Christians. They are among our most reliable allies in the free world and here in prison.

Spectator Christians are very like sports fans. They imagine themselves to be on the team. They cheer their side, wear the uniform (or at least a cheap imitation of it), claim the players' victories as their own, and regret defeats as if they have suffered a loss. They are the loud and highly visible public face of the faith just as sports fans are the loud and highly visible face of their teams.

Needless to say, they are not on the team, it is all a self-indulgent fiction. They are in the viewing stands. They do not suffer the blows on the field. They do not sweat through practice or spend countless hours preparing themselves mentally and physically for the contest. And when the day's game is done, the spectators do not return to the locker room to bandage the injuries. They exit the stadium and go back to whatever new distraction awaits them. They can neither win nor lose because they do not play.

The coaches and the owners are all too happy to indulge these make-believe players in the stands because they pay the bills. They are nice to have around so long as they do not become too disruptive on game day and they never, ever interfere with the real players while they are in practice or especially when they are on the field.

A modern basking-in-joy Christian finds the entire spectator approach to Christianity familiar and comforting. Now that "church[11]" represents little more than a specific building where they go to watch a well-choreographed program, the role of spectator seems to fit the venue perfectly. When the show is over, they go in peace with nothing more asked or expected of them. It hardly occurs to them that the Enemy has only ever called for players, never spectators.

While your Inmate is learning how to be a good spectator, he is also getting a lesson from the Assistant in our style of faith: moderation in all things, and especially in things having to do with the Enemy. One goes to chapel, of course, and is an upstanding member of the faith community. But it is quite unrealistic – unreasonable even – to build your entire life around worshiping and studying and serving the Enemy! Balance and moderation are called for in all things. And our Chaplain's Assistant is nothing if not a very balanced Christian.

He sports a "Christian attitude." He is pleasant enough to others and always has a nod and a smile. He does not engage in any of the home brewing, drug smuggling, cursing, gambling, or other low-grade temptations that are commonplace on the unit. And his Sundays – or at a least a good hour each Sunday – is dedicated to watching the show in Chapel.

But our assistant is no more dedicated to serving the Enemy than you are, Bentrock. He is dedicated to serving himself. Everything he does is built around him and his future. He became a Chaplain's Assistant because it was better than the laundry. He "serves" in extra chapel programs to get credit with the parole board. He works weekends with the volunteer programs because the food is good. And here is the real beauty of this tactic: he is quite sure he is on the fast track to heaven. He thinks his road is wide and smooth – and it is, but only because it is headed an entirely different direction.

I am sure you are beginning to realize how quickly and easily we can begin to transform your Inmate into a self-assured, even joyful spectator Christian. This transformation must be built on the foundation of inverted theology. Once the Assistant has firmly planted the idea that the Enemy is there to serve your Inmate and not the other way around, the rest is an easy coast down the hill to our wide and smooth road. In this context, moderation seems reasonable and right. After all, if you think of the Enemy as more genie than master, it is only polite not to rub the lamp too often.

Again, none of them would put it quite that way and you need to take care when whispering to your Inmate. You need to use the language of the Basking-in-joy

Christians about how the Enemy "wants you to be happy" and so forth. If his thoughts turn toward prayer, suggest fellowship instead. If his thoughts turn toward transforming into a "new creature," suggest that he is being insufficiently joyful and appreciative; that he is getting boring and dour; that he needs moderation in all things. Remind him that being a Christian is just one aspect of who he is and who he was meant to be.

Remember what I told you about hunting birds with a net. Do not rush to capture him, just get him used to hearing your voice in his ear once again. Do not suggest anything that he might see as an attack. It is all just friendly advice from the part of him who is more mature. And always steer him back to his new friend the Assistant.

As he becomes more relaxed with the idea of being a more "balanced and moderate" follower of the Enemy, we will open the next phase of our attack. For now, however, let's encourage this newfound friendship.

Watching Intently from the Stands,
Warden D.

Footnotes:
[11] Church is one of those words we have transformed from its original meaning to something entirely different. The power and meaning behind the *ecclesia* becomes weak and deflated when it is transformed into a synonym for a sixty-minute show in an undersized performance hall.

THE AWFUL NOISE

Dear Bentrock,

How can you possibly tolerate the awful sound? One of our free-world tempters was visiting this week, accompanying the free world delegation on Sunday, and he reported your Inmate was singing in Chapel! Not just singing, mind you, but singing aloud and with enthusiasm. It is little wonder you are struggling to make progress with him. You must stop that awful noise.

Remember the warning I gave you, and the difficult lesson you learned, when your Inmate began praying aloud? Singing in worship is even more dangerous. The ape-gods are distinct among the Enemy's creatures in their ability to sing. The entire purpose of this singing, as near as we can tell, was to give them a unique way to communicate with Him. When they are singing aloud, all other thoughts are blocked, and they are practically immune from distraction. When they are singing, they are completely engaged with the Enemy, especially if they are singing and moving their bodies simultaneously (a truly disgusting habit).

184184184 184 184
184184184184184184184184184184184184184184184184184184184184

The act of singing is as natural to them as breathing. If you ever encounter a group of young ape-gods (it is unlikely that you will because we do not begin to engage with them until they are older) you will often witness them singing with joy and abandon. I once encountered an event they call a birthday party[12] where one of my female prey had assembled a brood of young children. Suddenly there was an explosion of joy (it nearly crippled me) as the youngsters launched into song, screaming out the words and clapping hands in unison. It is no exaggeration to say that it was among the most terrifying experiences of my existence.

Fortunately, we have developed techniques to discourage this kind of behavior, especially in Chapel. As soon as the ape-gods are old enough to warrant our attention, we begin to teach them the difference between good and bad singing. We divide the species into those who are good singers and those who are not. The good singers have a reasonably broad vocal range and an ability to select and maintain vocal frequencies on demand (they call it singing "in tune"). The "bad" singers cannot. Few ape-gods are "good" singers, and even fewer are "very good" singers.

We then set about the business of making the bad singers self-conscious. It is one of the very first things most ape-gods learn when they come into our orbit. Even before they learn to be uncomfortable about their appearance or their station in life or any of the other fears with which we will plague them, we teach them to be embarrassed by their voice. This is no accident! If we can get them to stop singing, we cut off one of their most effective means of communing with the Enemy. So, at a very early age most of them are taught that they "cannot sing" (the phrasing is intentional).

For most, this will discourage their desire to sing to the Enemy and on the occasions when they do, they will be self-conscious, will mumble more than sing, and their thoughts will be fixed on how they sound to others rather than the expression of joy itself. We also do our best to ensure that singing in worship is as difficult as possible, but more on that below.

When it comes to the "good" singers, and even more the "very good" singers, we cannot so easily discourage their voices, but we do strive to distract them. We build on their vanity to emphasize that since they are good singers every song is a performance. If we do this well, from the moment they begin to sing they are busy critiquing their own voice and wondering how it sounds to others rather than being focused on communing with the Enemy.

The church-as-a-performance program is also immensely helpful here. The professional musicians who lead the worship aim first to deliver professional quality sound as they pursue their aspirations to become famous recording artists. They choose the songs and play them in the keys that make *them* sound best rather than choosing the songs and keys that are easiest for the bad singers to sing. Together, this helps exclude not just the bad singers but even most of the "pretty good" singers. It is only the "very good" singers with a broad vocal range who feel capable of fully participating.

Sadly, this singing business is yet another area where the Enemy has enormous advantages in prison. There are no professional musicians, the culture is one of sing-along rather than performance, and He has somehow (we do not know exactly how) created a place where it is uncommon for someone to be criticized for their lack of musical skill. This is why even a bad singer like your Inmate is free to join with enthusiasm.

You must put a stop to it. We have plenty of followers who visit the Chapel, at least on occasion. You should arrange for a few well-placed comments following next week's service. It does not need to be especially vicious, just a comment about how he sings "really loud" or how his voice "cracked" on the high note or something similar. The main point is to make him aware that others can hear him and have noted the quality of his singing. Our years of free world training should then reassert itself. He will remember that he is a "bad" singer, and his vanity will take over.

Let's end this awful noise before it does real damage to your efforts. An hour a week of singing with joyful abandon, of undistracted communion with the Enemy, will make everything we are trying to do indescribably more difficult.

Warden Deumus

Footnotes:
[12] The birthday parties are among their most amusing traditions. They gather on the anniversary of their birth to celebrate...*themselves*! The guests are obliged to bring gifts to the celebrant. One would think that if they were going to mark the occasion at all, it would be a day of thanksgiving oriented toward the Enemy or at least toward their parents. But no, they celebrate themselves.

FIGURE IT OUT YOURSELF

DEAR BENTROCK,

It is time for your Inmate to join the Assistant's Bible study group and it is your job to convince him. I understand that this is the most unnatural sort of act for our kind, but far better that he should study with the Assistant than continue with the group he met during the volunteer weekend. I will speak to Woertz and arrange to have him moved to a bunk that makes this easier and gives him a convenient excuse for making the change.

We have often wondered about the wisdom of the Enemy leaving his followers with a library of books that reveal Himself to them. If He meant it to prevent them from getting confused, then I must say that His strategy has failed miserably. The ape-gods are expert at arguing about the Enemy's books. What do they say? What do they mean? What do they say about Him? What do they say about them? Which books are even in the Library? For millennia they have argued endlessly about the books.

Now, it goes without saying, that I am no expert in His books. I have never read one and I never intend to. But I have been with these creatures for a very long time, and I have learned more than I care to know about them. As happens with so much else about the ape-gods, they seem to be very confused about the Library.

For one thing, most of them think of it as a single book even though the name they have for it is "The Library."[13] This is very odd, even by their standards. Even a foolish primate must realize that one will draw strange conclusions if one takes a library written by many authors, living in different places, writing in different languages, composed over many centuries, and pretends it is a single book with a single author. Even I know enough to realize the Library contains books of poetry, retold oral traditions, a smattering of tribal regulation, letters to friends, some history books, a few allegories, and several biographies. Some of the individual books are themselves multiple books bound into one. Reading the Library as a single work will inevitably make the average ape-god confused. (I should note here that this is entirely their own doing. Our hand is not in this.)

The scholars who study the Library cannot agree on its meaning any more than ordinary ape-gods who read it in a prison study group. They have written hundreds of thousands of books arguing about the Enemy's sixty-six books (or seventy-three books, or eighty books, or eighty-three books, depending on which tribe of followers you ask).

These days they seem especially excitable about the words they have translated "day," "grace," "faith," and "pre-destined." Of course, I have been with these creatures for a long time, and I can recall when they were especially excitable about entirely different words. (They spent two hundred years fighting about *homoousios*, and that word is not even found in the Library but is instead found in a description someone else wrote about the key points of the Library. You've got to love their foolishness.)

We certainly find this all very helpful for our work, but not chiefly for the reason you might expect. We do not care in the least – or even know in most cases – whether one tribe's interpretation is more correct than another's. They often accuse us of encouraging error, but it is disagreement, not error, that we most desire. Truth, error, it's all the same to us so long as they are arguing about it, creating divisions over it, and – most helpfully – they are distracted by it.

The Son, when he walked among them, was very explicit in clarifying that the entire point of all the various books could be summarized in two simple sentences[14]. But ape-gods are, by their nature, a curious sort. They cannot possibly accept that two sentences are all they need to know. They cannot even accept that what is explicitly in the books is all they need to know. They crave answers to questions for which they have been given no answers. So, they spend endless effort debating irrelevant questions and engaging in idle speculation about matters the Enemy has not chosen to reveal.

It may surprise you to know, for example, that they have constructed elaborate theories about when and how the current creation will end. They have no idea, of course, but the self-proclaimed experts of the books – they call themselves theologians though they seem to spend little time studying the Theos and a great deal of time arguing about other ape-gods' interpretations of the Library – are very confident in their theories (never mind that their theories are as diverse as leaves in a forest and cannot possibly all be true). They have constructed even more elaborate theories about the exact process by which the Son's mission reconciled them with the Enemy. Even we know this is a matter far beyond their understanding.

Before the Son walked among them, the ape-gods developed a habit of debating and interpreting the Enemy's laws. They created sub-laws; then guidelines to follow the sub-laws; then interpretations and explanations of the guidelines. They established practices to implement the guidelines and courts to enforce the guidelines. Since then, they have embraced a new and equally divisive habit. Now, they debate the rules and mechanisms of "salvation": what is required, what is not required, how it is achieved, who can be in the club, and a thousand other nuances (none of which they understand, at least as near as we can tell). And being the tribalistic sort of creatures they are, they divide into thousands of little groups, each of which adheres to one version or another of these speculative little theories.

As I said, most of this does not concern us – we care more about division and distraction than the truth or falsehood of the specific details. Still, one wonders: if a group of them should stumble upon the precisely correct answer, what would it matter? Perfectly accurate theology was most certainly not one of the Son's two sentences. (Laugh out loud, as the primates in the web say.)

While we have little ability to directly influence them when they are reading from the Library, you can accomplish a great deal of mischief by tuning the same filters and lenses I taught you to leverage for your Inmate's letters. With the judgmental types, for example, you can optimize their filters to see those sentence fragments that support their habit of judging others. (Some judgmental types will delight in sentences that endorse judging the "sinful" while others will delight in sentences that endorse judging the "judgmental" – either works equally well for our purposes.)

You can tune the filters to find support for a monastic lifestyle or a bohemian one. You can tune the filters to emphasize the necessity of good works or faith or both. You can filter the text to suggest that neither works nor faith are particularly important because salvation is an entirely arbitrary decision of the Enemy. With the properly filtered version in their minds, they will have plenty to argue and debate.

It is not that there is anything particularly unclear about the books of the Enemy's Library, it is just that our revisioning process works equally well on most material. As with your Inmate's letters, the lens and filter process relies upon distorting the mind of the *reader*. Even the clearest possible text is not immune, much less an entire collection of works spanning thousands of years, numerous authors, a variety of literary styles, written in multiple languages, and written for wildly divergent audiences.

There is, however, one great exception and it is why we must move your Inmate. When the ape-gods gather in prayer; when they read the Library with an aim to understand how they, personally, can better serve the Enemy; when they read with humility; when they strive to work out their own relationship with fear and trembling; and when they accept that some questions have not been answered; they are mostly immune to our mischief. Our methods are only effective when they read to support their own agenda and satisfy their own desires. If they are prayerfully reading to improve their service to Him, we are rarely effective.

However, the Assistant's Bible study is our kind of group. They encourage wild and speculative reading about things unsaid. They launch into deep theological debates about things they do not understand. They denigrate the way others read the Library. One of their members is fond of saying, "The Bible says it, I believe it, end of discussion," which naturally leads to endless hours of discussion about how others disagree. They read to gather evidence for their point of view rather than any real effort to become better servants. It is a terrific place for your Inmate to spend time. The other group, by contrast, is one of those prayerful, humble, fear and trembling study groups that are terribly counter-productive.

So, let's get him moved over to a Bible study group where we can train him to become a bona fide cell-block theologian. With time and effort, he may become a valuable tool for us.

W. Deumus

Footnotes:

[13] Editor's note: Deumus is obviously correct on this matter, the word "bible" means the Library, or the books. As for the rest of what he says here, I offer no warranty as to its accuracy.

[14] Editor's Note: Matthew 22:36-40, Luke 10:25-28, Mark 12:28-29.

MY WILL BE DONE

DEAR BENTROCK,

The news of a year-long setoff (a delay in his parole eligibility – it is so annoying that you were never taught basic prison vocabulary) has tossed your Inmate back toward self-pity. I think the entire episode will work to our advantage. The event has revealed what I have suspected for some time: when your Inmate prays "Thy Will be Done," he is really thinking "my will be done" at least on the things that matter most to him. He was on the road to becoming a full-fledged my-will-be-done Christian.

Do not be surprised. Many of the Enemy's followers are my-will-be-done Christians. There are entire my-will-be-done denominations, and they are growing rapidly around the world. It is all part of the magic genie view of the Enemy that I described previously.

With some of our prey, it is obvious that they follow the magic genie. They credit prayer for everything from finding a good parking spot to getting a reservation at a restaurant. They will often appear to other ape-gods as hyper-committed believers, but to us they are one step away from the pagan worshipers of my youth. For other prey, followers like your Inmate, the my-will-be-done attitude is more limited and more subtle, but the theology is the same.

This is, without question, a peculiar habit the ape-gods have developed. The teachings and traditions of the Enemy emphasize that there will be difficulties in the lives of His followers. He holds the view that allowing them to live as independent beings will help shape them into the type of creatures he wants them to become. Any one of them can see quite clearly – in the lives of His prophets, saints, apostles, and even the Son – that the Enemy's most trusted and dedicated servants usually find their journeys filled with pain and hardship.

Yet somehow, they have clutched an obscure and misunderstood sentence uttered by the Son to persuade one another that whatever they ask shall be given to them. So, they ask for stuff, lots of stuff. When they pray, thy will be done, what they often mean is something closer to: "thy will be done for things I do not care about, but on this matter that is especially important to me I am invoking the ask-and-it-shall-be-given clause, so in this very important case, *my* will be done." The thinking is one-step removed from the pagans who used to line up before our idols reciting incantations and offering gifts in exchange for a good harvest or a male child or whatever.

Of course, it is one step removed. The my-will-be-done Christians do not trade animal entrails for the expected blessing because that would be too obviously pagan. No, they trade *earnest faith* larger than a mustard seed for the blessing they expect to receive. And if that particular outcome is not part of the Enemy's plans?

Well, they think "thy will be done" is all well and good except when they have invoked the ask-and-it-shall-be-given clause, so, not in this instance, thank you Mr. Genie. They name it and claim it, as is their right under the contract.

Your Inmate is now nursing deep resentment that the Enemy has failed him because his parole was denied. He was willing to submit to what he perceived to be the Enemy's will on that gang business and in countless other little matters, but on this one thing, he was counting on the it-shall-be-given clause. From his conversations with the Assistant, we can guess that he had prayed most earnestly about it, and to hear him tell it, he prayed with abiding faith and confidence. Now he is left wondering what went wrong.

This is your moment. When a my-will-be-done prayer goes wrong, especially when it is a my-will-be-done prayer from someone who does not ask for things very often, the prey is always vulnerable. They will typically react in one of three ways. The first reaction, which we very much want to avoid, is that the prey will recognize that he has been treating the one he claims to serve as a genie who is at his command. He will realize the defect in his relationship with the Enemy, he will repent, and he will rebuild his relationship based on the proper foundation of Lord and servant. This is clearly the very worst possible outcome, and you must steer him away from anyone who might suggest this path. (Roach!)

The second reaction, which would be nice but is probably unrealistic in the case of your Inmate, is that the prey will get angry with the Enemy. He will conclude that either the Enemy is not real or (and this is preferred) that the Enemy is real but does not care about him, does not listen to him, and that the promise is empty. This reaction is most typical in ape-gods who are naturally prone to anger (I do not think we need to revisit *that* discussion!).

The third reaction, which is the one we wish to encourage here, is disappointment and distancing. Your Inmate is clearly disappointed, and rather than allowing him to dwell on the matter, you want to encourage him to "move forward." The longer he dwells on the matter, the more likely that either he or one of his fellow believers will recognize his own error. You want to keep this very simple: "Sometimes the Enemy says 'no' and there is no point thinking about it." Recommend this to his friend the Assistant, he will be glad to repeat that message.

Once your Inmate accepts this – and it should not take more than a day or two with him – you are ready to begin the distancing program. Every time he hears someone mention that they intend to pray for someone or about some important matter, you need to be at his side saying, "A lot of good that will do," or, "Don't expect too much." Subtly remind him that his own experience proves that prayer is pointless. Every time he encounters someone who has been let down after invoking the "it-shall-be-given clause," remind him again that prayer is pointless.

You are not only creating a rift between him and the Enemy, but you are also redefining the word prayer in his mind to mean "a request." All the other things he has learned about what prayer is meant to be will gradually get stripped away. When he thinks to himself "I must set aside time to pray this evening" just remind him that he already prayed during the chapel service this week, that he does not have any pressing needs at the moment, and the entire thing is a waste of time since it has little chance of success.

You should *encourage* him to say the occasional superficial prayer that he has memorized, and which means little to him. Frequently remind him to say that ridiculous little ditty he often recites at mealtime. Encourage the "let me pray for you" ninety-second quick stops for his friends at the chapel. But whenever he thinks to himself that he needs to set aside meaningful time to commune with the Enemy, just remind him that he has already been praying all day. Along the way, keep reinforcing the idea that prayer equals request.

This entire setback is also an excellent opportunity to return him to the mire of self-pity. Do not focus his attention too much on the unanswered prayer, but instead focus it on the unfairness of the parole system, the commissioners, and the warden. Why was he singled out? Others have been paroled earlier and with much worse records. He has not caught a case in more than a year – well, except that incident with the gang but obviously that was not his fault, and everyone knows it. Even his friend the magic genie could not help him because the entire system is corrupt and unfair.

Between the disappointment, the self-pity, and the feeling that he held up his side of the bargain, but the magic genie did not, he will naturally distance himself from the Enemy. In a few weeks' time, you will be able to encourage him to skip Chapel because he is "tired." At some point there will be a moment – it is impossible to know when – that one of his fellow believers will ask him to give a reading or share a testimony or some other modest task in service of the Enemy. At that moment, whisper in his ear, "Your head is not in the right place for this, maybe next week." When he turns down the request to serve the Enemy, even in a small matter, his distancing will be complete, and he will be ours again.

I cannot emphasize enough, however, that you do not want him to dwell too long on *why* the Enemy did not grant his request or *why* he believes that the Enemy was obligated to do so. If his mind lurches toward the painfully obvious Lord-servant relationship, the entire strategy may backfire. There is always a risk that my-will-be-done Christians who go through a disappointment like this one will reconsider their entire perspective and become genuine Thy-will-be-done Christians. That is something we very much need to avoid.

As an aside, I do find it amusing that when the Son uttered the misunderstood words about "ask and it will be given to you," in the very next moment he warned that the gate is wide and the road broad that leads to our domain. As usual, many of the ape-gods never read the next sentence. They stop when they imagine they have heard what they wished to hear: the part that seems to be all about a magic genie and unlimited wishes.

Following the Will of Our Master Below,
Warden Deumus

THE PROFESSOR

The distancing program will take time. You must be patient! While you are working on this, it is as good a moment as any to introduce a new source of doubt to your inmate: the old science verses faith trope.

Just because your inmate has only the most superficial understanding of the natural sciences does not imply that this cannot be an effective point of attack. Those who understand the least about the sciences are often the most eager to embrace doubts about the Enemy from a "scientific perspective" just as those who know least about history are champions of quirky conspiracies about how the Gospels are a rehash of the Osiris myth, and those who can barely speak one language fancy themselves experts on the "true meaning" of the Enemy's text. Ignorance does little to discourage your average ape-god from asserting expertise. Case in point: the inmate known as the Professor.

It probably goes without saying, but the Professor is not an academic of any sort. Before he joined our esteemed group in the Texas prison system he was, however, a math instructor at a community college. He adopted the nickname Professor shortly after he arrived here.

The Professor came to despise the Enemy as a teenager. He was not reared in a religious household, which is often a target rich environment from which we can recruit, but many of the adults in his life were followers of The Way. When he embraced the teen rebellion for which these ape-gods are famous, he quickly discovered he could offend, shock, and anger the religious adults around him by ridiculing the Enemy and those who followed Him. In college, he found a group of fellow-travelers who took pleasure in ridiculing their Enemy-following peers. He enjoyed the feeling of superiority he felt when he was in their company.

As usual, the Professor's views were reinforced when he saw high-profile political types touting their affiliation with the Church while also embracing self-serving positions no matter how intellectually incoherent. And, of course, he watched lots of television and movies, so he already knew most of the Enemy's followers were closeted deviants, corrupt narcissists, or hopeless and pitiable rubes. In other words, the Professor came to despise the Enemy in the usual way.

Most of the Professor's scientific arguments against the Enemy consist of little more than an eye-roll and a knowing smirk (he perfected this carefully practiced reaction while he was in high school). This sort of dismissive gesture is deadly effective with many of our prey and especially with those who feel intellectually inadequate. His more detailed arguments run along the lines of what I had previously encouraged you to teach your Inmate. The Professor will ask something like,

"Have you read Stephen Hawking?" followed by a ridiculous non-sequitur like, "Quantum theory disproves all of this." He is rarely challenged, and he knows enough jargon to confuse most of his peers.

A favorite argument of the Professor's, when he stops to engage with one of his fellow inmates, is to describe the size of things, the age of things, or the distance of things. He will offer something like: "Do you understand how old the earth is? It is four-and-a-half billion years old. The story of Moses and Abraham has only been around for the last 0.0001% of that." Or a favorite of his: "There are more planets in the universe than grains of sand in the Sahara Desert. Why do you think yours is so special?" (I often wonder why someone does not ask him how many tons of coal must be sifted to find a single diamond and if that somehow implies that a diamond is just another worthless bit of coal. But ape-gods are easily confused.)

He is also greatly exercised about the word "day" in the Enemy's writings. He has apparently concluded that the multi-billion years of creation and the word day are incompatible and that one need not look beyond the first few sentences to realize then entire book is therefore bunk. Or at least that is what he tells his fellow inmates. (I suppose he also believes that all meteorology is bunk since the weather forecast always includes a time for "sunrise" and "sunset." If meteorologists believe the sun actually "rises" then the entire discipline must be bunk, no? These ape-gods are incredibly gullible.)

The Professor likes to refer to the Enemy as "the flying spaghetti monster," which is something he picked up before he was incarcerated. If someone starts talking about religion – any religion – he will contemptibly mutter something about elves and fairies and unicorns and dragons and spaghetti monsters.

His views are completely incoherent, of course, and he persuades no one of anything, but persuasion is not his role. His entire purpose in our program – and make no mistake, he most certainly works for us – is to reassure people who are leaving the Enemy's camp that returning to us is no more consequential than denying the reality of Santa Claus – it may create some nostalgic sadness, but there will be no fewer presents on the holiday morning.

The Professor is latching onto one of our more effective recent marketing programs, the anti-theist movement. It is, as you will know, fashionable for ape-gods who work in the sciences to deny the existence of the Enemy. This is, of course, a new phenomenon. Until recently it was the Enemy's committed followers who led most of their scientific advances. (I know that this business of scientific advancement is not well understood by you or the rest of our kind since we have little use for a more detailed understanding of this very temporary "natural" universe. However, it has been something of a hobby of mine to track their progress.)

The anti-theist group has decided that rather than merely denying that the Enemy exists, rather than merely presenting their arguments for why they believe the natural world is the only thing exists, rather than merely trying to persuade those who will listen that there is nothing more to who they are than the sum of the bio-chemical processes in their brains, they have become determined to systematically discredit the Enemy's followers and everything they believe. They champion a process of "deconversion" and recruit followers who will also champion the effort. Unsurprisingly, they wrap their efforts in supposedly "new" scientific discoveries and the sort of rhetoric that the less educated ape-gods find convincing (flying spaghetti monsters and whatnot). It is especially popular among a particular type of teenaged boy with a desire to torment his parents and teachers.

Their effort has been helped along by two more recent phenomena among the ape-gods. The first was a broad reinterpretation of the Enemy's writings to make them obviously contrary to scientific evidence. This was led by some of our more helpful fellow-travelers embedded in the Enemy's ranks. In the mid-nineteenth century, some of these fellow travelers decided (contrary to millennia of tradition) that it was an article of faith that the earth was six thousand years old, for example. Early leaders of the Enemy's church, like that problematic fourth century monk Augustine of Hippo (the one they now call "Saint" Augustine) warned them against such nonsense sixteen hundred years ago and others even long before. But our fellow-travelers held sway and a very small faction of the Enemy's followers became known for insisting upon it. This sort of thing has provided an easy target for the anti-theists.

The second phenomenon that has been extremely helpful has been the way the ape-gods have become personally disconnected from the natural world. It has all become much more mysterious and abstract than it was in generations past. Few of them are connected to the natural rhythms of growing and harvesting, or husbanding herds, or even contending with the weather. Because their cities and towns are teeming with artificial light, when they look to the heavens, they see an orange hued darkness and a few dots of light. They no longer see a sky densely populated by innumerable stars or the clouds of the Milky Way or the constellations that inspired their predecessors. The natural world is becoming increasingly abstract and the property of experts speaking a language they barely understand.

We find this all very convenient. If the Enemy does not exist, or most likely does not exist, then the likes of us certainly do not exist. As I said, however, the objective of people like the Professor is not to persuade anyone of anything; the objective is to leave an impression that only fools, children, and uncivilized rubes embrace the Enemy's program. That is enough. Hence the eyeroll and knowing smirk is his best argument.

You will want to expose your Inmate to the Professor, at least to the extent that they become passing acquaintances. Your Inmate is moderately clever, however, (at least by the standards of our typical prey) and there is a risk he will scratch through the thin veneer of the Professor's world view. That could be counter-productive for both the Professor and your Inmate. So, expose him to a few eye-rolls and knowing smirks and perhaps an anecdote or two about the desert but avoid any detailed conversations. That should be sufficient for our purposes.

The Non-Existent Nemesis of the Spaghetti Monster, Deumus

THE HYPOCRITES

Dear Bentrock,

Your Inmate continues to make excellent progress under the able mentorship of the Chaplain's Assistant. If he continues traveling along his current trajectory, I see no reason why he might not become a leader in the chapel community and one of our most valuable assets. Still, do not get over-confident with these small victories. We have much work to do before he is a reliable ally for us, and the Enemy's tribe surrounds him day and night. For now, we can enjoy his transformation from an enthusiastic convert to a lukewarm Christian. If he remains this way the Enemy will soon enough spit him out[15]. But that has not happened yet!

I am pleased to see that he has also continued to embrace the Assistant's helpful perspective that the Enemy serves him and not the other way around. (Although he would never put it quite that way.) This transformation should help us in the months ahead (as he has already learned from his parole incident, the genie always disappoints). The next step in his journey is learning contempt for the hypocrites.

Now, I should say quite clearly that we do not want him to have contempt for *all* hypocrites, and especially not for himself or his newfound friend. And we certainly do not want him to have contempt for all types of hypocrisy, only a very narrow and specific type. As a result, this next move will require more than our usual sleight-of-hand, it will require you to encourage your Inmate to become the greatest hypocrite of them all as you persuade him to abandon the Church "because of all the hypocrites."

This entire focus on hypocrisy, it will not surprise you, has little to do with hypocrisy at all. It is mostly about old-fashioned envy and spite. In any church community, your average ape-god will find plenty of people they simply dislike for any number of reasons. Unfortunately, it is a rare Christian – even among the most lukewarm of them – who will admit they are leaving the Church because they despise and envy the people there. If they acknowledge their real emotions, even our most obstinate prey will be unsettled by what they see in the mirror. Hypocrisy, on the other hand, is wonderfully focused on the "other."

As always, we can find ample evidence to make our case with your Inmate. It is a weakness of the Enemy's approach that He will welcome almost anyone, no matter how flawed or immature, into His community so long as they are genuinely seeking Him. Even more, many of the Enemy's followers will welcome *anyone* into their community regardless of commitment, sincerity, or anything else (at least so long as they are from the right tribe).

The Enemy's Church is the only army the world has

ever known which will welcome spies and opposing soldiers into its ranks without so much as a loyalty oath or even a change of uniform. It is almost as if He does not recognize that He is fighting a war with us! We put this behavior down to simple arrogance. The Enemy's followers seem to believe that inviting our supporters into their midst will allow them to transform our followers without infecting their own ranks. Fools!

As a result, the chapel community here in our little prison system, just like churches across the world, is filled with hypocrites, unbelievers, and angry cynics. There is plenty of opportunity to train your Inmate to despise and envy the hypocrites around him.

One of the unique features of the prison chapel system is that the congregants, by necessity, are much more active in leading the so-called worship and teaching than they would be in the free world. (It is not as though they can import professional ministry staff each week – though that, too, could work to our advantage.) Despite our success in encouraging your Inmate to become a spectator, there are few places on earth where the church is less like a professional performance than here in prison. Each week, different inmates take turns sharing a "message" or a "reading" or a "testimony." Week after week, a parade of new faces come to the front to make their little contribution.

As they prepare for their part, each of the sycophantic ape-gods burrow into the Enemy's writings. Their nervousness encourages extensive prayer. The presentations usually feature halting, stumbling, awkward delivery, and very bad singing. Far from being less effective than a professional show of the sort we see in the free world; these do-it-yourself services generally spur a charitable instinct in the fellow inmates. They listen and encourage one another with a spirit of generosity born of the knowledge that they may be next in the spotlight.

The theology is often a bit sideways, the presentations are never smooth and professional, but no service in the free world is as devastatingly effective for the Enemy as those here in prison. But even with all this, we have certain advantages we can exploit.

You will recognize immediately that one great advantage of this DIY worship service is that those who stand before the congregation are ordinary peers. They are known to everyone in the audience. Their history, their failings, and their behavior is open for scrutiny from the entire congregation twenty-four-hours a day. What free world pastor or priest could withstand such scrutiny?

When they present with humility, and the audience listens with generosity it is, as I said, devastatingly effective. But when they present with arrogance, self-assurance, and a professional flair, they attract charges of hypocrisy like a magnet attracts iron. There is nothing that helps our effort to engage in anti-hypocrisy training like a showboating inmate preacher.

Fortunately, we have no shortage of those around here. They are glib, even gifted speakers. They can roll out a sermon with lyrical power and melodious rhythms that rival the most successful televangelists. They work the room with the Enemy's texts in one hand and a microphone in the other as their voices echo from the concrete walls and they make their pitch into the broken-down, donated sound system. And then they return to their bunks, all their personal failings and sinful habits on display for everyone to see. Hypocrites!

The showboating inmate preacher is larger than life for those few minutes on Sunday morning, but the next day he is just another shadow marching within the yellow lines or being tempted by the smuggled pornographic photo or the latest brew from fermentation bottle or the disappointing letter from home. "Hypocrites!" we shout into the ears of our prey as the showboating inmate preacher falls to one or another of the daily temptations in the unit.

For the halting, humble speaker on a typical Sunday, such failings are expected and generously accepted. For the gifted orator, however, we work diligently to shape their messages so that the charges of hypocrisy will stick. We tell them that they have a "calling" owing to their "gifts" (it rarely occurs to them that *everyone* in their little congregation has a calling from the Enemy and that the stumbling, stuttering speaking style is every bit as much a gift, at least when it is used in service of the Enemy). Once they are confident in their special calling, we then engage in a bit of harmless pronoun substitution.

The halting, humble inmate speakers will instinctively use "we" when speaking to their peers. They will talk about how "we struggle with" or the Enemy "calls on us" to do whatever exhortation is on tap for the day. It takes little effort, however, for us to encourage the gifted inmate preacher to make the move from "we" and "us" to "you." Now the soaring oration echoing from the prison walls reverberates with "who among you" and "the Enemy expects you" and so on and so forth.

It is a subtle change that most of the audience will not even consciously register, especially when it is cloaked in those beautiful rhythms. But it is a change that underpins the charge of hypocrite. And for people like your Inmate, who is a poor public speaker, who is shy and uncomfortable standing before his peers, it will take only the smallest nudge from you to encourage his contempt for the showboating inmate preacher. "He is a hypocrite. Even the Son derided religious hypocrites," you can remind him. And if someone as advanced in the faith as this great orator, someone who has a "calling" as he is quick to remind everyone, is full of hypocrisy, what does that say about the Enemy's entire program?

At this point, I imagine you are scratching your head in disbelief. After all, nearly every useful thing the ape-gods do is an exercise in hypocrisy. The fitness instructor is a hypocrite. The parent is a hypocrite. The spouse is a hypocrite. The doctor is a hypocrite. The politician is a hypocrite (a minimal qualification for holding office!). Anytime the ape-gods attempt to do something good and useful, anytime they attempt to live according to their aspirations, they will routinely fail and will be open to charges of hypocrisy. It is who they are.

And yet, we have been extremely successful in limiting the charge of hypocrisy to the religious realm (and occasionally politics, just for amusement). Even more, we have focused it on the Christians. You will rarely hear other faiths derided as hypocrites, but it is routinely applied to the Enemy's followers.

Hypocrisy in daily life is routine, ordinary, and not worth mentioning. Hypocrisy in the faith is appalling and calls into question the validity of the entire enterprise. The ape-gods' greatest hypocrisy is being uniquely outraged by hypocrisy in the Church.

Our deception is effective because of that little pronoun shift. "We" becomes "you" and the hypocrisy magnate is energized. The lack of humility in the presenter, coupled with old fashioned envy that he is gifted and admired, helps the charge to stick.

Once you have raised the ire of your Inmate toward

the showboating inmate preacher, it is easy enough to expand it to others in the chapel community: music leaders, small group leaders, the guy in the next seat who is striving to read and understand the Enemy's writings. The charge of hypocrisy is available for any of them and – as with any human endeavor – it will be accurate.

"And with all these hypocrites around," you should whisper to your Inmate, "what does that tell you about the Enemy? Perhaps He is not there at all," you can suggest. "If He is there, perhaps He is distant and does not engage with people like us. One thing is certain, if the people He has 'called' are such hypocrites, there is not much to this Church business."

Start developing his outrage about hypocrisy. Do not push it on him too aggressively. Take your time (remember, the birds in the forest). You are working to discredit the faith. The purpose of this exercise is to amplify his suspicions that this entire faith journey is nonsense.

Warden Deumus

Footnotes:
[15] Editor's Note: Revelation 3:16

COUNTERFEITERS AND THE LONG CON

Dear Bentrock,

First, you are quite correct that there are many examples of the Enemy's communities that most certainly do *not* welcome anyone into their ranks. Those churches are dominated by our own followers (a fact they do not recognize). Unsurprisingly, those churches are much more concerned with keeping their local tribe homogeneous and keeping real followers of the Enemy out.

It is amusing to send a newly released inmate to one of our pre-selected beautiful suburban churches or, even better, to a long-established small community church. The parolee is quickly informed – in subtle and obvious ways – that this particular community is not a good "fit" for him and he is shown the door. We have unraveled the faith of countless enthusiastic Christian ex-convicts this way.

I did not mention it because it was not relevant for your Inmate at this moment, but it is something his assigned free world tempter will pursue when he is released from prison. Even if, as looks increasingly likely with your Inmate, we are successful in pulling him back from the Enemy, we will as a matter of routine practice send him to one of these churches just so he can experience the rejection. It is a beneficial reminder that in the "real" world the Enemy's followers want nothing more to do with him than anyone else does. Each parole system tempter is provided with a list of reliable churches to which they may steer their prey.

Returning to the purpose of this letter, however, I had mentioned in my previous note that the chapel community here has its share of hypocrites, spectators, and angry cynics just like free world churches. While this is true, we also have something here that is far less common in the free world: parishioners playing the Long Con as counterfeit Christians. I think this may be the ideal path to encourage your inmate to follow.

What sets the counterfeit Christian apart from other cynics, spectators, and hypocrites is that he *knows* he is not a follower of the Enemy, and he has no intention of ever *becoming* a follower, but he is nonetheless a faithful participant in the Enemy's community. Most often he does not even believe the Enemy exists, but he makes a purposeful decision to attend church, to be part of the community, and to pass himself off as a sincere follower, because he believes it will be beneficial to his career, his personal life, and his reputation. As I said, this is much more common here in prison than out in the world.

There was a time when playing the Long Con was commonplace in free world churches as well. In the days when being a "good Christian" was an essential, or at least valuable, qualification for professional and social advancement, plenty of our free world prey were expert at dressing up as a dedicated person of faith and convincing others that they were firmly in the Enemy's camp. They would cultivate a church-going reputation over years and decades, often taking roles as leaders in their faith community, and all the while having no more intention of serving the Enemy than we do. These days, most ape-gods find very little value in that sort of thing and so it has mostly fallen out of fashion[16].

Here in prison, by contrast, being a dedicated member of the Chapel community is still seen as a valuable qualification. It helps with parole, it is useful in extracting sympathy from volunteer organizations and family members, and it provides access to air conditioning for a few hours a week during chapel services. It also makes inmates eligible for the coveted jobs working for the Chaplain. Your Inmate's pal the Assistant is an excellent example of someone who understands these benefits!

Helping your Inmate evolve into a counterfeit Christian will allow the seeds you have been planting and nurturing these past months to fully bloom. As a moderate follower of the Enemy who has the "appropriate balance" in his life and who now understands that religion "has its place" but cannot be all-consuming; as a dedicated attendee of the weekly show who prefers to be a spectator; as a person who has learned to recognize and despise the hypocrites (especially those who are the most fervent followers of the Enemy); as one who has come to believe that the Enemy's role was mainly to serve the ape-gods and not the other way around; as one who has seen first-hand that the Enemy does not keep his promise to "ask and you shall receive"; as one who doubts the truth of the entire tale (on the basis of sand in the Sahara and a knowing smirk); and most especially as one who, thanks to the mentorship of his close friend the Assistant, can see that there are nonetheless obvious benefits to remaining affiliated with the Enemy's church; your inmate is a prime candidate to settle in and play the Long Con.

There is, of course, patient work to be done before he fully rejects the Enemy. Teaching him to play the Long Con will support that process. First, you should help him concentrate on how being part of the chapel (and Church) community offers practical benefits for him. This is the cornerstone of counterfeit Christianity. With all the doubts and disappointments swirling in his head, it will make him feel magnanimous when you suggest, "At least this religious stuff has helped you become a better person." Remind him that he now has better friends, he is altogether more agreeable, he is less trouble to the prison staff, his mother is happier with him, and the air conditioning is very welcome. Help him see that even if none of this religious business is true, that does not mean it is not valuable and useful. (You do not need to assert that it is false, just suggest that *even if* it is false the idea holds. It is far better from our perspective to keep him in what they mistakenly call an agnostic state of mind.)

As one of our followers who puts on a Christian costume, your Inmate will enjoy many of the benefits of being a genuine part of the Enemy's family. Most obviously, the prison system will regard him as less threatening. That is good for the parole board and equally good for his day-to-day life in here. It will also keep the gang off his back (as I said, retreating now is not a viable option for him). As he grows into the role, his remaining faith will wither away. But coach him to remain vigilant!

The Long Con demands that he fully commit to his new persona.

To anticipate your concern, yes, it is always a risky strategy to leave your prey in the midst of the Enemy's camp. I generally prefer to do this with ape-gods who have never truly surrendered to Him. But while it is easier and safer to start with an unbeliever, converting your Inmate into a counterfeit Christian is not as risky as you might think. In our experience, the Enemy has little patience for people who cynically use Him and his Church as tools for individual development and personal advancement. The Spirit stays far from them and the likelihood they will be drawn back into His circle is very low. It is ironic that a committed counterfeit playing the Long Con is more firmly on the road to our Domain than almost any other type of ape-god even though his physical body is firmly and reliably planted in a pew every Sunday.

Not all ape-gods are good candidates for this sort of work. They must be self-centered enough, ambitious enough, and desperate enough to submit themselves to the Enemy's services and ceremonies just so they can gain the personal benefits they seek. They also must be willing – this part is essential – to only engage in unacceptable "sinful" behavior in secret. They must be expert at hiding their true nature, especially from their friends and family.

This is not as difficult as it might appear. Most of the ape-gods divide the behavior into acceptable and unacceptable sins. Your Inmate will have free rein to engage in all manner of acceptable sins like white lies, serial monogamy, taking advantage of others in business, and living a wantonly materialistic and self-centered existence, but he will need to steer away from public displays of the unacceptable sins like pornography and excessive cursing, anger and violence, adultery, theft, and addiction. Most importantly, he needs to adopt the crocodile smile and ready handshake that the Assistant so expertly demonstrates. What these have to do with being a follower of the Enemy is beyond my understanding, but for some reason the ape-gods equate the things.

To be effective in playing the Long Con they need to embrace the Enemy's language, abide by His guidelines, and offer an expertly crafted outward appearance. In the old days, local salesmen and business owners were among the most gifted practitioners as they reliably played their counterfeit Christian role to secure a solid base of trusting customers. These days, as I said, it is mostly politicians who are experts in the art of the Long Con, at least in the free world.

I think your Inmate has shown a promising tendency to be able to run the Long Con. His admiration for the Assistant, and the way his chapel habits rebounded so quickly after his disappointment with the parole board even when his faith did not, both suggest to me that he has what it takes. As always, I will leave it to you to decide how best to play this. You understand his state of mind better than I. Let's keep working on all of this. His faith is retreating quickly. He is nearly ours again.

The Always Authentic,
Warden D

———————————————

Footnotes:

[16] The exception, of course, being politicians. Many of them continue to find it helpful to portray themselves as members of the faith – especially since it appeals to spectator Christians who vote in large numbers. Many politicians are expert at pretending to follow the Enemy while, in fact, remaining reliable soldiers in our militia.

FOR THE CHILD

Dear Bentrock,

I find it amusing that the ape-gods always seem surprised when they are finally forced to confront the inevitable consequences of their actions. I find it an especially curious defect for a species which prides itself on its ability to anticipate and shape future events. As anyone could easily see, the divorce papers that arrived from the attorney's office yesterday were as predictable and certain as vomit after too much drink. Yet somehow your Inmate was still "shocked" and "devastated" by their arrival. Shrug!

This marriage was set to end in divorce long before the Inmate arrived here. Its foundation was built for this specific purpose. The couple entered the deal believing the endorphin stew they were feeling would last for decades, or at least years, and certainly more than a few months. Each entered the union with entirely selfish motives – as most couples do – on the strength of the fact that the other person made *them* feel a particular set of emotions that *they* enjoyed. They each reasoned that the other would be a good partner for *them*. They both believed that it would improve *their* long-term happiness. And both believed that doing the necessary things to make the other feel this way was an acceptable price to pay, even if it was annoying sometimes. In other words, it was one of our standard-issue marriage foundations based on little more than a feeling of "love" and the hope by each party that it was advantageous for them. It was designed to fail.

Along the way they have both been unfaithful, unkind, impatient, proud, envious, self-seeking, often angry, occasionally vengeful, distrustful, and frequently cruel. All in all, a fairly typical modern couple. Mentally and emotionally, they had become unmarried long before your Inmate's stint in prison intervened.

When they got married this couple had one other, less common motivation: the child. With the baby due, both said to themselves and to friends (though never to one another) that they were at least partly getting married "for the sake" of the child. It was the one unselfish thing about the entire union. They did not admit this to one another because it would have risked the suggestion that they were not marrying for "true love" in our carefully crafted meaning of the term. Now, thanks to our colleagues in the free world, his wife has asked for a divorce and, as she explained on the phone, it is all "for the sake of the child." The marriage did not fail, she did not abandon him, she is just doing what is best for the child. But of course.

"For the sake of the child" is one of our more useful phrases. It expresses, at its core, a selfless desire among the ape-gods to put the welfare of their children first. It often competes, however, with the everyday selfish desires of a typical human. With our usual sleight-of-hand, we can help our prey learn to use this phrase to make even the most selfish desires sound virtuous. Desire a new house? The new neighborhood is better "for the children." Want a new car? It is safer "for the kids." Feeling decidedly uncharitable with the paycheck? A "responsible parent" would save it all "for the children's welfare." Want to sell drugs on the street? You've got to provide for your kids! Want to jump into a relationship with a different man or woman? It is better for the children than seeing their parents unhappy and stuck in a loveless marriage. (Yes, that really works! We can massage the phrase enough that the prey believes their own personal happiness is being pursued "for the sake of the kids.")

Your Inmate's divorce is just another useful example. Our free world colleagues have been whispering to the wife for many months that her daughter would be much better off with a "stable father figure" in her life. She now genuinely believes (at least after a fashion) that her daughter will be better off no longer seeing her father but instead being parented by the boyfriend. She believes that the best thing "for her daughter" is to see her mother in a "healthy and happy" relationship. And while she has not yet explained it to your Inmate, she has every intention of completely disconnecting herself – and her daughter – from him. It is nothing personal, it is only for the sake of the child.

For now, we need to maintain careful balance with your Inmate. Reinforce the messages that true love does not exist and stoke his anger. We do not want him to slide back into the mire of self-pity, and we certainly do not want him to fall into despair while he is making such good progress becoming a counterfeit Christian. Remind him that this is just another example of how his prayers have gone unanswered. It is especially important that you remind him of all the reasons he "knows" that there is no point turning to the Enemy at times like these.

It is unfortunate that your Inmate was not fully expecting this. We must do our best to soften the impact (yes, I know that is difficult for you). If we play our hand well here, we can keep him pointed in the promising direction he was headed before the news arrived.

For the Sake of the Inmate,
Warden Deumus

THE MOSQUITO SYNDROME

I HATE ROACH! HE IS A FILTHY, DISGUSTING... [EDITOR'S note: At this point Deumus launches the foulest verbal assault I have ever read. It runs for several pages, before his anger finally subsidies. I will not reprint any of it here.]

Be that as it may be, we must face facts: the Roach not only shook your Inmate from the Assistant's spell, but he has succeeded in having the Assistant moved to a different unit altogether (something the current Chaplain had been planning for months). Your Inmate has once again slipped from our grasp, and we have simultaneously lost one of our most effective and reliable servants. I absolutely *hate* Roach.

This all started with that letter from the soon-to-be-ex-wife. There are moments when that woman's anger and cruelty seems boundless. (In different circumstances I might find this admirable.) What did she hope to gain by sending your Inmate photos of his daughter and the new boyfriend out for dinner on Father's Day? The divorce papers and the phone call were obviously insufficient to satisfy her spite. Capturing that Father's Day card in the frame was bound to send him over the edge.

As I have told you previously, when it comes to her sort, we can equip the prey with our armor and point them in a general direction, but the destruction they unleash is chaotic and beyond our control. Unfortunately, the Enemy often uses the uncontrolled actions of our soldiers for His own purposes, and that is what he has done in this case.

With his wife's letter in hand, your Inmate leapt back into the mire of self-pity. The Assistant, who is far too self-centered to be of use to us at times like these, retreated to his other friends and interests to avoid becoming entangled with your Inmate's sorrow, anger, and depression. It is a weakness of our side that we almost exclusively employ fair-weather friends as influencers. (For obvious reasons, we do not have the sort of soldiers who will stick to something through good times and bad.) When they retreat, the Enemy will often send one of his own onto the field and, sadly, He specializes in foul-weather friends. In this instance, he sent the Roach.

As always, much of what was said is hidden to us. It is apparent, however, that over these past weeks your Inmate has been persuaded to reassess everything he learned from the Assistant. It was always a danger to leave him in the midst of the Enemy's forces, and I warned you about the risk you were taking. Now the consequences will be yours.

What is most troubling about the transformation that took place, especially in the first few days after Roach intervened, was seeing the bouts of laughter through his tears. This can only mean one thing: Roach showed him the ridiculousness of what we had taught him.

It's possible that your Inmate was confronted by his

own hypocrisy and the foolishness of despising others for theirs. It may be that Roach showed him how he was treating chapel like a personal entertainment venue. Most disconcerting of all, your Inmate may have come to realize that he was acting as though the Enemy was his personal genie. Whatever the cause (there is likely more than one), your Inmate was spotted laughing at himself, the Roach was seen embracing him as a father would embrace a son, and the Assistant has now disappeared.

I would say we are back to where we started after the volunteer weekend, but all evidence suggests we have been set back much further. Roach has poisoned your Inmate with one of the most pernicious ideas he has been spreading around the unit. He has convinced your Prey that, "Joy is not an emotion you experience; it is an attitude you choose." He read this in some ridiculous book somewhere. It may not be a new idea, but it is as destructive as ever for people like your Prey.

I fear your Inmate may now be inoculated against self-pity. He has decided that he will choose joy, pray for contentment to accept his circumstances, and praise the Enemy in all things. Roach has explained to him that the Enemy's promise was that all things will "work for good" not that all things will work out the way His followers find most desirable. Roach explained that if serving the Enemy is your Inmate's true goal, and if he trusts in the promise, then he must have faith in things unseen including the ways that his own setbacks and difficulties may be used for good.

As they talked, your Inmate realized he was suffering from what I call the "mosquito syndrome." I noticed the phenomenon long ago when I was observing one of my prey trying to sleep. He was terribly tired and wanted nothing more than rest. In the early hours he was awakened by the sound of a single mosquito buzzing in his room. He tried to swat it away in the darkness but moments later the buzzing returned. The prey swatted again and again to no avail. Finally, he jumped from the bed, lit the lamp, and spent the next hours attempting to locate and kill the pest. As morning arrived, the prey found himself more tired than ever while the mosquito remained safely hidden from sight.

I thought the entire episode was profoundly odd. The prey's greatest desire had been to get some rest. At any time, he could have chosen to ignore the mosquito, wait a few minutes until the insect extracted its drop of blood, and then resumed a peaceful night's sleep. But he did not. He became filled with rage as he thrashed about in the dark.

Was the drop of blood so precious, I wondered, that he should sacrifice the sleep he so desperately desired? Of course not! But, as I have learned, these ape-gods will often sacrifice what they most desire to avoid some immediate discomfort – no matter how minor.

Now, I fear your inmate has learned to stop flailing at mosquitos in the dark; to recognize the obvious truth that if he believes the Enemy's promise that He will use all things in your Inmate's life for good, then even setbacks are a cause for thanksgiving; to understand he can *choose* joy instead of self-pity.

Your Inmate also now appreciates how close he came to abandoning the Enemy's side. He suspects our hand in this and he even cursed Our Master's name aloud. As I told you, if you throw the net, you must hit your target. You missed spectacularly. Now your prey will be more wary than ever. He will be hyper-sensitive to your approach. In the weeks ahead, you must be as subtle and crafty as the most skilled tempter. But now more than ever you cannot afford to step back! He is becoming more deeply embedded in the Enemy's militia by the day.

In Everlasting and Faithful Service of the Great Master Below,
Deumus
Senior Warden,
Texas Incarceration Division

DANGEROUS MONOTONY

DEAR BENTROCK,

What is especially troubling about this most recent episode, is that your Inmate may be re-discovering the idea of contentment as a virtue. If he does, we will be perpetually operating on the Enemy's front lawn.

It has been one of our great successes to persuade the entire race of ape-gods that restlessness is a virtue. Endless striving and ambition are virtues. Discontent itself is now a virtue of sorts while anyone who shows signs of contentment is often denounced as complacent and even lazy. It should be obvious to even the most thick-headed amongst them that contentment is not remotely connected to these other behaviors, but we have succeeded in attaching them.

The old writers used to encourage *practicing* contentment as a spiritual exercise. They pointed out the obvious, that "tying happiness to the unpredictable actions of others or the chances of fortune" was a recipe for perpetual discontent and that discontent was a vice.

The monotony of prison life, coupled with the

coaching from Roach, has led your inmate to a program of seeking to be content in what the Enemy has placed before him. He is breaking free from the idea that his happiness depends upon anything that others control. Worse, he is breaking free of the idea that his personal happiness ought to be his objective.

We must go back to fundamentals, back to the seven essential messages. The Enemy has destroyed nearly all of these with your Inmate, but I have an idea that may allow us to reenergize one of the essential messages. I will review the strategy with our technical experts before sharing it, but I believe I may have identified a fruitful new line of attack.

One thing is clear: the prey is escaping, and we must shift our strategy. I will write more soon.

Discontentedly,
Warden Deumus

THE MOST DIFFICULT DEMAND

Dear Bentrock,

Your Inmate scarcely even hears your voice anymore. If you are going to get through to him at all, you must learn to speak the Enemy's language. Obviously, I cannot possibly train you in these advanced techniques through a letter, but I believe we can cover enough to get started.

It is intolerably frustrating that the Training Division does not include more instruction on how to approach committed Christians during the prison training program (not that it would have done any good for you!). Unfortunately, they still think this is a place to send novice tempters because they will be among "thugs and thieves" who are "already halfway down the road to Our Domain." It is infuriating.

You must understand that the traditional vocabulary of temptation cannot penetrate his armor and it has become counterproductive. You should *immediately cease* using any of those techniques. He clearly recognizes your hand in his life, and he is developing a robust immunity to your methods.

I have reviewed your Inmate's case with experts from the Advanced Intervention Division and we have discovered several areas of weakness in his armor. For now, we will target the area that looks weakest: forgiveness. I should have seen this months ago, but the cursed Roach was distracting me. We are headed back to Essential Message Number One, "you are here because of what others did to you," but we are going to shroud it in the Enemy's own language. Bear with me while we delve into one of the most difficult demands the Enemy places upon his followers.

I had written earlier that when he walked among them the Son had summarized the entire Library in two sentences. The second sentence, the one about loving the neighbor, has always been difficult for the ape-gods. It was difficult for them when the Son was among them as well. When he taught them how to pray, He gave them a simple list of six things to bring before the Enemy each day (they call this the "Lord's Prayer"). Interestingly, among those six items there was only one where He thought it necessary to provide further explanation: forgiveness.

The Son told them that it was their obligation to forgive others. He emphasized the point both in the prayer he taught (where they ask to be forgiven in the same way they forgive others) and in the parable He shared immediately after teaching the prayer. (I know, this is all very difficult for you to read, and it is difficult for me to write, but it must be done.) He concluded his parable with a warning that if they do not forgive others then neither will the Enemy forgive them!

It is the only place in His entire teaching where He introduces what seems to be a specific *quid pro quo* with the vermin. We think He did it to emphasize the importance of the thing. Yes, there are other requirements – the first sentence about loving the Enemy and putting their faith in the Son – but those are not obligations of the same sort. They are just natural outcomes of realizing who they are, realizing who the Enemy is, and deciding to follow Him. But this forgiveness business is a very specific requirement that comes with an ominous warning if they fail to follow His command.

Now, we have theories on why this ultimatum was laid down. The most accepted idea is that unless they do this it creates an impenetrable barrier to being transformed into the sort of creature He wants them to be. Regardless of the reason, however, it is a specific and uncompromising demand he has made upon them. The only one, really. And it is an area where your inmate has been lagging.

Here, then, is your new line of attack. Encourage your Inmate to read the sections of the biographies from Luke and especially Matthew that discuss this matter. Your voice will get through since you will be speaking the language of the Enemy. Point him to those passages (tell him Matthew chapter six and eighteen, he will know what that means).

The following day, begin to introduce to his mind a list of people he needs to forgive. We know many of the people who have wronged him in his life including: his father who left when he was young, his brother who turned on him the moment he was arrested, his former friends and "business partners" who let him take the blame, his wife (what more needs to be said here?), the gang in prison, that old high school principal who set him on this road, and the drug supplier who gave him no way out when he wanted to start over before his daughter was born. Oh, and let us not forget the Chaplain's Assistant who, as he now realizes, nearly succeeded in separating him from the Enemy.

Do not bring these to mind all at once but introduce their names individually week after week. Because you are talking about forgiveness, his guard will be down. Once you are in, remind him of the reasons he is so angry and hurt by them. Emphasize that if he "truly wants to forgive them," he must "fully confront" the memories of what they did to him. That is nonsense, of course. He does not need a full recitation of their crimes, he does not need to re-live the pain, in order to forgive. Fortunately, he does not know that. He is inexperienced in forgiving others, and he will be easy to deceive. Meanwhile you can pursue your true objective: to reawaken the anger he felt toward them when he first arrived here. All this can be done in the guise of forgiveness.

If you are subtle and persistent, I am confident you can uncover the well of hate and anger that remains deep in your Inmate's soul. As these emotions are brought to the surface it will startle him. When they do, you must move swiftly to keep him from turning to prayer. At the first sign of anger, reassure him. Trot out our proven phrases like, "some people are difficult to forgive," or "it takes time to forgive" (which is the cousin of our "Always Tomorrow" deception that you *should* have used during the volunteer weekend), or "forgiving does not mean forgetting" (which is especially useful in encouraging him to regularly return to the memories and ruminate on them).

Encourage him to discuss openly with some of his friends the effort he is putting into this. Have him say things like, "I am working on getting better at forgiveness." As always, you want to discourage him from talking about any specific examples. Convince him that these are private and would just embarrass him in front of his peers. It should not be difficult since many of the memories are both painful and personally embarrassing. Above all, repeat our tried-and-true phrase that "forgiveness is a *process*." The entire idea here is to set his expectation that it will take years to achieve genuine forgiveness, and this is to be expected.

As you are cycling through these messages, you should also be emphasizing the idea that forgiveness is an *emotion* more than an action. (This part should be familiar ground!) When he sets his mind toward forgiving someone, quietly ask if he "feels" like he has truly forgiven them. The feelings will lag – they always do – and they are irrelevant to the task, but it will give him reason to pause. Then suggest that if he does not *feel* that way, he is *not ready yet* and that this is to be expected since forgiveness is a process. Tell him the anger he still feels is perfectly normal and he must just give it time.

Obviously, you can see where all this is going. We can keep him working on the forgiveness process for years searching for some particular *feeling* that may never come and all the while pushing off the one obligation the Son gave him. At the same time, you have a perfect opportunity to repeatedly encourage him to relive the most painful and difficult moments in his life.

As he becomes discouraged – and he will – remind him to re-read that parable. Remind him that he is failing at this terribly important task. Suggest to him that he certainly should not discuss this with the Enemy since he is disobeying the Son's command. With a bit of luck and a lot of persistence, you can drive a new wedge between them.

We have identified one of the weakest parts of his armor. I think this new line of attack may prove his undoing.

Unforgivably,
Senior Warden Deumus

THE MAGIC FISHING BUDDY

DEAR BENTROCK,

I am encouraged by the progress of your forgiveness attack. We see a growing distance emerging between your Inmate and the Enemy. While we have the advantage, I want you to take on a new task with your prey: shrinking the Enemy to human size.

It all comes back to that "personal relationship" idea that has been popular among the Enemy's followers for the past century or so. We suppose that at its essence there is nothing the Enemy would find offensive about the idea of a personal relationship with the ape-gods. The Son called his disciples "friends," and he *does* encourage them to bring all manner of human foolishness to him in prayer.

When the typical ape-god hears that phrase, however, he does not think of the Almighty accepting him into His circle, he thinks about a kindly grandpa or a fishing buddy. Those are the sorts of personal relationships our prey can imagine. It has become increasingly popular to talk about the Enemy (and, for that matter to speak to Him) as if He were just another neighborhood friend.

We know better, of course. Even we, beings far more powerful than any ape-god could imagine, fear the Enemy and His servants. Until the day that Our Master is finally victorious, we must always work in the shadows and hide from His gaze.

Not so for the ape-god who has an imagined a "personal relationship" with Him. This sort of ape-god believes it is appropriate to speak to Him, and about Him, as if He were just another guy they "hang out with" as they like to say. To them, He is not thought of as the Almighty Creator and Sustainer of the universe, He is just a guy with whom they have a friendly and comfortable "personal relationship." The Son as fishing buddy. Even better, the Son as *magic* fishing buddy!

Now, we have no idea why the Enemy indulges this sort of thing, but it seems that He does. What we have noticed, however, is that this ridiculous familiarity is useful in cutting the Enemy down to human size in the minds of our prey. In little more than a century their attitude has transformed from cowering in fear of the angry deity watching them dangle above the flames by a thread,[17] to chatting with their magic fishing buddy with no more deference or respect than they would show a casual friend. And why not? They have a *personal relationship* with Him.

Both errors – the angry and distant deity ready to cast them into the flames and the magic fishing buddy – are equally useful for us. The preachers who specialized in portraying the Enemy as an angry master pushing hopeless souls into the fires of Our Domain encouraged countless ape-gods to flee the Church. The fishing buddy trope has been equally useful. The prey who imagine the Son as a magic fishing buddy feel no more obligation to him than they do to any of their casual friends. Their relationship is at least as much about what He can do for them (the genie phenomenon) as anything they can or should do for Him.

After that unfortunate situation with the Roach, your Inmate firmly rejected the magic genie version of his faith, but that does not mean we cannot try again from a slightly different angle! For the moment, he has reset his understanding and his expectations of his relationship with the Enemy. Your Inmate is firmly in the Lord-servant mindset. We can whittle away at this, however, by pushing the personal relationship idea.

Emphasize to him that he needs to work on his personal relationship with the Enemy. Tell him that thinking of the Enemy as an Almighty Being who is holy beyond his comprehension is simply a *defect* of his spiritual maturity. The Father should just be "dad" and the Son should just be "friend" and the Spirit should just be ignored. Encourage him to engage in pseudo-prayers where he speaks to the Enemy in casual language about trivial things ("Friend, this job is exhausting today, give me grace!" or, "Dad, I need a break from this CO.") And when he settles in for a proper prayer, just remind him he has already been praying all day, so no need!

We find that if we can persuade our prey to adopt this language and this attitude, they begin to forget all about the Lord-servant relationship and they quietly slip back into the magic genie mindset without acknowledging or even realizing it. We also find that people of this sort are wonderfully effective in trivializing the Enemy among unbelievers. The unbelieving ape-gods know nothing about the idea of the "personal relationship," but they see and hear the followers speaking to the

Son as if he were a magic fishing buddy. From their perspective it seems ridiculous to be called to serve and worship and live for a being like that.

Even a devoted follower of the Way can be habituated to adopt this sort of language, and with these ape-gods the language they use shapes their thinking and their thinking drives their actions (or inaction). It will not be a quick or simple transformation for your Inmate, especially after his experience with the Assistant, but over time we can make progress with him.

I will also search for a few free world churches that specialize in the kindly grandpa/fishing buddy approach to the Enemy. Your Inmate will be released eventually and that would make a nice first stop on his return trip to prison.

Personal Regards,
Deumus

Footnotes:
[17] I presume Deumus is referring here to the famous 18th century sermon by J. Edwards. -Ed.

FAMILY VISIT

DEAR BENTROCK,

Our moment has arrived! I will be calling in favors from several of our free-world colleagues to ensure the upcoming family visit goes well. We expect his mother to be driving up with his wife and daughter as well as his brother. It will be the first time all of them have visited and, if we play our cards well, we will not only push him back into the mire of self-pity, but we can also undermine his relationship with the Enemy. In this single family visit we have all the tools we need to drag him back to the lowest point of his pre-conversion state. (Families are often our best allies in stalking our prey!)

Your first and most important job is to set his expectations as high as possible. The visit is only a week away, so you need to work expeditiously. He has been fantasizing about this visit since he arrived, and while previous visits from his mother and his wife have been somewhat disappointing, this particular visit has already taken on significance beyond anything it deserves.

From your Inmate's perspective, this is the moment

for him to unveil – to his entire family – the new Enemy-following version of himself. The "new Inmate" will share his joy and his new outlook on life. You must build up in his mind an expectation that their reaction will be similar to that of the father in his newly-favorite story, "the prodigal son." Tell him he should expect that they will welcome him with open arms, that they will congratulate him on his transformation, that they will make plans for rejoicing and beginning a new life once he returns from prison.

It is important that you have him picture separate conversations with each of them. He should imagine that his mother will embrace him as the son, and the man, she always knew he could become. His wife – at least in his imagining – will tell him that she loves him and wants him back. His daughter will admire him. His brother will be terribly proud of him. All of them will welcome him joyously. Replay portions of this fantasy reunion in his mind every day for the next week until the conversations are almost scripted for him. The more details the better.

Naturally, none of those things will happen. Your Inmate has been so busy focusing his letters on his own "new life" that he has missed entirely the real reason for this visit. He thinks they are coming to see the new man. My intelligence from our free world tempter network assures me that they are actually arriving with a truck-load of dreadful news. His mother is dying. She has been hinting at this these past months, but between his conversion and his beating and his enthusiasm for getting involved in the Chapel, your Inmate has completely missed her hints. That is why his brother is coming for the first time – it is not to see *him* but to serve as an escort for *her*.

His wife, meanwhile, will be bringing the final divorce papers for him to sign. She intends this to be her last visit. That should not come as a surprise to him – he had agreed to a divorce many months ago – but he has been imagining that once she sees the "new man" he has become she will change her mind. Our free-world colleagues assure me that she will do no such thing. She is pregnant and living with the man who is fast becoming a father to his daughter.

It is plain to see why we wish to set his expectations as high as possible. The greater the mismatch between what he believes will happen and what will actually happen the greater the chances that we can deal a single fatal blow to his faith, his confidence, and his future. That must be our plan.[18]

I am preparing his wife and his brother with messages from our free-world colleagues. As you know, his mother and daughter are beyond our reach so we will do our best to encourage the visitors with whom we have considerable influence to accomplish our work.

We will be reminding both his wife and his brother of the many instances in the past when your Inmate promised he would "turn over a new leaf" only to go right back to his old ways. We will be telling both (in different contexts) that the best and most humane thing they can do is be honest and firm with him: "tear off the bandage quickly," and "do not give him false hope," and all the other platitudes we use to convince people that acting with cruelty is humane. I expect both will be happy for the advice. They each harbor great anger toward him, and the cruel-is-kind message should be a welcome suggestion for those two.

Beyond setting unreasonable expectations, you need to help him prepare his "speech." He is nearly bursting with desire to tell them all about his new relationship with the Enemy. Rather than discouraging this desire, you should support and reinforce it. You should remind him that his wife, his brother, and his daughter are not in the Enemy's camp. Suggest to him that it is his role to bring the "good news" to them during this face-to-face visit. Help him practice repeating some of the things he heard from the Chaplain, from his fellow Christian Inmates, and from the volunteers. In other words, help him prepare to deliver a *sermon* when his family arrives. And be sure you encourage him to give his "testimony" including the parts about joining the gang and all the rest.

On these matters, he has lost all perspective. The audiences with whom he has shared his experience are all inmates, prison staff, and prison volunteers. They find this sort of discussion commonplace. They have heard many stories of prison gangs, and transformations from drug dealer to Christian. Here, in this prison context, he is praised for his courage and honesty. He imagines his family will react the same way. They will not. They will be disgusted to learn he joined a prison gang. They will think his beating when he left the gang was not an act of courage but was instead just another example of him making a mess of his life, getting into trouble, and breaking the rules. It will be yet another case of him falling in with the wrong crowd followed by the usual destructive consequences.

And his transformation from drug dealer to Christian? He has conveniently forgotten that he has been denying his drug dealing ways with his family for years. The only thing they will hear when he makes that confession is that he is "finally admitting" what they always suspected: he was never the unfortunate victim of a bad group of friends. He was, all along, the career criminal the police accused him of being. As for his much-heralded conversion, his family only sees a guy in the same white prison uniform, locked in the same cell, serving out the same sentence, but now with a new vocabulary. In other words, they do not see any change.

But as I said, he has lost all perspective. Within the prison context everyone can see a profound change in your Inmate. From his family's perspective it all looks the same through the visitation glass.

If we play this right, he will walk away with the two most important women in his life about to exit for good, his family will dismiss his well-practiced sermon as just another scam, they will be genuinely shocked by the revelations about his past, and it will cement their view that he is a hopeless bungler, beyond any sort of practical redemption (his religiosity notwithstanding). This is our moment to snatch him back from the Enemy for once and for always!

Happy Hunting
Deumus

———————————

Footnotes:
[18] You will, of course, recognize that there is nothing about this strategy that is unique to getting out of prison. It is precisely the same strategy we follow with free world converts to The Way who are returning to their family and friends after their initial transformation. It is especially effective with former addicts, newly-sober alcoholics, or pretty much anyone who has left home and had a conversion experience with the Enemy.

AN UNTIMELY INTERVENTION

Dear Bentrock,

There is no need to cower in the shadows, the Enforcement Division will not be coming. There was nothing you could do to prevent the failure of his family's visit from having the desired effect. The Enemy's servants intervened the day before they arrived. Your Inmate was prepared for what he would face, and the disappointment – though profound – has done little lasting damage.

There are times when even a well-crafted plan like this one fails. The wife and the brother dutifully played their parts. Indeed, his wife exceeded our expectations by spontaneously announcing her pregnancy and describing how well her boyfriend cares for your Inmate's daughter (cruelty-is-kindness at its finest). But none of it was enough. Your Inmate was prepared.

You must learn to accept that since your Inmate joined the Enemy's side, he enjoys the care and protection of the Enemy's servants. The problem we faced in this instance was the Chaplain. (He is the source of endless frustration for us in this unit and we are doing all we can to have him replaced.) Apparently, the mother had contacted the Chaplain ahead of the visit and gave him warning that she would be sharing news of her illness. (It is terribly frustrating that she is beyond our reach.) The Chaplain took it upon himself to spend an hour with your Inmate in counseling and prayer. After that, there was little chance of success.

I am loath to admit this, but our carefully crafted family visit seems to have left your man more firmly in the Enemy's camp than before. He has lost his wife. He is losing his mother. His brother remains a skeptic of his "new life." Most importantly, he now realizes that the relationship with his daughter will never be what he hoped and envisioned. The (mostly imaginary) life on the outside in which he had placed so many of his hopes, has all but vanished.

But he was prepared. He had asked the Enemy for guidance, we suppose. The Chaplain must have told him what to expect (again, we cannot see what happens in that room). Whatever the case, his reaction was the very worst possible. He prayed with his mother for a peaceful and pain-free passing. He confessed the truth (which was hardly news to her) and he sought her forgiveness. He even – and this was a shock to all of us – told her where he had hidden the stolen money and asked her to return it. Then he prayed with his soon-to-be ex-wife and asked for *her* forgiveness. (The man has no self-respect.) Even worse, he forgave her. Then he prayed for his daughter and his brother.

When he returned from the visit he headed immediately to his vile group of "prayer warriors" and even Woertz was locked out for more than an hour. By the time your Inmate emerged, the worst had happened:

your Inmate had allowed himself to be stripped of the last pieces of our armor, pride, and hopelessness. I fear he is now nearly as lost to the Enemy as Roach.

We will not surrender, however! Your best strategy for now is to step away for a few days. Once you have returned, you should begin to press on his sadness over his mother, over his lost marriage, and over his daughter. His surrender to the Enemy will not shield him from sadness.

Perhaps you can help him convert that grief to self-pity. Dust off your list of "if-only" taunts. Remind him how terribly unfair it is for someone as young as his mother...you know the drill. Even the Enemy's most faithful servants can get bogged down in the mire of self-pity from time to time, especially if they let their guard down.

I will also be taking steps to work on an early release for him. Our best bet from here is to get him out of this environment and back into the free world where our job is so much easier.

I won't pretend that this situation – *your* situation – is not dire, but all is not lost. We have had great success in pulling inmates back into our fold by getting them refocused on life beyond those gates and getting them back to the familiar temptations that brought them here in the first place. That will be our emphasis now.

Warden Deumus

JAILHOUSE CONVERSION

Dear Bentrock,

This is a week filled with encouraging news! Your Inmate's mother is dead. She is out of his life for good. No more problematic letters, no more encouraging phone calls, and most importantly no more prayers! This is just terrific news. (Your Inmate is terribly sad about it, of course, but it does not appear that he is heading back to the mire of self-pity anytime soon so I do not think that will affect our work one way or another.)

There is, however, even better news on the horizon for your Inmate (though perhaps not such good news for you): I have been notified by the Department of Corruptions that he is due to be released shortly. We have been working on this for several months and now it looks as though it will finally happen. He is about to become more vulnerable than ever.

For you, this means the end of your time with the Inmate. It also means your performance will be judged by Our Master and consequences will be meted out. As we both know, your first outing as a tempter has been disastrous. I cannot imagine the outcome will be good for you.

Still, all may not be lost. You have made some noteworthy progress using my clever forgiveness attack, so that is a small point in your favor. And you still have several weeks before he is released during which you may be able to lay a strong foundation for your successor in the Parole Division. If you do this well, you may yet be given another chance (though certainly not here in the prison system, as I have had my fill of your incompetence).

As we prepare him for his life outside of prison, we need to follow our standard pre-release protocol. Once he has settled into his free world life, we will share our Essential Messages for Parolees. As of now, however, our objective is to sharpen his desires for things he left behind and, most critically, to make his expectations as unrealistic as possible.

First things first, wait until he gets the news from the Warden's office. Naturally, he will be overjoyed. Given his ongoing affiliation with the Enemy, he will inevitably head straight to the Roach to offer thanks and to seek advice. This will work contrary to our purposes, but it is of no consequence. Even the most committed followers of the Enemy quickly turn away from Him when things are going well.

It is one of the many odd features of the ape-gods that they instinctively turn toward the Enemy when things are going badly, but when they are being showered with "blessings" they look mostly to themselves. We have never been able to fully explain this habit, but it is as predictable as the sunrise.

When this news reaches your Inmate, he will quickly begin to shift his focus to constructing his plans and racing toward the next oasis. He will be proud of himself for being selected for parole. He will imagine it is something he has *merited* owing to his good behavior and how *he* turned his life around. In only a few hours you will see him transform from a repentant and lost sinner whose hope is placed entirely in the Enemy to someone whose outlook resembles those "winner's circle" ape-gods I mentioned in one of my early letters to you.

To be sure, the attitude will not last. We cannot rely upon it in the same way we do with our "successful" free world prey, but for those delightful few days after receiving this news, you can expect him to disconnect from the Enemy and become as full of himself and his plans as any high-flying executive in the free world.

This is your opportunity to plant a crop of expectations that will lead to devastating disappointment. Begin where he is most vulnerable: his daughter. Suggest to him that this is a new start for them. Help him to imagine a life of sunny afternoons in the park, of school dances and proms, of learning to drive and providing sage and greatly appreciated advice. Build the fantasy. Once these images are firmly in place, expand the fantasy to include his brother (with whom he will be staying upon his release). Help him to imagine a new career and a new place to live. Build an oasis with as much detail as possible.

Let your Prey lead the exercise. Let his mind alight on a subject and then make subtle suggestions to amplify the thought and expand the image. He will paint most of the picture all on his own. Just keep encouraging him.

Eventually his mind will turn to the Enemy. Do not be concerned, this is just another aspect of his life for which you can help him establish unrealistic expectations. Suggest to him that "with his experience" he will be able to help many others, especially young people, by sharing his "testimony" before they take the "wrong" path. Help him build a fantasy in which he is a sought-after guest speaker for the at-risk-kids program or a youth group leader. Let him create an imaginary church in which he is a respected leader in the community just as he is here in the Chapel. Suggest that he might even become a pastor and lead a congregation! Let him imagine that he will no longer be a Private in the Enemy's militia, he is about to become a General (or at least a Captain). Remember, for these few days he believes nothing is impossible.

While you have his ear, take the opportunity to revisit the deceptions you introduced before his unfortunate weekend experience. He is not nearly so immune to these temptations as he imagines – especially in this irrationally optimistic frame of mind. Rekindle his fantasy life. It is suddenly all within reach! Naturally, you should keep it within the bounds of his newfound faith so as not to arouse his defenses. You need only help him imagine the idea that he will find a new wife, and the many years of our training will do the rest. (Do you now understand why that was so important?)

As his joy begins to fade – typically in two or three days – the last thing you ought to bring to his mind is money. Remind him why it is the one thing he can count on and why it must be his focus in the months ahead. Play to his vanity and suggest that his financial success will "allow him to do much good" for the Enemy. It does not matter. Just get him fixated on the importance of money and the idea that, like it or not, he must put his faith in it. That is "just how the world works."

The money discussion will lead him nicely into stage two of his pre-release program: anxiety. He will begin to worry about all the things that kept him awake when he first arrived here. Follow the same program I taught you. Keep it vague, keep a few in reserve, put just enough pressure to deliver a feeling of discomfort and unease. Will he be able to live with his brother? Will his daughter accept him? Will his ex-wife cooperate? Will he be able to find and keep a job? What about his old crew? Will he slip back into his old ways?

Keep it vague, keep him anxious, and when it occurs to him that he is becoming filled with anxiety, you may use one of my favorite little torments for followers of the Enemy: remind him of the Son's instruction *not* to worry about tomorrow! Point out that his anxiety suggests he is not a very good or faithful Christian after all. This will give him yet another thing about which he can feel anxious.

When he is inclined to seek out his Chapel friends for comfort and advice, remind him that in just a few weeks they will no longer be around to help him. No more Roach, no more Chaplain, no more prayer warriors, no more study group, no more choir, nothing. So, there is no point leaning on them now because none of them will be here tomorrow. He is on his own, a lonely super-hero standing against the night: Ex-Convict-Man.

Okay, I am exaggerating, but just a tiny bit for effect. In truth, you are tilling the soil for the Essential Messages for Parolees, one of which is "Never let your guard down in the free world, the system is not to be trusted."

As I said, your Inmate has never been more vulnerable than he will be during these weeks approaching his release. Now is the moment to set impossibly high expectations and rekindle his old habits. (It would also be a good time to call up a memory of how much he enjoyed getting high. As I told you, timing is everything. Now you can see why we kept this one in reserve!)

While we have no intention of trying to separate him from the Enemy in the ways we previously attempted, we have every intention of helping him realize he is far too busy for all that right now. If you incorporate his Enemy-serving fantasies into his planning, he will scarcely notice that he has stopped praying, stopped worshiping, and stopped relying upon the Enemy for his hope.

These few weeks, coupled with the first few weeks after release, are our single most successful season for snatching inmate prey back from the Enemy. We are so successful that the ape-gods even have a phrase for it. They call it a "jailhouse conversion" when an inmate begins to follow the Enemy in prison but returns to his old ways shortly after release. Fools that they are, they attribute jailhouse conversion stories to inmates pretending to convert in order to gain leniency or favor. It never occurs to them that the jailhouse conversion phenomenon usually has little to do with the conversion and everything to do with the success of our pre-release procedures.

Be warned, however, that it is still possible your Inmate will arm himself against our pre-release program. It is simple enough to do. He need only recognize, and acknowledge, the perilous position in which he finds himself. He need only accept that opening the prison gate is not a door to salvation but a door to temptation. His first reaction on hearing the news could be thanksgiving followed directly by a fully warranted fear of the spiritual dangers that lie ahead. He could turn to the Enemy and deliberately, patiently, and carefully focus on establishing a post-release arrangement that guards against falling into his old patterns.

He could easily do all these things, but he won't. None of them do. He will be seduced by the fantasy that the next oasis is finally within reach. In just a few short weeks the prison system will fling him into the swamp of free world parole. If you do your job well, he will carry around his neck the millstones of impossible expectations and barely contained desires only recently rekindled. And in a few short months he will be just another jailhouse conversion story.

Good Luck,
Warden Deumus

PS As I expect this will be our last correspondence, I will close by noting that I will not miss our little back-and-forth. I have found it tedious trying to conduct tempter training via letter. I have found it even more tedious reading the endless excuses for your failures. I wish your next supervisor – if you survive long enough to have another supervisor – better luck and I trust you will be tasked with a much easier assignment, like looking after a politician or a celebrity.

SENTENCING DEFERRED

DEAR BENTROCK,

I have spoken to the review board, and they agree that your failure with the Inmate has been comprehensive. When he arrived at this prison, he was on the fast-track to our Domain. He is leaving here a committed soldier in the Enemy's militia. I had warned you that this would not be an easy assignment, but I had also made clear that you would be held fully accountable for your results. You have been sentenced to the usual liquidation ritual.

I have further discussed your fate with Secretary Alastor and with management at the Enforcement Division. It is the decision of the committee to defer your liquidation and to instead continue your assignment with this individual as he returns to the free world.

You should not interpret this as a vote of confidence in your abilities and you should certainly not consider it any sort of charitable gesture! In truth, you have made such a mess of the situation that it would be all but impossible to persuade any experienced tempter to volunteer for this duty. So, you will follow this out to its conclusion. If you succeed in returning him to our path, you may yet avoid the punishment which you have already earned.

Because your incompetence has reflected poorly on me as well, I have the undesirable task of continuing as your coach while you pursue this ape-god in the free world. We are bound together in this matter.

Serving the Master Below,
Deumus
Former Warden,
Texas Prison Division

PART III

THE FREE WORLD

THE PAROLEE

Dear Bentrock,

In a previous letter I characterized your Parolee as "committed soldier in the Enemy's militia." Yesterday, that is exactly what he was. When he stepped off the bus in Houston today, he was transformed into a washed-up ex-convict lost in unfamiliar terrain. He has been dropped, alone and unarmed, behind enemy lines – behind our lines. Your moment of advantage has arrived.

One of the strategies you effectively prosecuted when he was in prison was to help him construct a diabolically unrealistic fantasy about life after he was released. This will now begin paying dividends. There was no loving family awaiting him at the bus stop. His daughter did not run to him with open arms. Indeed, she does not even know he has gotten out of prison. (Her mother and new father thought it was better not to "confuse" her by raising the subject – for the good of the child, of course.) His old crew is nowhere to be seen. The only person there to meet him was one of the Enemy's volunteers with a bag of toiletries, a bottle of water, and a few snacks. The joyous day has arrived, and once again the oasis was a mirage.

Your Parolee is heading to his brother's house, but his brother does not want him. Yes, the brother said all the right things to the lead voter on the parole commission, but it was out of obligation to his late mother rather than any genuine desire to have your Parolee in his home. If this follows the usual course, and I expect it will, your Parolee will be out on his own and living in tent city in no time. For now, we need to revisit the essential messages and modify them for life in the free world.

You will no doubt have recognized that many of the Essential Messages we plant in prison are just variations of the seeds we routinely plant in our free world prey. For your Parolee, who has left prison determined to live a life in service of the Enemy, it will not be so easy to capture his attention and plant the free-world versions of our Essential Messages. Nonetheless, when you see weariness and doubt, you must always be ready to whisper these in his ear:

1. You deserve happiness.
2. Your situation would be so much better if others treated you fairly.
3. No matter what people say, you will never be trusted or forgiven for your failures – by anyone.
4. Your past actions are no worse than anyone else's.
5. A better future requires changing your circumstances not changing who you are.
6. Never let your guard down in the free world, the system cannot be trusted.

7. The one thing you can trust is money. It is the only thing that will never let you down.

It will be obvious to you that these Messages are tailored for a particular category of free world prey: the down-on-their-luck types[19]. The "successful" free world types will receive messages about how they "deserve your success and have merited it," how "the only thing you can trust is your own abilities," how "happiness is proof of a life well-lived," and so forth. Given your Inmate's situation – this applies to most of the ex-convicts – the down-on-your-luck ape-god messaging seems to work very well.

We wish to especially push messages one, three, and six during these first few weeks. I would encourage you to adjust message number one to say, "The Enemy wants you to be happy." This will play best given his current mindset. If you are subtle, you will be able to slip this into his meditations. If you accomplish nothing more than firmly embedding the idea in his mind, the next two weeks will have been a success.

You will instantly recognize that message one is only a short step from the magic genie deception that we nearly had your Parolee adopt when he was in prison. In the magic genie version of Christianity, the ape-gods imagine that the Enemy serves them. In the "you deserve happiness/the Enemy wants you to be happy" version of Christianity the Enemy is not exactly their servant (they would never put it quite that way) but He so desires their happiness that He nearly acts like one. It fits well with the kindly grandpa / fishing buddy image we have been advocating.

The genie-following congregations are expert at pulling excerpts from the Library to make their case that the Enemy's top priority is the ape-gods' near-term happiness. While this can be useful, I would avoid this strategy with your Parolee. He has demonstrated an inclination to look up the verses when he hears others use them. Unfortunately, that will never serve our agenda. So, I would steer clear of those for now. Indeed, I am not even going to recommend that we point him to a magic genie church (I have something different in mind for him).

Messages three and six may seem redundant, but they are distinct, and both are useful in these first few weeks and beyond. Message three, you will never be trusted or forgiven, is especially useful to prevent your Parolee from forming meaningful relationships (except possibly with "his own kind").

You should be watchful for opportunities to point out examples of message three whenever they arise. His interactions with his brother will be fruitful in this regard. It is, in fact, true that his brother has not forgiven him and does not trust him so there will be an abundance of evidence at your disposal. The important thing here is to regularly remind him that what he sees from his brother is the way "everybody" regards him.

You are, of course, setting the foundation for new sources of anxiety and anger. You want him to feel like his life and his reputation are unrecoverable, that the damage is as permanent and noticeable as his prison tattoo. You want him to believe that there are no second chances. You want him to believe that the skepticism and hostility he feels from his brother is unanimous here in the free world. Every time his brother makes a snide comment or gives him one of those accusatory looks, just keep generalizing the lesson. Do not allow him to imagine that what he hears from his brother is personal (which it is) and not universal (which it is not).

Given his mindset, he will feel obligated to forgive his brother for the "unfair" treatment he has received. So, before he heads to prayer, you should suggest to him that he does not need to forgive his brother as an individual, but that he instead needs to forgive "all people" who are "blinded by distrust and unforgiveness."

This is a useful strategy that will apply well beyond this particular matter. Recommending to your Prey that he forgive categories of people rather than actual people reduces the act of forgiveness to a sentiment rather than an action. It is not forgiveness at all. (This should build upon some of the work we started a few months ago in prison.)

Message six, that the system cannot be trusted, should aim toward two distinct aspects of his life that will overshadow all others for the next few weeks: the parole system and the everyday government bureaucracy. Do not let your Parolee forget, even for an hour, that he remains under the supervision of the criminal justice system for these next two years. The parole system itself, with its arcane rules and its routine demands, will provide ample ammunition for your work. So, too, will the everyday government bureaucracy. From getting his driving license to his social security card to getting registered for medical care, he will face innumerable obstacles. All of these will be made far more difficult by his inability to find transportation to and from the suburban location of his brother's house.

As he navigates these little tasks he will be threatened at every turn. Each person he speaks with – from the parole department to the employment office to the licensing bureau – will helpfully explain the penalties in store if he violates one rule or another. Register to vote? Back to prison. Fail to find a job? Back to prison. Fail a urine test? Back to prison. Fail to make your parole meeting on time because the bus was unreliable and late? Back to prison. And so it will go, day after day. (You should also, of course, encourage his brother to make similar threats.)

In a week or two, when he begins to meet with prospective employers, we will have another avenue to sow frustration and cynicism. The bureaucracies will steer him to the employers known for hiring ex-convicts. You should steer him to better jobs elsewhere. Let him experience the realization that – outside the small group of curated employers – he is not good enough to flip hamburgers or remove trash, much less practice the mechanic skills he learned in prison. The system cannot be trusted, and nothing will go according to plan.

Meanwhile keep repeating "the Enemy wants you to be happy" and "you deserve to be happy." Force the incompatible reality of his daily threats and frustrations onto the imaginary vision of happiness he "deserves" and believes he was promised. Remember, you are not doing all this just to enjoy the spectacle of his personal suffering (as enjoyable as that may be)! You are doing this to drive a wedge between your Parolee and the faith he has adopted.

Let us concentrate on these messages for now. In a week or so we will start sending him to Church. That is always great fun. I have just the place in mind.

Just Another Word for Nothing Left To Lose,
Deumus

Ps Your Parolee has just left one of the loneliest places on earth: prison. Few inmates discuss their loneliness, but it is an essential feature of every passing week. We are also aiming to make the free world feel as lonely as the place he just left. Far beyond all the disappointments of his imaginary oasis that vanished the moment he stepped off the bus, is the devastating realization that he is still completely alone ("and always will be" you may helpfully add when the thought crosses his mind). We do not have this luxury with all ex-convicts, but given the death of his mother, his brother's antipathy, and his ex-wife's hostility, this is fertile ground for your Parolee.

Footnotes:

[19] I should note here that being a "down-on-their-luck" ape-god is, despite the title, not a temporary status. They are a classification of prey who live in the bottom half. Few of those who dwell here ever escape the category. We employ the phrase down-on-their-luck to encourage false hope when it suits us. When we wish to make them feel hopeless, we simply call them the poor or the underclass or the disadvantaged.

UNGRATEFUL GRATITUDE

Dear Bentrock,

The tension between your Parolee and his brother is thickening by the day. This is an excellent development. Your Prey has become an ill-mannered, ungrateful, and burdensome houseguest. At least that is how his brother sees things.

In your Parolee's mind, the description could scarcely be more inaccurate. As he sees the world, he and his brother are getting along as well as can be expected, he is striving night and day to be the perfect house guest, and he feels deeply grateful for his brother's generosity.

Both versions are true, in their own way. Your Parolee is, in fact, striving to be a good houseguest. He is exceptionally polite, conscientious in keeping his little space clean and neat, cautious about asking for even the smallest thing, and he profusely thanked his brother and sister-in-law for their generosity when he arrived last week. But a week is a long time, and your Prey suffers from the common ape-god habit of exhibiting ungrateful gratitude. It has now become a wellspring of resentment for his brother.

Exhibiting ungrateful gratitude is a common practice among most ape-gods. It is characterized by the recipient of a gift *feeling* very deep and sincere *emotions* of appreciation but *acting* in a way that is contrary to the sentiment. (Yes, this is a habit with them in many aspects of their life!) As with so much else, the ape-gods recognize the behavior in others but cannot see it in themselves.

Ungrateful gratitude is something we have encouraged and nurtured among the ape-gods. We intended it as a means of undermining their response to the Enemy, but it has the added benefit of creating discord between individual humans like your Prey and his brother. It all starts with us shaping their perception of how humans can, and ought to, express gratitude. Since gratitude is a variation of love, it is obviously just another emotion. When they feel this emotion, we explain, the correct and right response is to *tell* the giver they are appreciative. The more deeply and sincerely they communicate the sentiment, the deeper their expression of gratitude. It is merely this. Nothing less, but certainly nothing more. And your Parolee has deeply and sincerely expressed his gratitude. Job done.

The difficulty is that this sort of gratitude seems, even to them, empty and hollow – at least when they see it in others. When they give a child a birthday gift, for example, if the child regurgitates the token words of thanks, the child is said to be grateful. If they do so with excitement and enthusiasm, the child is credited with being *very* grateful. But even an idiot ape-god cannot help but notice that the way the child behaves in the weeks and months that follow is the true measure of gratitude.

Is the toy discarded in a box? Hardly grateful. Is it abused and quickly broken? Completely ungrateful. Alternately, if it is used often and well cared for the child is obviously grateful. If it is displayed prominently, shared with other children, and if the child often tells others about the person who gave the gift, the child is genuinely *very* grateful, the gift is treasured, and the giver is deeply appreciated! These are all just naturally occurring expressions of genuine gratitude.

Humans instinctively understand that genuine expressions of gratitude play out long after the initial emotional response has passed. When child says all the right words to convey appreciation but then quickly abuses and discards the toy, it is not real gratitude. Even though few ape-gods hold themselves to this standard, they recognize the difference between genuine and empty expressions of gratitude when they see it in others.

It is just this sort of behavior that is on display with your Parolee. After all, if he were genuinely grateful, he would be caring for the gift. He would be seeking opportunities to help with the upkeep of the house (not just his tiny corner of it). He would work to improve the house – caring for the yard, cleaning the common areas, perhaps completing some of the overdue repairs his brother has left undone. He would, at a minimum, be working with great urgency to secure an income so he can contribute to the expenses. He is doing none of that, and his brother has noticed (even if he never notices the same behavior in himself!).

There is also something else at work here: in his heart your Parolee believes his brother was obligated to provide him a place to live. He believes he is entitled to it. He believes it is the least his brother should do. There is no better way to undermine gratitude than to suggest to our prey that they are entitled to the gift. No ape-god with even a modicum of self-respect would allow himself to feel grateful for someone giving him something to which he was entitled!

As I said, the main purpose of our program of ungrateful gratitude was to undermine the prey's response to the Enemy. The sort of conflict between your Parolee and his brother was simply a secondary benefit. When it comes to how they respond to the Enemy, our program of ungrateful gratitude has become the prevailing custom among His followers.

Christian ape-gods delight in expressing thanksgiving and appreciation for "all He has done for me" when they think of forgiveness and all the rest. They sing about it. They write books about it. They pray about it. They even wear clothing with slogans that tell others about it. They express their gratitude with feeling and conviction – especially in the days and months following their conversion to his side. And once they have deeply and sincerely expressed their gratitude? Job done! (Other than to repeat the thanksgiving exercise from time to time on holidays and special occasions or when the gratitude emotion unexpectedly surges while listening to a song or a sermon.)

As for the business of actively improving His Kingdom – caring for the yard, cleaning the common areas, perhaps working to complete some overdue repairs, much less helping to maintain someone else's tiny corner of it – well that is another matter altogether. These might be nice and good and helpful things to do, but they are hardly *necessary* or *essential* aspects of the gratitude they *feel* towards the Enemy. Certainly, none of them are rushing forward with great urgency to secure an income so they can contribute to the Kingdom[20]. These might be good and useful things, but almost none of them would imagine that this, and not the earnest words and songs of thanksgiving, is the real measure of the gratitude they feel towards Him.

Moreover, just like your Parolee with his brother, many of the Enemy's followers secretly think that they are *entitled* to the forgiveness and grace He offers them. Indeed, most of them secretly believe that *everyone* is entitled to this. Well, everyone except the "really bad" people – like your Parolee.

Even those who do not harbor this hidden thought are inclined to feel that the Enemy is somehow *obligated* to offer it. They do not have a fully-formed theology along these lines but in their minds the train of thought runs something like this: He created them, so He has an obligation to care for them and He created the likes of us, so He has an obligation to rescue them from our kind (chuckle). Besides, this forgiveness business is just who He is, so He more or less *must* get on with it and not make it too difficult for a simple ape-god like themselves. So, yes, "Thank You! But really, You were going to do this anyway because that is just who You are." (Though they would not put it quite that way.)

So here we are. Your Parolee is enjoying the benefits of his brother's house. He has already expressed his gratitude most sincerely, last week, when – coming off the bus from Houston – he deeply and sincerely felt that emotion. But he believes that he is more or less entitled to this sort of treatment since his brother is family and like any brother he is more or less obligated to provide a place for him. In the meantime, his brother is getting more resentful by the day as he sees little evidence of real gratitude from your Prey. As I said, the tension is rising, and it is all very excellent indeed!

There is, however, one worrying sign: your Parolee continues to exhibit signs of genuine humility. It is something that has been a concern since his days in prison following the family visit. I had dismissed it then because even the proudest of ape-gods can appear humble when he is behind bars. It is in the nature of the place – with its rules and constraints and penalties – that the prey will put on a mask of humility just to get along. However, I had expected to see your Inmate's old pride-filled personality begin to reassert itself by now. So, it is a bit worrying.

In any case, we should not overact to this last point. While it is somewhat troubling, you should give it a week or two before raising the alarm. Redouble your efforts on message one, you deserve happiness. This should help to reawaken his pride and will also serve to inflame the tensions with his brother.

With My Usual Gratitude,
Deumus

PS Do not forget to use the tensions with his brother to remind him of message three: you will never be trusted or forgiven for your failures. He will be out looking for a job this week. It is useful to keep this message in his mind.

Footnotes:
[20] We have seen some of them provide the Enemy

with a ten-percent share of the income they secured for entirely self-centered purposes, after tax, in a good year. So perhaps that counts as a genuine expression of gratitude, though the usual reluctance they feel when offering that ten percent looks a great deal more like paying a bill than an outpouring of thanksgiving!

SEND HIM TO CHURCH

Dear Bentrock,

The time has come to send your Parolee to church, or more precisely to send him church shopping. I am aware of the dangers in this for us, but it must be done. With or without our prompting, his thoughts are beginning to gravitate back to the Enemy. He is longing for the spiritual connection that he found in prison and he is keenly feeling the disappointment of his new freedom. He has even resumed his prayer practices – albeit sporadically. In short, your Parolee is headed back to church one way or another, so it will be beneficial for us to help steer the process as much as possible.

It has worked out well for us that he landed in Houston after prison and not back in Beaumont. Had he returned home, he would have gravitated to his late mother's little congregation and that is just an awful place! Fortunately, that is not an option for him, and he now feels lost in his new city. To be sure, it would have been equally effective to thrust him into a small town with few church options beyond the closed, homogeneous little tribal churches that mostly want nothing to do with people like him. Nonetheless, the big city, with its expansive menu of church choices, offers its own opportunities.

The main thing we wish to accomplish here is to have him concentrate on *his* criteria for a "good" church. We want to help him build a mental checklist for what he hopes to find. In some respects, it does not even matter what items are on the list. The main thing is to for him to be the one who is passing judgement. He must think of himself as a sort of quality control inspector filling out his little report card. We want his relationship with this new community to begin based on the notion that he is the customer, and the church is the service-provider (though he would not say it quite that way).

While the specifics of his checklist are not terribly significant, the overall theme is important. You want your Parolee looking for a church that is the best fit "for him." You want to encourage him to look for a place where he can feel most comfortable and most spiritually nourished. He should be seeking a place where he feels welcome and where he fits in well. Of course, you want him to seek a place where he "enjoys" the service. The details do not matter, but the overall theme – that the priority is him and his enjoyment – is essential.

You should be able to whisper these things to him over the next days and have him launch his search for the perfect ex-convict/good fit for him/place where he is comfortable/good music and preaching/very enjoyable church. Propose that he borrow his brother's computer to look around on the web – that should keep him stuck in it for a while.

You should also suggest that he visit one of the local churches from the list I provided you. I am assured that any of those places will make him feel out of place and unwelcome. We previously sent one former inmate to that second church on the list and achieved a wonderful result. The first week he was greeted by someone who asked, "May I help you?" We prompted him to return a second week and the same woman approached him after the service to helpfully explain that she did not think the church would be a "good fit" for him. He persevered for a third week – at our prompting, of course – and the woman explained sternly and before the service, "We do not think this is the place for people like you." Despite our best efforts we could not get him to round four of the insults and awkward stares, but the church secretary had accomplished her appointed task. He stopped looking for a new church "home." So, let's give that one a try!

With a bit of luck and persistence we may be able to guide your Parolee into the tribe of Christians who do not attend church. This is a large and reliable group of supporters for us. They describe themselves as "spiritual but not religious," or characterize their view as "believing in Christianity but not in organized religion." We can always use another CHINO (Christian in Name Only) who claims to follow the Enemy but whose faith consists primarily of the conviction that the Enemy *must* be happy with him because he is a "good person," and he has repeated the sinner's prayer incantation on several occasions so what more could possibly be expected? That is nearly always the final landing place for prey who follow the road to being a spiritual-but-not-religious-Christian. (Well, not the *final* landing place, but the final stop-over before they come to us!)

If we are unsuccessful in our initial attempt to put him off the entire church-attendance idea, you may wish to recommend that he try the big stadium church across town. He can be anonymous there, so that may help him feel comfortable. The place is firmly wedded to the magic genie theology with which we nearly seduced him in prison. It is worth another try now that he is in the free world and safely away from Roach. Also, they put on a rip-roarin' show each Sunday so at least he will tick the enjoyment box on his report card! (That is a little Texas colloquialism I picked up.)

The one thing we must guard against is that his thoughts veer in a thy-will-be-done direction. We do not want him to start seeking guidance from the Enemy. As I have told you before, should your Parolee ask the Enemy for help, He will send it – He always does. We also do not want his mind to gravitate toward the wrong sort of criteria! We do not need him seeking a church where he can best serve the Enemy, where he can grow and mature, or where he can assist and contribute to the community. If it occurs to him that the entire purpose of the Sunday show is to worship the Enemy and that the entire purpose of his participation in the community is to serve and grow, he will likely discover that his selection of a particular church matters less than his attitude when he walks through the door. This would be very unhelpful.

Finally, you should discourage him from theology shopping if the idea crosses his mind. For many of the ape-gods, theology shopping is a useful pathway because in practice "finding a church with good theology" mostly means finding reasons to criticize other followers of the Enemy (and engaging in their uninformed and speculative little theories). Since you were never able to transform your Parolee into a cell-block theologian, however, he has never embraced the view that Christianity is mostly about the doctrinal tribe to which one belongs. He remains hopelessly stuck in the two-sentence version of the faith. If your Parolee begins to think about the various church doctrines, we will accomplish nothing more than sending him back into daily reading of the Library – something he has thankfully stopped doing now that his study group is a distant memory.

So, let's send him church shopping before he gets serious and turns to the Enemy for help.

Your Personal Shopping Assistant,
Deumus

UPSIDE DOWN

Dear Bentrock,

All other things being equal, we would rather your Parolee had not gotten a job quite so soon but working on the dock at the second-hand store is as good a place for him as any. It is demeaning in its way – at least you can encourage him to believe that – and it exercises and develops few skills to help him build a better future. More useful from our perspective, he will be surrounded by a shop full of other parolees and most of them are our sort of people. We will find plenty of opportunities to influence him while he is there.

As an aside, you did well when you sent him to five car dealerships in a single day. It was an especially nice touch to convince him he should go "in person" rather than apply electronically. It created an opportunity for him to be rejected face-to-face five consecutive times. That was a delightful, confidence-shattering, anger-stoking experience that we can put to good use.

I especially appreciated the maintenance manager who spent thirty minutes asking about your Parolee's skills and getting his hopes up before explaining that it was company policy not to hire ex-felons and that your Parolee should have thought about that before choosing a "life of crime." I do so love when an ape-god decides to give an impromptu moral lesson to an ex-offender.

Now he is back with his own kind in his little ex-convict oasis at the secondhand store. The days of rejection have taught him that he will never be trusted, and he will never be forgiven for his failures, even (especially?) by people who know nothing about him except that he is an ex-convict. Now is the time to start working on essential message number four, your past actions are no worse than anyone else's (and certainly no worse than those of the arrogant auto dealership manager). Press the point with him. Make him angry. Have him imagine all sorts of things about the manager. Remind him of the crooked businessman stories and assure him that the "guy is probably a thief, and who is he to criticize you?" Take advantage of this moment to reiterate that he is all alone, that the world does not trust him, and that he cannot trust the world.

With this new job now in hand, his parole officer will remove a little pressure and he will have a bit of money. On the surface it will appear that things are looking up for your Prey. But make no mistake, his sincere expressions of gratitude to the hiring manager at the secondhand store were just another white lie. He is embarrassed and insulted to be working there. The salary is a "joke" (I personally heard him muttering as much). He believes it is unfair and "nearly pointless" to even take the job. (You should encourage his brother to sneer and shrug when your Parolee shares news of his new career.)

It is now an opportune time to reawaken his pride.

Remind him that he deserves to be happy, that he is *entitled* to it! (You may also suggest that if the Enemy *wants* him to be happy, He sure has a peculiar way of showing it.) Frequently remind him of his humiliation at the auto dealership. If you do this often enough it will become like his prison tattoo: always visible just below the thin fabric he uses to hide it. Likewise, help him to dwell on the humiliation he feels when his brother sneers and shrugs. We can use these incidents to feed his anxiety and his anger for many years.

I am sure it will not be lost on you that this feeling of humiliation has uncovered a lack of humility in your Prey. A genuinely humble follower of the Enemy cannot be humiliated. He is immune to it. He may be disappointed, to be sure, but not humiliated. The emotion of humiliation can only burn when it is fueled by the oxygen of pride. Your Parolee's reaction is a reminder for both him and you that his old pride may have been dormant these past many months, but it remains very much alive. So, reawaken it! Compliment his "justified" anger and remind him that it is only natural for someone with a decent amount of self-respect. Let him see just how little of the transformation into a "new creation" actually occurred during his spiritual retreat with the State of Texas.

These career disappointments and humiliations will be a central feature of our work with him in the months and years ahead. We follow this same program with most free world prey, from the very wealthy to the dock worker at a secondhand store. It is among our most routine free-world temptations to pitch the "you are too good for this job" idea and help our prey feel underappreciated, rejected, humiliated, prideful, and angry with their careers. The workplace is one of the very best venues to sow the sort of discontent that serves so many aspects of our agenda.

Now that I think of it, given that your entire short career has been in prison, you may not be familiar with our Success Platform. Nearly every aspect of our work here in the free world rides atop our definition of success. I had best take a brief detour to give you some background.

Here in the world, we define success following a very specific and clear hierarchy of criteria that drives every aspect of ape-god behavior. It starts with the simple idea that "Results matter." We have ingrained this into every aspect of their culture. What counts above all else are the Results. Whether it is measured by profits or popularity or anything else, the *successful* ape-god is, first and foremost, the one who gets Results. If you do not deliver the Results, you failed. Period. It is the first rule of business, politics, the arts, even pastoring one of the Enemy's little congregations.

A very distant second in the hierarchy is How the results are achieved. As long as the ape-gods stay within some very broad (and somewhat flexible) boundaries, the way they achieve the results is unimportant. As we have discussed previously, it is assumed that everyone lies, deceives, "pushes the boundaries" of legality, exploits other ape-gods (within reason), cheats on occasion, and generally engages in "whatever it takes" to achieve Results. If you are delivering Results, however, pushing the already-malleable boundaries is necessary and commendable.

A distant third – so far down the list it barely even matters – is an ape-god's Intent or its motivation for doing a thing. Humans will, on occasion, give some credit to someone who is pursuing something for "noble" reasons (the definition of noble is more or less down to individual taste), but for the most part in our Success Platform an individual's Intentions are irrelevant. Greed can be good and selfishness a virtue if it gets Results.

This is our Success Platform, and it informs every corner of their little societies – even with a lowly, washed-up, ex-convict like your Parolee. Like most modern ape-gods he is looking at his situation and seeing failure. He has little money, no respect, and humiliation all around. With just the slightest prompting from you – and probably without any encouragement at all – he will begin to look at his situation and ask himself how to refocus his efforts to get Results. He will forget all about intentions and he will compromise as necessary on the means so that he can get the outcome he deserves. As much as anything, it was this that landed him in prison, and it will be this that steers him back.

Of course, our Success Platform is just Enemy's design turned upside down. In His program the top priority, the thing that matters above all else, is the Prey's *Intent*. Are they seeking His Kingdom first? Are they putting His glory above all else? Is the objective they are pursuing intended to be wholly and completely for Him? If the answer to this is no, nothing else matters.

A close second in His program is *how* they pursue their goal. Are they treating their fellow ape-gods as they would treat themselves? Are they pursuing their Kingdom-building goals in a way that brings honor and credit to Him? Are their behaviors and the practices consistent with those He set out for them? Can anyone watching clearly see by the way they act that they are His followers? Even the best intent is insufficient if the way they pursue their goal is inconsistent with His design.

A distant third – so far down the list it barely even matters – is the question of Results. He tells them not to concern themselves with results. He tells them that if they seek Him first then the results will come. He tells them that they are meant to be building a Kingdom that is not their own. He has explained candidly that they will *not* reap what they sow, and they need to be content with the idea that others will take in the harvest from their labors. That is His version of success. It requires humility and a steely-eyed focus on Him and His Kingdom rather than themselves and their little kingdoms.

Fortunately, our version has won the day. Even the Enemy's close followers are ignorant of the inversion trick we have played. They are a Results-oriented people, and this attitude serves as a barrier between them and the Enemy throughout their lives. Your Parolee is no different. Like the rest of them, he believes he ought to be a Results-oriented ape-god, and in the "real world" that means making some compromises.

As you can see, this unimportant little job, coupled with the petty humiliations he has suffered, are accelerating our program. I think he is halfway home to our side.

Delivering Results for the Master Below,
Deumus

PS I am pleased to see how little progress he has made toward finding a church. For each of the past few weeks he has wandered into a different venue and spent the entire hour critiquing the people, the music, the building, the sermon (at least the few bits he heard), the liturgy, the dress code, and even the coffee. His mind has not settled long enough to spend even a few minutes worshiping the Enemy. He walks through the doorway intent on completing his mental report card and each place has fallen well short of making the grade. It is excellent progress. You should try again to suggest that he go to our preferred church, number two on the list. That place may finally break his desire to keep searching.

NOT PERFECT, JUST FORGIVEN

DEAR BENTROCK,

I do so love bumper-sticker theology. Your Parolee has latched onto the idea that "Christians are not perfect, just forgiven." By this he means that his growing list of personal failings are to be expected – even from a "good" Christian like him – and he should not expect too much of himself. He is only human after all! But he may rest confident knowing that he is forgiven, because he always *feels* appropriately guilty and says he is sorry, and that is the important thing.

Armed with this bumper-sticker assurance, he is well on his way to stuffing his quickly shrinking Christianity into a little mental box, the Faith Compartment, where it will remain safely tucked away until Sunday morning (if he ever finds a church that makes the grade). In other words, he is following in the footsteps of a great many free world followers of the Enemy. They find it far too bothersome to have Him invading every corner of their lives, so they compartmentalize and do not think too much about Him or His program except during select parts of their day or week.

As you have watched him at work, you will have noted that your Parolee's job is most certainly not an area of his life cluttered by thoughts of the Enemy. (What a wonderful change from the days when he was singing hymns in the prison laundry!) Following his workday, he heads home to "unwind" with whatever distraction device catches his attention (after all, he has earned it). These unwinding hours are another time where there is little room for the Enemy! Then there is socializing time with his work colleagues. You may be sure nothing is leaking out of the faith compartment during those after-work gatherings! Much of his remaining time is consumed by the daily interactions with his brother and sister-in-law. Since they are not religious folks, he reasons, it would be rude to discuss the Enemy with them.

This leaves him with a few minutes during the day, just before bed, plus the designated time on Sunday morning (if he can ever find a decent church!), to engage with his faith. It is a nice, neat, and increasingly compact little compartment that suits us very well.

It is always astonishing to me how even the Enemy's followers cannot grasp the simple truth that in all they do they are either working for Him or for us. There is no third way. When they are working for themselves or for some other cause or person, they are inevitably working for us. It is only when they seek Him first in all they do, that they are truly working for Him. And that is why the compact and hermetically sealed little compartment is so delightful. In those moments when the box is opened, they are working for Him. The rest of the time they are working for us.

By the way, I should acknowledge your initiative in helping your Parolee "misplace" his well-worn copy of the Library. He had not opened it even once these past two weeks, which was encouraging, but even I was surprised at how quickly he gave up the search yesterday when he could not find it. Within minutes he had returned to his familiar distraction device, reassuring himself that it would surely turn up tomorrow.

Speaking of tomorrow, I believe we have arrived at the appropriate moment to share our Always Tomorrow idea with him. It tends to be more effective in the free world than in prison in any case. Try it tonight. Suggest that perhaps it is time for him to stop trying to find a new church and to concentrate instead on building a life for himself in the free world. Remind him that he is busy and that it is his obligation to make the most of his freedom by concentrating on his new job and his free world life. Tell him that, of course, he really *should* get back to the Enemy's business and he most certainly *will* when his schedule permits him to do so (that is the sort of good Christian he has become), but there is plenty of time for all that in the future. There is always tomorrow.

You may finish with the suggestion that even the Enemy would probably prefer that your Parolee not spend too much time attending to his spiritual matters just now. He has a great many demands on his time, a great many stresses in his life, and he is only human. After all, Christians are not perfect, just forgiven.

Perfect But Not Forgiven,
Deumus

COUNTERATTACK

Dear Bentrock,

I knew the Enemy would launch a counterattack, but I did not think it would be so comprehensive or deadly effective. He has pushed forward on every front. Your Parolee is once again recommitting himself to the Enemy and he is now armed with a range of new defenses to resist us. As I have warned you so many times, when the humans call out for help the Enemy always answers.

Your mistake here, Bentrock, was overplaying your hand with the Always Tomorrow story. It was partly your inept delivery and partly poor timing. Regardless of the cause, he was taken aback by his own thoughts (your whispers), and it disturbed his conscience. He cried out for help and now help has arrived.

The Enemy's counterattack started with the little group of ex-convict Christians at the secondhand store. They had been there from the beginning, but your Parolee had not noticed because he was too engrossed in his own humiliation and disappointment. With his gaze turned back toward the Enemy, he quickly recognized that the Enemy's followers were literally all around him.

They immediately welcomed your Parolee into their little gaggle, as they do. The old woman parolee has been especially troublesome. I think she reminds him of his late mother. Her faith is strong, and, like his mother, she is one of the rarest of ape-gods: a genuinely humble human.

The first casualty was ungrateful gratitude. It started to unravel the moment he said, "Good morning, how are you?" and she answered with a broad smile that revealed decades of dental neglect and her well-practiced quip: "Well, I'm not in prison!" It is her way of summarizing that everything in her life is far better than it was, and far better than she deserves (she sincerely believes that rubbish).

At that moment, your Parolee's mind was flooded by memories (the Enemy's doing) of his experience in prison when he had finally resolved to "choose joy." He had nearly forgotten the idea entirely. Now, in an instant, he had been transported back to the weeks following his encounter with the Roach. Like stepping outdoors for the first time in months, he suddenly realized that the air he had been breathing was tainted and stale.

The experience was simultaneously physical, mental, and emotional. "I'm not in prison!" was the ridiculous, nonsensical, declaration of an old woman with low expectations and no self-respect. For several long moments, your Parolee fumbled for the correct reaction before mumbling what he realized was the only appropriate response: "Amen."

Your Parolee now, for the first time, noticed the genuine gratitude with which this woman embraces her low-paid, inconsequential little job. She had been invisible to him these past weeks. Now she was impossible to ignore.

The woman is happy to explain to anyone who will listen that she is "blessed" to have this job, blessed to have the "wonderful friends" and a "church home," blessed to feel alive and mostly healthy, and blessed to have "everything I need." She is content. She is grateful. She believes these so-called blessings are far more than she deserves. She delights in sharing all of this with anyone who will listen. And should a briefer explanation be required, a damaged smile and a simple, "Well, I'm not in prison," does the job.

The gaggle has also introduced your Parolee to a reformulated checklist for finding a church. As it happens, the secondhand store Christians attend several different churches. One attends a traditional Roman church, another a house church, still another a so-called non-denominational church, and so forth. When he began asking his colleagues for recommendations, our deception was revealed.

One young woman explained that she loved the church she attended because she found that it allowed her to "worship" most effectively. Another man explained how he especially appreciated the way his church had "so many opportunities" to serve. A third talked about how his church was a place where he found he could "grow" and become more Son-like.

By the third conversation it had occurred to your Parolee that his thinking was upside down. Everyone in the gaggle was attached to their individual church because it was a place where they could best serve and worship the Enemy. It had nothing to do with how well the church served them.

It appears, at least for now, that your Parolee will begin attending church with the old woman. This is obviously what the Enemy had intended all along. In His typical fashion, He has connected two ape-gods who could not have less in common. Separated in age by four decades, separated by race, without common interests or experience (other than his short stint in prison and her very long one), the only thing tying them together is this common faith.

That is His point. I have seen the Enemy do this sort of thing many times. When he forms a bond between followers of The Way who have little else in common, the relationship is extraordinarily effective in helping both build their faith. Sadly, they will discover soon enough that they have a great deal in common. Most ape-gods do once they peel away the superficial skin of habits and hobbies and heritage. It all reminds me of a time when I watched Him push together a similar pair with the words, "woman behold your son..." (best not to think of that!).

The secondhand store Christians also place a troubling emphasis on "practicing new habits" and being "mutually accountable" as they like to say. As I explained to you in those early days with your Prey, the seed of every vice is a temptation, but it is watered and fully blooms through habit. Unhappily, it works in both directions. The seed of every virtue is an act of grace, but it is watered and blooms through habit. As the old follower of the Enemy Thomas from Kempen taught them, "Fight bravely, for habit overcomes habit." This is what these secondhand store Christians are determined to do.

As the current circumstance demonstrates, the

Enemy can be clever in His counterattacks. Your Prey called out for help and the only thing the Enemy offered was a gaggle of secondhand store Christians and an old woman's declaration of joy. It was enough. Your Prey now has a new church, a new militia of prayer warriors, and a renewed perspective. The simple and joyful declaration, "Well, I'm not in prison," undermines all our Essential Messages. (If you do not see how, I suggest you revisit them.)

As if this was not enough, your Parolee received a letter from Roach this evening. It contained nothing of consequence except the closing salutation, "Until we meet again, in this life or the next." The Enemy slipped in the one message that would help set your Parolee back onto the narrow path. He has become re-centered on the idea that he is playing for eternity. He has been reminded that none of the worldly things we offer are more than future piles of rust and dust. He is nearly lost to us. It is time to alter our approach.

Deumus

PS Do not be fooled by the simplicity of the Enemy's counterattack. Yes, it was merely a couple of well-chosen phrases and giving your Parolee the eyes to see people who were already there and ears to hear what they had been saying all along. But the suddenness and breadth of it is a surprise. Typically, the Enemy's response is more subtle and more measured. I must assume that He is preparing your Prey for a more serious challenge that lies just over the horizon.

It is one of His great advantages that He often seems to know what is coming long before we do. (Some say that He knows all that will happen in the future, but we are assured that this cannot be the case as He has predicted our Master's defeat and we are all quite certain the final battle will be decisively ours.) You must remain at the ready. If your Parolee is to encounter more difficulty in the coming days, we must be prepared to exploit the weakness when it arrives.

WHAT HAPPENED TO THE WALLPAPER?

DEAR BENTROCK,

I see that the Parolee has adopted the very troubling habit of turning off his television. Based on your last report, he has now gone a full two days without ever turning it on. This is no small matter! You must quickly return him to the habit of watching.

I trust I do not, at this advanced stage in our relationship, need to reiterate the point about distraction. With the Enemy surrounding him at work, television is one of the best remaining weapons in our arsenal. When your Parolee returns to his brother's house, television acts as a sort of always-on wallpaper that serves as a constant diversion for him. This is true for most of the ape-gods. There may be "nothing to watch," as they say – but there is always *something* happening on the screen. The motion and colors of the rapidly changing images catch the ape-gods' attention as reliably as a spinning lure on the end of a fishing line grabs the attention of a lake trout. Even more than this, television serves our agenda on multiple levels. It has become invaluable to our work.

Beyond basic distraction, television provides a rich and reliable source of mental clutter for our prey. It is only when the screen is completely off, as it has been with your Parolee these past two days, that the prey begins to realize the way the visual clutter on the screen becomes mental clutter in his mind. Images and audio (when they bother to turn on the sound) pour into their minuscule brains where they are left half processed and half ignored. At night their dreams are filled with television muddle as their brains work to sift and catalogue the flood of information that poured into them during the day. This electronic wallpaper literally distracts them day and night, waking and sleeping, pushing out the kind of thoughts that might bring them closer to the Enemy.

It goes without saying that the programming itself is delightfully supportive of our efforts. I have written previously about the angertainment programs and the excellent work they do to further our agenda. Then there are the low-grade invitations to lust and envy which are always useful. I am also especially fond of the limitless variety of trinkets and services on offer during the commercial breaks that help keep money at center of their thoughts. Television advertising makes the bazaar at Vanity Fair look like a neighborhood lemonade stand. All of this is useful to us, but the real value in the programming is the way it insists upon depicting the "real life" of the ape-gods.

Years ago, we began a campaign among the artistic types to ridicule the art, literature, and especially video programming that portrayed an "idealized and unrealistic" version of the world. The campaign succeeded beyond our fondest hopes. Programming that represented the ape-gods at "their best" (as the Enemy might describe it) became the subject of relentless derision. They were Pollyannish (see what we did there?). They were not real or authentic. They were childish. They were foolish. And anyone who enjoyed them was an unenlightened rube.

Well, your typical ape-god does not wish to be a rube, so in no time they were racing to create and consume a flood of realistic, gritty, honest depictions of themselves. Thanks to our efforts, the video that streams into your Inmate's cell night and day now depicts them as they really are: habitually killing one another, cheating one another, fornicating with one another, and generally embracing their role on this earth as greedy, prideful, lustful, deceptive little primates.

My personal favorite innovation of recent years has been the "reality" video programming that provides unscripted, as-it-happens video diaries of ordinary ape-god behavior: following the police through a city, watching our prey get dropped onto an island or stuffed into a small house, or whatever. The conflict, lust, pride, and deception caught on camera validates the realism of the scripted programs. This is who they are. It is just "real life" caught on video and broadcast for all to see.

Except, of course, it is another of our lies (based on a kernel of truth). In the television version of the world the most common occurrence in any police station is homicide. The average executive cheats and embezzles, the typical spouse is sleeping with the neighbor, the average public official is corrupt, and the most common first date is two drinks and a bit of copulation (which is nearly always "amazing"). It is nonsense, of course, but it is our nonsense. The too-good-to-be-true characters of yesteryear have been replaced by the so-despicable-it-must-be-true characters of today. The selfish, narcis-

sistic anyman who dominates the screen is our example
of "real" life.

There is reality in all this, to be sure, but it is so
stretched and misshapen that it is unrecognizable to any
outside observer. Most executives are boring, honest,
and stay late at the office. Most spouses rarely commit
adultery (we're working on that). Most public servants
are modestly paid bureaucrats carefully guarding their
pensions. Most first dates are a coffee followed by an
awkward hug and a wave. Our prey certainly do not go
around wantonly committing homicide, though it would
make our work much easier if they did. (In truth, we had
them killing one another at much higher rates back in
the Middle Ages – and in those days we had to really
work to get our prey enraged enough to dispatch their
neighbor, in hand-to-hand combat, without the benefit
of this impersonal point-and-squeeze, kill from a
distance rubbish.)

Which most closely resembles reality? The question
is irrelevant. Art (to dignify this beyond its worth) is
always a tiny and distorted window into a place and a
moment. The question is whether the places, moments,
and distortion the ape-gods depict will highlight the
worst aspects of their nature, their most admirable qualities, or their aspirations for who they might become.

When television is dominated by impossibly high
standards of personal virtue, the ape-gods attempt to
mimic it and fall short. When it is dominated by impossibly low standards of personal vice, no matter how low
they fall they succeed. It is obvious why we prefer the
latter. (Some years ago, one of their more observant
thinkers described it as "defining deviancy down." The
description now seems quaint. The modern ape-god
responds: Deviancy? What is deviancy?)

And just for our fun and pleasure, we succeeded in ensuring that the Enemy's followers are nearly always depicted on television as closeted deviants, corrupt narcissists, or (most commonly) hopeless and pitiable rubes. Did I mention that your typical ape-god does not wish to be a rube?

Do I need to make my case further? Pushing an endless feed of this pseudo-reality to your Parolee is invaluable, especially with the Enemy's servants surrounding him during the day. Even if he does not believe that the version of life depicted on the screen is true, it lowers his expectation of himself and others; it reduces his defenses against our suggestions; and for good measure it ensures that he views the Enemy's followers with a useful suspicion. Television gives us all this and constant distraction as a bonus!

Let us assemble a list of upcoming programs that will pique his interest. Get some of our followers at the secondhand store to begin discussing them. We need to re-open this carefully distorted window to the real world before he gets comfortable living without it.

Deumus

THE UNDESIRABLES

DEAR BENTROCK,

Your Parolee is wandering further from our reach each day. We no longer have the luxury of subtlety or patience. It is time to set our most reliable and trusted snare: It is time for romance.

Let me be clear, I am not advocating the sort of fantasy-driven pornographic escape you trained him with in prison. There may be a time in the future to lure him back into the fantasy-depravity-disappointment cycle, but his faith is too enthusiastic, and he is too determined for that to be effective at this moment. Our trap needs better bait than mere lust.

Before attempting to set this snare, you need to understand an essential truth about your Parolee: he is an *Undesirable*. He has been all his life – or at least since puberty. He knows this to be true with as much certainty as anything he knows about himself.

In this respect, he is hardly exceptional. Most ape-gods count themselves among the Undesirables, at least during most of their lives. It is a uniquely human defect that most ape-gods harbor a secret conviction that they are unappealing to members of the opposite sex.

The reasons why they believe this are as varied as the race itself. Often the belief stems from a perceived physical flaw of one sort or another. They imagine themselves to be too short or too tall; too fat or too slight; too dark or too pale. They fear they have too little hair in the right places or too much in the wrong places. They might think one bit of their anatomy is too big or another too small or too asymmetric or whatever. The variety of things that make the ape-gods believe they are unattractive is astonishingly varied.

Beyond physical characteristics, there is an even more diverse assortment of emotional and mental traits that they imagine have made them an Undesirable. They perceive themselves to be socially awkward and unappealing for a countless number of reasons. They believe they are too talkative or too shy; too needy or too aloof; too academic or too simple; too ambitious or too lazy; the list is nearly endless.

Then there are the incidental traits based on where they were born, how they were raised, or even their occupations. Some are burdened with ancestry from one of the ever-changing list of currently reviled tribes or nations. Others have the wrong accent or come from the wrong side of the tracks, as they like to say. One ape-god might see himself as an under-educated might-have-been while another imagines he is book-smart-prig no one would desire.

I could continue for countless pages and not exhaust the list of reasons these animals use to convince themselves, with our encouragement of course, that they are an Undesirable. And should we find someone who is not "too" anything? Why we just remind them that they are "too ordinary" to be appealing. In no time they also rush headlong into the cave of perpetual insecurity. (Imbeciles!)

We spend years carefully curating these feelings – with the invaluable assistance of the many ape-gods who do our bidding. The very first sustained encounter most humans have with one of our kind is when they are teenagers, and we busy ourselves tempting them into one sort of self-loathing or another. A well-timed embarrassment here, a public rebuke there, a bit of demeaning criticism from an admired man, or a dollop of gratuitous ridicule from a popular woman is all it takes to set in motion a lifetime of self-doubt.

As always with this type of thing, we insist that our prey keep these feelings *secret*. Thus, while most of them feel they are Undesirables, they believe that almost no one else feels that way because all of them are keeping this fact secret. And as a precaution in case the specific insecurity begins to unravel, we helpfully remind them that the mere habit of feeling like an Undesirable all these years *makes them* undesirable because no one likes a mate who is needy and insecure!

The result of all this is that most ape-gods, most of the time, believe that they are genuinely considered romantically undesirable. Even those we fail to persuade when they are teenagers, will gladly reclassify themselves as an Undesirable at the first signs of aging or injury or personal failure.

It is *this* characteristic of the ape-gods, the fact that most believe themselves to be Undesirables, rather than lust itself that we use to tempt them into all manner of destructive sexual sin. Arrange for someone of the opposite sex to show interest in an Undesirable, to suggest that they may actually be *desirable*, and most humans will gladly sell their soul for the momentary feeling that they are truly wanted by another.

Surely even you must recognize that we could never accomplish our program of infidelity and casual sex with lust alone. We may have successfully sold the lie that sexual gratification is a basic human need, but it is not, and in their hearts most individual humans recognize the lie. (It is only as a collective group that they have ever truly embraced our deception.) Few ape-gods will surrender marriages or children or careers or reputations for the promise of occasional hydraulic hijinks. But offer them the promise of escaping the ranks of the Undesirables? They will slap a soul-for-sale sign on their backs with little more than a moment's hesitation. (The hydraulics merely serve as reassurance that the other person *genuinely* regards them as desirable.)

Like most of them, your Parolee is a lifelong member of the Undesirables – even more so after the cruel business with his now ex-wife. He is convinced that women could not possibly be attracted to him, especially if they really knew him.

Your task, then, is to work with some of our colleagues to find a woman who can convincingly persuade him that she genuinely desires him for who he is, failings and all. This should not be difficult. Once we find the right bait, the snare will be set.

But listen to me clearly, Bentrock, you cannot once again take short-cuts. This cannot be the solicitation of a prostitute or an addict. It will be too obvious to him that the woman is insincere, that she is feigning desire to get something in return. The woman must be a credible partner who appears genuine.

Now do not get me wrong, the work you did with his fantasy life was not irrelevant, but as I told you at the time it was aimed primarily at teaching him to dehumanize his intimate partners and to diminish the significance of the act. That, after all, is the entire aim of our work with lust and pornography. Nearly all temptation to sexual sin, especially among followers of the Enemy, begins with an appeal to their insecurities not to their libidos.

In fact, I will share a little secret of ours: nearly all pornography is designed to appeal more to the insecurities of the Undesirables than to their libidos. Whether it is aimed at women or at men, the underlying message of every erotic film, book, and even image is the same: the person (object) depicted is burning with desire for someone *just like you*.

Erotica aimed at the males pitches the idea that the fantasy partner so desires *someone like you* that she literally cannot keep her clothes on. Erotica aimed at the females pitches the notion that the fantasy partner is so overwhelmed with desire for *someone like you* that all other women will be invisible to him, he will give up all he has, and he will change everything about himself just to be with you. In both cases, the fantasy is the same: you can be desirable.

That is why it makes no difference what sort of physique we highlight in these works. Women representing most any variant of physical type will hold the same pornographic appeal. Men can be rich or poor, tall or stocky, old or young and still have the same effect. The only reason we portray a particular body type is to create unrealistic images that further the insecurities of our prey.

You will recall, when I was instructing you on how best to steer your Parolee's "fantasy life," that I told you "it is crucial that you emphasize the idea that the people who appear in his fantasies secretly *want* and *desire* exactly the sort of thing he imagines." I trust you now see how these tactics converge.

It may also start to become clear why the Enemy insists that His followers let the "old person die" if they wish to follow him. It is no use for them to rage against their libido, for example, and leave their desirability cravings intact. We just shift tactics slightly and pull them right back onto the wide and straight road.

It is time you put your Parolee's lifetime of insecurities to the test. We have many servants who are happy to desire him as and when necessary. Even *I* desire him (and believe he will make a delicious and hard-won meal). Let that fact make him feel wanted.

Deumus

THE ONLY DESIRABLES

DEAR BENTROCK,

Given the urgency of the situation, of *your* situation, I cannot imagine why you would waste time asking me about academic issues! Your question has no relevance to your Parolee, unless you are plotting to secure an already-attached woman to be his romantic snare? If this is what you have in mind, you must immediately change course. It adds layers of complexity and risk to our task that we cannot possibly accept given the circumstance. (Do I really need to remind you that, like all these fragile creatures, he could die at any moment?)

As a quick answer to your question, it is a simple enough matter when we wish to set a romantic trap for one of our prey who happens to be in a relationship and feels desired by their partner. We merely transform them into an Only Desirable, which is the next best thing to being an Undesirable.

First, let me remind you that no matter how desired an ape-god is by their partner, they are shackled to our definition of a good and satisfying "sex life" and their own hydraulic habits are inevitably failing to deliver at the impossibly high standard we have set for them. Second, the perspective of all ape-gods is shaped by a lifetime of teaching them to rush toward the next oasis and to have contempt for contentment. In every ape-god pairing, then, they are failing to achieve a good and satisfying sex life and it is all feeling a bit stale.

Still, in a strong relationship they often feel desired and desirable. To combat this, we introduce the idea that they are *only* desirable to their partner. We re-energize their anxieties and remind them of the attributes that made them feel undesirable in the first place. We then suggest that their partner may overlook these, but no one else ever would. We spend time reinforcing this message and once it is firmly embedded in their minds, we then suggest to them that their partner's opinion should not be trusted or valued.

Yes, I know this is ridiculous. Why should an ape-god in a marriage, for example, be bothered by the idea that they are only desirable to their partner? And yet they are. Both males and females, are equally susceptible to the idea. And once we have firmly implanted the notion that they are an Only Desirable (and that even this is not to be trusted since their partner is probably "just saying that" but does not "really mean it"), they are every bit as vulnerable to one of our romantic snares as any unattached Undesirable.

Breaking the bonds between the partners is also generally a simple matter since we have very helpfully redefined love to mean the stew of emotions I described previously, and these will have long since subsided. It takes little effort to combine the elements and complete the trap. They are now an Only Desirable, they no longer "feel" the love, the sex life is sub-standard according to our experts, there is a new and better oasis just over the horizon, and they only live once.

All of that said, you must not – under any circumstances – target a woman already in a relationship to snare your Parolee. The process I have described above often takes months or years, and prey are frequently pulled back by the powerful emotion of nostalgic loss that I mentioned in my earlier letter about love. An Only Desirable is unreliable bait for your snare and the situation is too urgent to risk another failure.

Stick with an available, unattached female for this trap. Do not concern yourself with finding the perfect mate who can pull him away from the Enemy. We need a temporary distraction. Now is not the time to be choosey.

Director Deumus
Texas Parole Services

PS If the Enemy derails the Undesirables stratagem, I am inclined toward a less subtle, more direct approach. My patience is wearing thin.

AS WE FORGIVE THOSE

Bentrock,

I can only assume that the Enemy had planned all along to connect your Prey with the young woman from the secondhand store Christians. I can assure you this romance will not last. He is a convict, while she is just an ordinary "recovering" alcoholic with an illegitimate child from an unremembered seed. Let them wallow in their mutual failures.

In the near term, the natural flood of endorphins and hormones will keep your Prey from being caught in our romance snare. We must move on and return to the matter in the future, after this ridiculous pairing has dissolved. In the meantime, the Enemy has granted us an advantage. With your Parolee busy falling "in love," his defenses against pride will be at an all-time low. This is a new opportunity to strike.

For reasons we do not fully understand, the act of falling in love also creates a surge in territorial behavior especially among the males. It creates a barely control-lable desire to demonstrate personal prowess and "success." While the precise causes of this behavior are unclear, we suspect it has to do with their shared animal biology (filthy hybrid creatures). Regardless of the reason, your Prey will be on alert for any incursions into his new "territory" with this female, and he will have an instinctive desire to "win," especially when she is present. We can use this to our benefit.

As you have observed, your Parolee is delighted with the idea that he is finally a Desirable. Even more, he is surprised that this particular young woman would ever desire him. He thinks she is "beautiful" and "kind" and all other manner of revolting and ill-suited adjectives which he has been heard spewing out to anyone who will listen (and a good number of people who were not listening at all). Their mutual affection is further intensified by their resolution – following the Enemy's command – to deny one another hydraulic gratification.

To be sure, this is what deferred sexual gratification was meant to accomplish. An ape-god overcome with passion is also overcome with a desire to be patient, kind, long-suffering, and all the rest. The obvious design of the Enemy's program was to allow passion to temporarily create in the ape-gods the attributes of real love while deep affection has time to grow, and commitment solidifies. Passion deferred has this effect. Passion indulged dissipates the temporary feelings of love before deep affection and commitment can take root. Given their mutual vow to adhere to the Enemy's program, however, it is obvious that they are going to deny themselves the usual carnal delights (at least for the moment).

As I said, however, we can use this to our advantage. Your Parolee is on guard and expecting us to stoke his lust in an attempt to break his resolve. You should engage in a small amount of that sort of temptation just as a distraction. While he is praying and seeking assistance to guard against lust, however, we will be attacking from an entirely different direction: pride.

I have received intelligence from our former colleague Woertz that one of the leaders of the prison gang – the one who broke your Parolee's jaw – has recently been released to Houston. I believe we can combine some of our various strategies to deliver your Parolee back into the hands of the gang. If we play it well, he need not even slide fully back into gang life. We only need him to begin to dabble in it. Once he has flirted with his old gang brothers for a few weeks, we can notify the authorities and catch him out on a parole violation. It may not be enough to return him to prison (and to be clear we would prefer that he remain in the free world), but it should be enough to strike a fatal blow to many of his new relationships and to his resolve.

The idea here is simple enough. You should begin by reminding him daily of his obligation to forgive others and then begin to remind him that he still has not fully forgiven his old prison gang brothers. Bring the gang to mind frequently in the coming days and especially the "brother" who gave him his beating. Once the idea has settled in with him, we will help him discover that his old prison gang brother has returned. That should be enough to spur his desire to meet up with his prison nemesis.

Now, before you bring up the point, I am perfectly aware that he "counted it as joy" when the beating happened. One thing you will learn about the ape-gods, however, is that they are volatile creatures, especially when it comes to pride. A beating counted as joy one day becomes an intolerable humiliation the next. The memory festers like an infected wound. Left untreated it can poison the entire body. In the many months that have passed, he has often felt remorse over the "weakness" he showed. The wound has been left untreated because he has kept these thoughts secret, ashamed to admit that what he once trumpeted as joy had become anger and, on some days, even hatred. With his falling-in-love hormones raging, it is an ideal time to remind him of it.

When the groundworks are fully laid, we will suggest he meet with the gang brother "in person" to offer forgiveness. Once they are together, our plan can unfold.

As I have emphasized so often in the past, even though the Gang Leader is a dedicated soldier for our side, we cannot control this sort of prey. We may point him in a general direction, but beyond this his actions are chaotic and unpredictable. This does not mean, however, that we have no influence. I will work with his tempter to make a few suggestions. We will encourage him to believe that the very best revenge for your Parolee would be to have him abandon his faith and return in humiliation to the gang. At the very least, we will suggest, the Leader ought to take the opportunity to further humiliate your Prey by allowing him to grovel for forgiveness!

As you will have already realized, no matter how the meeting goes, our efforts will be advanced. The Leader is expert at vice signaling[21]. I expect he will put on quite a show for your Prey. Your Parolee will either be enticed by what he sees (in which case we have him back) or filled with anger by the encounter (in which case he is halfway home) or appalled by the sin (in which case he will once again fail to forgive, we will be able to ridicule his lack of faith, and in a few months' time, we will do this all over again).

As he approaches the encounter, you should do your best to remind him of the lessons you taught him years ago about respect and especially about self-respect. Having these ideas race through his mind in advance of the meeting will enhance the likelihood that there will be a clash. Do not hesitate to remind him of how this all would look to his new "love." Run through the many, many humiliations he has experienced with his ex-wife, with the gang in prison, and with so many others since he has been released.

I need not remind you, Bentrock, that we have nearly lost him to the Enemy. If this last gambit fails, we may have to wait years before we have a new opening with him. Do not keep anything in reserve. Push on every fear and failing he has been carrying. He believes he is going to do the Enemy's work. Follow the plan and he will fail spectacularly.

Sincerely,
Deumus

PS To anticipate your objection and save us both another round of pointless correspondence, yes, there is an infinitesimal risk that he will "turn the other cheek" and invite more abuse. It is my experience, however, that the Enemy's followers think of this more as a metaphor than a command. They might embrace the *idea* of turning the other cheek, but they almost never do so. When they are hit, they hit back just like every other ape-god. This is a near certainty. Their tendency to hit back is even more reliable when the falling-in-love hormones are raging. There is no need to worry.

Footnotes:

[21] You may know that the ape-gods often delight in deriding one another for "virtue signaling." This is what they call the practice of engaging in behavior which makes it obvious to others that they are trying to "do the right thing" whatever that may be – from driving an environmentally friendly vehicle to expressing disdain for another ape-god's cruel comments.

Vice signaling, by contrast, is usually welcomed with smirk of approval. These ostentatious displays of what the Enemy would call sinful behavior are intended to signal to others that the person shares and endorses others' vices and desires. It proves to all witnesses that the vice-signaler is "courageous" enough to thumb his nose at convention and tradition. It says, "There is no need to pretend around me, I unapologetically do what I want to do, and so should you."

MEMORANDUM FROM THE SECRETARY

TEMPTER BENTROCK:

You are hereby ordered to report to the Tempter Training Division for immediate reeducation. I must formally notify you that earlier this evening your Parolee slipped forever beyond our grasp. He is now with the Enemy – slain by a former gang brother following yet another blundering and ill-advised attempt by Deumus to reclaim his soul. Moreover, he was killed at the worst possible moment, cut down while offering forgiveness to his enemies.

It defied all logic and experience that Deumus would suppose your man's former gang brothers would welcome your Parolee back into their ranks. It is even more puzzling that he did not anticipate that the Enemy would be closely guarding your Prey in the days leading up to the encounter. Even if the Enemy had let His guard down – which is unimaginable given the stakes – your Parolee had long-since moved beyond clumsy attempts to appeal to his pride.

I can only observe that it fits with Deumus' long

pattern of incompetence. This same incompetence led to the prison system being the one place in the modern world where the Enemy continues to make progress and where our own success rate has been declining. The Master has long grown weary of Deumus' inability to accomplish the simple task of maintaining his inmates' current direction, especially when nearly every human we sent him was already on the fast track to our Domain.

It is no longer of consequence. The Master has sentenced Deumus to liquidation which, as you know, is a process that will be completed over several centuries. He has already begun the slow and agonizing annihilation procedure at our Master's hands. The only reason you are not suffering the same fate is that our Master has focused his wrath on Deumus and you are too unimportant to attract his attention.

For your own part, there is nothing further you need to do with respect to this incident. I have dispatched our public relations team to the scene. They will be working to recast the events as another example of a former inmate murdered after returning to life in the gang. Memories of your Parolee's faithful service to the Enemy will be swept away by accusations (from the gang and the police) that he was there with criminal intent. His was just another jailhouse conversion, a burst of piety signifying nothing. His killer will be placed into long-term segregation in the prison system to ensure that the story of your Parolee's sacrifice is lost.

For the moment, there is little we can do with respect to his daughter. She witnessed his execution and she saw this man she scarcely knew sacrifice his own life for hers. The impression will last a lifetime. As is our usual practice, we will enlist her mother, her uncle, and the other adults close to the girl in our effort to rewrite her memory of these events. The ruse will likely fail. In the years ahead we may discover that we lost two souls this evening.

The Master has also ordered that the entire management team for the Texas Department of Corruptions be replaced. Along with the other tempters in the prison division, you will be retrained and assigned to a different department upon completion of your training. That is all.

Serving the One True Master Below
Alastor
Secretary General
Tempter Enforcement Division

PS On a personal note, Bentrock, I would strongly encourage you to apply yourself to your studies with all the diligence you can marshal. I have reviewed the case files and your correspondence with Deumus. Most of his instruction to you was well grounded in many centuries of experience and success. Some of it even showed considerable insight. As it happens, however, the Master has directed his wrath at Deumus, so your own part in this matter will be overlooked. You will not be so fortunate in the future.

EPILOGUE

AN INMATE'S FINAL LETTER

Editor's Note: The Inmate left this letter for his daughter, who has graciously allowed me to reproduce it here. I believe it is self-explanatory.

DEAR _____,

I'm not very good at writing so please excuse me for the spelling and grammar mistakes (my friend Steve is helping with this so you can blame him too!). Steve says I should just write from my heart and not worry too much about how it sounds.

I am writing this letter from prison. I am supposed to get out next week, but before I do, I wanted to write this letter while everything from this terrible experience is still fresh in my mind. I plan to give it to you when you get older. Who knows what the future will bring, but I do not want to see you make the same mistakes I made. One day I'll give this to you, when the time is right.

First I want to say, from the bottom of my heart, I am sorry. If I had known that my decisions would leave you without a father I would have made different choices. I can tell you truthfully that I did not do all of what they say I did, but that doesn't matter. I did plenty of illegal stuff that would have landed me here sooner or later, and for that I don't have any excuse. Please believe me when I say that I would never, never have purposely hurt you. You mean more to me than anything in the world. I am sorry.

I fell out when you were only two years old. You could barely talk. Now you are going to school! I've missed so much. I did not get to see you much while I was here. Your mom said it was too far to drive with a baby and I understand her perspective. Now she is busy with your brother so she doesn't have time. But don't be mad at her for this, it is my fault. She should never have had to drive all day just so you could see your dad. That's on me and me alone.

Prison is a horrible place. Never do anything that will bring you here. I have hated it every day. Out in the world it is so easy to get involved with things that seem like easy money, especially when all your friends are doing it. But it is NOT WORTH IT! I was just a teenager when I got involved with drugs. I was never much of a user, but I thought selling it would be an easy way to make some money. It was for a while, but all the time I was selling drugs I never thought about the people whose lives I was hurting. I used to call the addicts my "regular customers" like I was selling hamburgers. I know now that I was helping them ruin their lives. I used to tell myself that if I don't sell it someone else will. That is probably true, but I have learned that I have to answer for my life and not for someone else's.

I want you to know that I love you. I used to say that to you all the time when you were a baby, but at the time I did not know what love was. Now I do. I learned about this thing they call agape love. It means loving someone no matter what, not because they deserve it or because they make you feel like loving them but just because you decide to love them no matter what. That is what God does for us. He loved me even though I was a prisoner and had spent my life hurting others. He forgave me. The day I realized that was the best day of my life. (I won't lie, there were lots of tears shed that day in the prison. Not just mine, but other men too. They were tears of joy. It is difficult to explain.) Before that day I thought there was no hope for me. I thought no one would ever love me. Not even you.

My greatest prayer, and I pray this every day, is that you will find the love of Jesus that I found. I plan to do everything I can to help you find that while you are still young. (I don't want you to have to come to a place like this one to find Jesus!) Your grandmother did everything she could to try to bring me up in the church, but I was too hard-headed to listen. It was my pride that steered me down the wrong path. I was so busy trying to "be someone" that I forgot that I already was someone...at least in God's eyes. I realized that if I was someone to Him then why should I ever care about what anyone else thinks? Pride was just the Devil's trick. He was playing on my fears.

Your grandmother was a wonderful woman. You will never get a chance to know her because she passed a few months ago. They say she died from cancer but I think it was at least partly from a broken heart. I was a disappointment to her, because of my criminal ways I guess, but mostly because I rejected God. I am at least thankful that she died knowing that I had come back to God just like the prodigal son (Luke 15:11-32). I know I will see her again in heaven. I miss her a lot and I prayed so hard that she would live long enough to see her one more time after I got out. But I guess it was not in God's plans.

I do not know what the future will bring. I am excited about getting out of here but I am scared. Steve says that is normal. It is not that I am scared of the world, I am just worried that I will be tempted back into my old ways. I am praying every day that God will put the people in my life to help me stay on the good road. I want to do that for you and for your grandmother. Mostly I want to do it for God. I want to show Him I have really changed. I want to live the way He wants me to live. I learned here that the greatest among us are the ones who serve others. That is who I want to be. By God's grace that is who I will become. I guess that by the time you read this we will both know if I made it (ha ha).

I am getting paroled to Houston so I am still not going to be able to see you too much. I am planning to get a job and save my money and then move back to Beaumont when I get off paper. It will only be two more years so it is not too bad. But I am going to come see you as much as possible.

Anyway, I guess none of that will matter by the time you read this. The thing I really just wanted to say was that I love you, I am sorry, I am going to do everything I can to be the best dad I can be. I am living my life trusting in God. I am praying for you every day.

Before I finish I wanted to share my favorite Bible verse with you. Some free-world volunteers who came here to prison shared it with me and I wrote it down. It is Romans 15:13, "May the God of hope fill you with all joy and peace as you trust in him, so that you may overflow with hope by the power of the Holy Spirit." I pray that you will grow up knowing that we serve "the God of hope" and that if we trust in Him he will fill us with joy and peace.

Love Dad

PS Steve says Hi and says that he hopes that by the time you read this you will have grown up to be happy and filled with joy. He is never getting out of this place but hopes that maybe one day you will come with me to visit him.

AUTHOR'S NOTE

I hope and pray that this little book will offer some encouragement to readers who are incarcerated as well as those in the free world. I pray it will help them to recognize and combat some of the deceptions and temptations they encounter from the lips of the Deceiver. I appreciate that it is old fashioned to discuss demons and temptation (it was old fashioned in Lewis' day as well), but those who have lived through the struggles of trying to faithfully follow The Way will know all too well that they are real enough. Yes, there really are dark forces working, often with the enthusiastic assistance of fellow human beings, to divert us from the path to a new life in Christ Jesus.

I have tried my best to be prayerful and listen to the prompting of the Spirit when writing this book. If there are any useful insights or spiritual truths contained in these pages, you may credit Our Lord for his guidance as I would certainly not be able to discern them on my own. In the places where I have gotten it wrong (and I am sure there are many) you would be safe to assume it is my own hard heart and hard head which prevented me from following the guidance I sought through prayer. I ask for your charity in these instances, and I welcome correction.

Houston, Texas
July 2021

ACKNOWLEDGMENTS

I would like to thank those who encouraged me in this project and especially those who prodded me to keep working on the many occasions when I became frustrated and discouraged and wanted to cast it aside. I am beyond grateful to those who offered prayers on my behalf.

I wish to especially thank the men and women – both inside prison and in the free world – who read early manuscripts and provided valuable feedback. Thanks to Carol B., Chad H., Chris S., David B., Dennis W., Dennis F., Gerald P., Giovanny C., Guy M., Jennifer H., Jennifer M., Jerimiah B., Jim A,, Kevin T., Rob R., Tom B., Vance D., and Vince L.

Finally, I am beyond thankful for my wonderful wife who reminds me daily what Paul meant when he explained that love is patient, love is kind, love does not envy, does not boast, is not proud, is not self-seeking, is not easily angered, keeps no record of wrongs, always protects, always trusts, always hopes, and always perseveres. She has encouraged me along the way and graciously tolerated the many months of lost weekends and evenings while I worked on this project as the COVID pandemic was raging and we were sequestered and working from home. I thank God that He has blessed me with an amazing partner I do not deserve.

A LOOK AT: WHEN THE WOLF COMES KNOCKING

BY KEN PRATT

Some wolves attack when their prey is at its weakest. Some charge fiercely. Others...knock softly.

When Greg Slater returned home from college for winter break, his whole world changed. After rescuing his high-school sweetheart, Tina Dibari, and helping sentence his best friend, Rene Dibari, to life in prison, Greg fell in love for the first time.

Fifteen years later, life isn't easy, but Greg and Tina are working on their marriage. But an old fear has come back to haunt them…

Rene has escaped prison, and he's thirsty for revenge.

As shocking truths unfold, Greg and Tina face a ripple in their faith and in their *home*. Tina starts doubting her faith and seeks comfort in a friend with lustful intentions. Meanwhile, Greg struggles to navigate this new unrest in their relationship.

Unfortunately, evil stops for no one, and three very different wolves are after the Slater family.

Will Greg and Tina's love be enough to keep them together, and—more importantly—will their faith hold true when the wolves come knocking?

AVAILABLE MARCH 2022

ABOUT THE AUTHOR

Joseph "J.B." Cyprus is a pseudonym for someone who is not famous and whose real name would certainly not help sell books. He lives in Houston, Texas, is an executive in the renewable energy industry, a part-time venture capitalist, a repentant former management consultant, and a veteran of the US Military. Most of all, he is a person who strives and often fails to faithfully follow Jesus. He wrote a book about temptation and sin because it is the one theological subject about which he knows a great deal.

J.B. holds an MBA from one of those snooty, over-priced Ivy League universities and an undergraduate degree from a somewhat less snooty public university. He was born in the Northeast US and has lived in Michigan, Florida, Pennsylvania and North Carolina before settling in Texas. He has also lived or worked in several countries in Europe and in Asia. He is married and has two adult children.

J.B. has spent more than a decade as a volunteer in both the Jubilee Prison Ministry and the Kairos Prison Ministry and has served at numerous Texas prisons.

All proceeds from this book go to help support prison ministry programs.

Made in the USA
Monee, IL
06 March 2024

54176589R00204